A DISGUISE FOR DEATH

'Bless me, Father, for I have sinned...'

It has been twenty-three years since Aoife Cusack last attended confession, but now she desperately wants to atone for her part in a heinous incident that led to the deaths of six people. Recently released from prison, Liam Sullivan, Aoife's ex-boyfriend and leader of an IRA cell, has written a best-seller about his part in the Windsor bombing of 1981, and Superintendent Gregory Summers attends one of his readings. With old scars opened by Sullivan's profiteering, the situation soon turns violent, involving Summers in one of the most complex cases of his career.

A DISGUISE FOR DEATH

A DISGUISE FOR DEATH

by

Susan Kelly

Magna Large Print Books
Long Preston, North Yorkshire,
BD23 4ND, England.

British Library Cataloguing in Publication Data.

Kelly, Susan
    A disguise for death.

    A catalogue record of this book is
    available from the British Library

    ISBN   0-7505-2539-8

First published in Great Britain in 2005 by Allison & Busby Ltd.

Copyright © 2005 by Susan Kelly

Cover illustration © The Old Tin Dog by arrangement with Allison & Busby

The moral right of the author has been asserted

Published in Large Print 2006 by arrangement with Allison & Busby Ltd.

Magna Large Print is an imprint of Library Magna Books Ltd.

Printed and bound in Great Britain by
T.J. (International) Ltd., Cornwall, PL28 8RW

Prologue

'Bless me, Father, for I have sinned. It is twenty-three years since my last confession.'

The priest's voice, through the wire mesh of the confessional box, was gentle, even humorous. 'Welcome home, my child.'

Father Michael settled himself more comfortably, his unforgiving wooden seat cushioned by an embroidered kneeling pad and buttocks which had grown fleshy in middle age. No wonder he hadn't recognised the voice. This would be a long session, but few people came to confession on a Monday evening – leaving, as it did, six whole days for sinning again before communion on Sunday.

The church had been empty when he'd walked through after supper, half an hour ago, which was no doubt why the repentant sinner had chosen this night.

Many priests didn't bother to hear confessions on week nights any more, but Father Michael was old-fashioned and thought that absolution should be there when it was needed. Besides, he liked the peace of the confessional where he could be alone with his thoughts, or even catch a nap, although once he'd snorted to an abrupt awakening in the middle of a confession and realised that he'd missed the juiciest bits; which was a pity since, given that he recognised the voice as that of young Jack Dellaglio, they would have been juicy indeed.

The dim shape on the other side of the barrier had been silent now for some minutes, gathering thoughts, rounding up memories. It must be hard, Father Mike reflected, to remember the venial sins of more than two decades – the white lies told, the prayers missed, the hours spent in idleness or gluttony – but he doubted that it was trivial sins that had brought this person here this day.

The silence was not yet oppressive but he said, 'Start with the big thing, my child, the thing that has kept you from Christ all these years.'

The words fell out in a rush, as if he had opened the door of an overstuffed and badly ordered cupboard:

'I have done murder, Father.'

The priest caught his breath. In thirty-five years of missionary work among the English, he had heard the usual tales of adultery and theft, of old women mugged and young ones seduced. He'd thought to have heard it all, but he had never before heard those four words:

I have done murder.

An admission that he could do nothing

8

with, not in this world, since privacy was sacred to the confessional. There would be no citizen's arrest; all a priest could do in such circumstances was to urge the confessor to go to the police and turn himself in. What he *could* do, if the sinner were truly repentant, was to grant absolution and he felt a surge of excitement in his breast, a feeling of power. The gates of heaven were presently closed and locked to his visitor and he – mere Michael Patrick Dooley from Limerick – was the custodian of the key.

But his sinner had other ideas.

'No. I can't do this!'

He heard a flurry in the darkness, saw a figure hastily rising from where it knelt.

'I'm sorry. I can't. It's not yet time.'

'Wait!' He rose involuntarily to his feet, faster than he had moved in ten years, his arthritis whining complaint. 'There is no sin so great that God will not pardon it.'

He went unheard. The door banged on the other side of the confessional and he heard footsteps scurry across bare flagstones, almost a run.

Father Mike left his cubicle slowly, curious, yet reluctant to break the anonymity of the sacrament. The cool oblong of the nave was empty. The only change from when he had passed through earlier was a fresh candle burning in front of the statue of the Virgin.

He felt deflated.

'Though your sins be scarlet,' he murmured, 'they shall be white as snow.'

He crossed to the door and stood for a moment in the porch. There was no one in sight. Somewhere nearby, he heard a car start, an engine purr away. At some time in the last half hour it had begun to rain heavily and the handful of gravestones reflected the clouds above, equally grey.

He would hear no more confessions tonight. It would be a black sin indeed that would bring someone from his fireside on such a night as this and his parishioners were not black-hearted.

None of them had done murder.

He locked the door. If they needed him, his regulars knew to ring at the priest's house.

He turned back and genuflected towards the altar, his right hand moving automatically to form the cross, and, after a moment's thought, snuffed the solitary candle out, lest it start a fire.

A drop of wax fell on his dusty black skirt and set.

That night's visitor would need more than a votive candle to enter the Kingdom of Heaven.

Chapter One

Gregory Summers stood staring at the plate-glass window of Goodrich's, the independent bookshop in Northbrook Street, Newbury. The object of his interest was a poster, advertising a reading and signing that night by best-selling author Liam Sullivan of his autobiography, *Behind the Wire*.

Greg didn't have as much time for reading as he'd like, or for keeping up with the latest from the world of books, but he'd have to have been living in a cave not to have heard of this one.

Sullivan had been interviewed on *Start the Week* and on breakfast television, where the female presenter had smiled at him and fiddled with her hair while her male counterpart looked nervous. Richard and Judy had famously refused to have him on, which was better publicity than if they had.

He had talked to *The Times*, the *Guardian* and the *Telegraph*. The launch party for the book had been held at the Groucho Club in Soho and attended by luminaries of the sport, fashion, television and film worlds.

All of which made Gregory Summers angry.

Sullivan was an IRA man, dyed in the wool. He liked to boast that his grandfather had been shot by the Brits in Dublin during the Easter Rising in 1916. It was in his blood and he had waded in the blood of others in the late seventies and early eighties. He'd been convicted of masterminding the deaths of six people in the Windsor bombing of 1981, and no one doubted his involvement, if not as principal, in earlier atrocities.

He'd been caught shortly after the Windsor bombing and sent to jail. Most decent people assumed that they'd thrown away the key, but he'd been released after nineteen years.

The Good Friday agreement had given an amnesty to sectarian killers in the hope that the troubled province of Ulster could make a new start after thirty years of civil war. Sullivan and his gang – as murderers of British civilians – didn't fall into that category, but they'd kept their noses clean in jail and expressed remorse which, Greg was sure, was as authentic as the Tooth Fairy.

And now he'd written a book about it and people were queuing up to buy it. It was being serialised in the *Sunday Times*. There was a law against profiting from crime but somehow that didn't seem to apply to writing books.

Greg didn't approve of murderers, what-ever their motives; he didn't approve of mur-derers who wrote books about their crimes and made a fortune; he didn't approve of the people who bought the books and so encouraged them. All in all, he was a giant puffball of disapproval and he thought he had better huff off home before he exploded.

The poster had a sticker along the bottom with the words 'Sold Out' written on it. Not that Greg would have dreamed of going, of dignifying a criminal in that way.

Wild horses wouldn't get him to Goodrich's that night.

As he let himself in at his front door in Kintbury half an hour later, his girlfriend Angie called out, 'Supper in five.'

He looked at his watch. It said six-fifteen and he had no reason to question it.

'Bit early, isn't it?' he ventured.

She appeared in the kitchen doorway, a thin, fair woman, neither plain nor pretty, understated in jeans and a vest top. He wouldn't swap her for Michelle Pfeiffer. She was now twenty-five to his forty-nine, so he was no longer twice her age. Yippee.

He was never sure if having a much younger partner kept him young or made him feel every one of his years.

'I have to be at Goodrich's at seven-thirty,' she explained, 'for a reading.'

'Liam Sullivan?' She nodded and he frowned. 'Why?'

'I'm a psychology student,' she reminded

him. 'I'm interested to see a man who could kill random strangers in cold blood, for mere politics, find out what makes him tick.'

'I doubt if the best psychologist in the world could tell you that, my darling. Such men are a mystery.'

'I have to start this big third-year project in the autumn. I thought I might do it about serial killers and Dr Burnside said it was a good idea.'

'Sullivan's more of a mass murderer,' Greg objected. He didn't have many areas of expertise but homicide happened to be one of them and he wasn't going to let the opportunity slip, especially if it meant putting one over on Dr Sideburns.

'Pedantic much! Third-year project on mass murderers.' She turned back into the kitchen.

'It's sold out,' he said, following her.

'I bought a ticket yesterday.' The microwave pinged three times and she took a bowl of pasta out, transferring it hastily to the breakfast bar and blowing on her fingers. 'Ooh! Hot! I bought two tickets. Wanna come?'

'Er, yeah, okay.'

The first person Greg saw on entering the bookshop was PC Chris Collins, standing in uniform with his colleague, Constable Tom Reilly, in front of a sign that said Gay Section. Both men wore body armour but that was standard practice in these violent times.

He remembered that Goodrich's had requested a police presence that evening.

Liam Sullivan had a lot of enemies.

He said, 'You might want to stand somewhere else, Chris.'

Collins started at the sight of the head of Newbury CID. He looked round furtively and whispered, 'Are we expecting real trouble, sir? I thought it was just a nice bit of overtime.'

'I'm here in a purely private capacity,' Greg assured him.

Collins looked disappointed. Greg and Angie went to the refreshment table where she exchanged their tickets for two glasses of white wine. It was already half past – it had taken them a while to find a parking space – but there was no sign that the event would start soon, despite the capacity crowd.

It occurred to Greg that he should stay on the alert, since a policeman was never truly off duty. He let slip a small sigh and Angie glanced at him. 'Let's find a seat,' he said.

Easier said than done, but they eventually squeezed on to a couple of chairs about halfway back after Greg had glared at a fat man long enough to get him to shift over and make room for them. He sat sipping his wine and surveying the crowd but he saw no one who troubled him: nobody who looked agitated or, conversely, eerily calm.

15

He tried to relax, taking Angie's hand and squeezing it.

'Isn't that your mate from forensics?' she said suddenly.

Greg looked where she was indicating. A short, plump man of Asian appearance had just come in, accompanied by a beautiful woman in a cherry-red shalwar kameez, topped with a black linen jacket, her sleek dark hair folded into an immaculate bun. Deepak Gupta and his bride, Indira, recently arrived from Mumbai. Greg caught his eye and wiggled his fingers in greeting. Deep wiggled back and, leading Indira to a solitary free chair at the back, squatted on his haunches beside her.

It was almost eight when Sullivan made his appearance, walking out of a door marked 'Private' and straight to the front of the room, flanked by three very different women. Greg recognised the small, dumpy one as the manager of the shop. The second, who was young and very fashionable – all pelmet skirt and long tousled hair – he guessed to be a PR girl from the publishers. The third he clocked immediately as a professional bodyguard; a good one, too, not obvious, blending in. Anyone less familiar with the breed would take her for Sullivan's sister or girlfriend.

Angie was leaning forward, her tongue protruding slightly from her pursed lips as it did when she was concentrating. She fumbled in her bag for a notepad and pencil and Greg wondered what observations she would make. He examined the man too, knowing that killers did not reveal themselves in any obvious way.

Sullivan was in his late forties but looked younger, his black hair only a little troubled by grey – less so than Greg's own, if he was being honest. A good tan gave him a healthy glow, no prison pallor here, but then he'd been out for two or three years. He was thin, which reminded Greg that he had been on hunger strike at one stage but had failed to carry it through to the end. So he would kill for his cause, he thought cynically, but not die for it.

He wore cream chinos and a black T-shirt with short sleeves revealing decent biceps but no tattoos. Greg had once been told by an RUC officer that the IRA would brook no delinquent behaviour, turning away thieves and vagabonds from their elite ranks. They wanted no troublemakers and he didn't know if that made him want to laugh or cry.

Sullivan and the shop manager sat behind a table on which copies of The Book were piled. The publicist perched on a chair to one side and didn't know what to do with her hands. The bodyguard retreated to the back wall where she stood with a clear view of the room, her arms folded. Her eyes moved smoothly over the crowd, rather as

Greg's had earlier, lingering once or twice but clearly unworried.

'You're late, Paddy,' a male voice called from behind Greg's right ear. 'We've been cooling our heels.'

Sullivan half rose in his chair and unleashed a smile of great charm from his typically thin Celtic lips, his blue eyes crinkling crows feet. 'I am that,' he said. His voice was melodious, with only a trace of accent instead of the grating Ulster tones Greg had been expecting. 'And I apologise. Thank you all for coming and for waiting so patiently.'

The bodyguard, meanwhile, stared intently at the man who had called out for perhaps ten seconds, then looked away, as if he was of no account. Her eyes were tawny, glittering jewels. Greg heard the unimpressed heckler say derisively, 'Ooh! I'm *so* scared.'

Sullivan opened the book and began to read.

'I was five years old when I first learned that I was living in an occupied country...'

At least he would be on the spot if there was any trouble tonight, Greg thought. There must be many people who wanted Sullivan dead, not least the families of his victims. He had an image of a would-be assassin bursting through the door at any minute, waving a gun.

Good job that sort of thing happened only in books.

'Are we done?' he asked an hour later.

Sullivan had read to them from the early chapters, recounting his middle-class childhood in Bangor, twenty miles from Belfast, a good education at a private Catholic school. None of which gave any real clue – or not to Greg – as to what had made him go out one day at the age of twenty-five to kill half a dozen strangers who had done him no harm.

The question and answer session had been subdued, as if the audience were afraid to ask what they really wanted to know. Greg had remained silent, knowing that if he got started, he might never stop. *How can you live with yourself?* was only the beginning, followed by, *What would you say to the families of your victims?*

'I want to get a copy signed,' Angie said, answering his question.

'You're buying one? Can't you borrow it from the library?' He heard his own voice rising in dismay.

'That could take weeks,' she said patiently. 'There'll be a wait. It's top of the bestseller list.'

'It's £17.99!' he squawked in disbelief.

'Less than the cost of lunch for two at Pizza Express,' she said, 'and it's my money.'

'I'd rather have the pizza,' he grumbled, but he fell into place next to her in the signing queue, unwilling to let her confront

19

the murderer alone. They shuffled forward two steps every minute for the next twenty. Outside it was growing dark and he wished they were elsewhere, taking a walk in Goldwell Park, hand in hand in the dusk.

When they finally reached the front, Sullivan grinned up at Angie. She reciprocated automatically but Greg felt that her smile was forced. Many dark-haired Irish people had piercing blue eyes, but his were pale, Greg noticed, watery, like an autumn sky.

'Who's it to?' he asked, opening the next book in his pile and cracking the spine audibly.

'A simple signature will be fine,' she replied.

He glanced at Greg. Did he recognise him as a policeman? His sort usually could; but he'd been caught because an undercover officer had penetrated deep into his Active Service Unit. Now that was someone whose memoirs would be worth reading: a true hero.

'There you go, sweetheart.' He handed the book back and turned to the next in the queue, reaching mechanically for another copy. 'Who's it for, mate?'

Only then did Greg realise that Deepak Gupta was standing behind him.

'Could you make it out to Eileen Harris?' he said, in a normal, pleasant tone. As the Irishman started to write, he added, 'Peter

Mitchell, Adam Mason, Donald McLaverty, Sharon Pearson and Sangita Gupta.'

Sullivan's cheerful face closed up. He was suddenly ugly. He slammed the book shut, half rising in his seat, and the bodyguard stepped up to the desk, glancing from one man to the other. Greg saw her right arm flex for action.

'That was all a long time ago, mate,' Sullivan said softly.

'Not for the families of your victims.' Deepak didn't lower his voice but spoke out clear and loud. 'For the parents, the brothers, it's like yesterday. *Mate.*'

'Step back from the desk please, sir,' the bodyguard said in a reasonable tone, her hand rising to form a psychological barrier between the two men.

There was total silence in the crowd as the reality of what they were witnessing became clear to them. The two policemen had their hands to their batons, ready to draw them at a second's notice.

Greg laid a hand on his colleague's shoulder. 'Leave it, Deep,' he said, adding words which he'd never thought to hear come out of his own mouth: 'He's not worth it.'

At least he now knew what Sullivan would say to the families of his victims:

It was all a long time ago, mate.

The younger man allowed himself to be led away, shaking under Greg's guiding fingers.

Behind them, Sullivan sank back on to his chair and went on with his signing as if nothing had happened. The bodyguard and policemen relaxed, the two constables casting curious glances the way of their superintendent and the swotty little scientist from forensics who looked like he wouldn't say boo to a goose.

Deep made a visible effort to pull himself together and remember the social niceties. 'You've met my wife?' he said. 'Indira.'

'We have met once,' she said in her precise English, offering Greg her hand to shake.

'How are you, Dr Gupta?'

The bodyguard sidled up to them before she could reply and spoke to Deepak in a low voice.

'I think you ought to leave … sir.'

Greg showed her his warrant card. 'We'll leave when we're good and ready, thank you … miss.' She grimaced and walked away. 'That's a nuisance,' he said. 'I was going to suggest we get out of here. Now we have to hang about to prove that we can.'

'Oh, grow up!' Angie said. 'Let's go to the pub.'

'Good idea. Let me buy you both a drink, Deep.'

'Okay. Thanks.'

He tried to smile and his wife took his hand. She said something in Hindi and he nodded. Greg thought that she had asked if he was all right. They exchanged intimate glances of affection. Greg knew that they'd met for the first time only days before their wedding in Mumbai, five months earlier, although they had written many emails beforehand. Now he was a witness to their falling in love.

The sight touched him.

'The Windsor bombing?' Angie asked gently. 'Was she your sister, Deep?'

Gupta looked into his pint of bitter for a moment before answering. 'She was eighteen. I was nine and I adored her. She never acted like I was a nuisance kid brother, not like a lot of teenagers. She was due to take her A levels in three weeks and she had a place at medical school. We were all so proud of her. She and her best mate, Rachel Goodman, decided to give themselves a Saturday off from studying and catch the bus into Windsor, have a wander round the shops and sights, lunch in a pub.'

'The Angel,' Greg recalled.

'Yeah. Nice place. Then. Good pub lunches. They pulled it down after. She was killed instantly when the bomb went off. Rachel had gone to the toilet, got off with a few cuts from flying glass. She never got over it, though, didn't sit her A levels, or go to Oxford like she planned.'

'Survivor's guilt,' Angie murmured.

'And Mum and Mrs Goodman never spoke to each other after. Each of them insisted that the trip to Windsor had been the other daughter's idea.'

'Interesting,' Angie said. Greg shot her a look. Now was not the time for her to play the amateur psychologist. 'And desperately sad,' she added, repaying Greg's look with a sardonic one of her own.

'Mum heard three years later that she'd committed suicide – chucked herself under a train.'

Greg said, 'So there were more than six victims.'

Deepak nodded and took a long draught of beer. 'There are the parents who lost a daughter, me who lost a sister, my children who lost a wonderful aunt.'

Greg glanced at Indira's trim figure. 'Are you ... expecting, Dr Gupta?' he asked, uncertain if she would find the question indelicate, even if she was a paediatrician.

She flushed. 'No! I have to requalify, rebuild my career in England. Then we will think about a family.'

'Boy and a girl,' Deep said stoutly. 'Both doctors.'

They all laughed uncertainly and Indira said, 'Do not "count your chickens", Deepak,' as if she found the expression rare and comical.

'And that bastard made the bomb,' Deep

went on, 'and had his floozy plant it, and now he sits there with his fucking book – sorry, darling – like he has the right to exist. And he's nothing. Did you see him? He's rubbish.'

'He will pay for it in the end,' Indira said serenely, 'one way or another, in this life or his next.' Which reminded Greg how little he knew of their religion and its beliefs. Deepak was inclined to make fun of the idea of reincarnation but he offered no objection to his wife's words now.

Greg's problem with reincarnation was that the people who believed in it seemed to take it for granted that they would come back into a comfortable life in the West, whereas it seemed to him, statistically, that they were likely to be born into poverty and misery in the third world: an AIDS baby in Africa, say, or a little girl in rural China, doomed to die within hours because she was the wrong sex.

Indira raised her glass of apple and mango juice. 'Let's drink to the future. Yes? Superintendent? Angelica?'

'To the future,' they said, clinking glasses.

'To the future,' Deep echoed, unconvincingly.

'And at least he'll be out of Newbury by tonight,' Greg said. Angie cleared her throat. "What?' he asked.

'He told the *Telegraph* he was moving to Berkshire, renting a house on the downs.'

25

Greg groaned. 'He didn't specify where, for obvious reasons,' she continued, 'but he said he wanted somewhere quiet to work on his next book.'

'He can do that?' Indira asked earnestly. 'There is no mechanism for keeping undesirable aliens out of this country? Why do they not deport him?'

Angie shrugged apologetically. 'He was born in Northern Ireland. That makes him a British subject.'

'The irony being,' Greg put in, 'that he's devoted his life to trying to change that fact.'

'Well isn't that peachy!' Deepak said. He drained his glass and got up abruptly, his voice aggressive. 'Who needs a refill? Angie?'

'White wine spritzer, please.'

'Superintendent?'

'I'm driving.' Greg indicated his half pint of beer. 'I'll nurse this.'

Gupta turned to his wife but she shook her head without speaking, her large dark eyes saying all she needed to. As he shouldered his way to the bar, ignoring the plea in her look, the other three exchanged worried glances.

'So how are you liking England, Indira?' Greg asked, to change the subject.

'I'm getting used to it,' she said. 'It is not altogether what I was expecting.'

'England in the twenty-first century is very different to the image the rest of the world has of us,' Angie put in. 'I sometimes think people arrive expecting us to be in doublets and crinolines, saying "Prithee".'

'Or at least to be polite!' Greg said.

'Yes,' Indira agreed. 'I was taught growing up that the English are the politest people on earth. This does not seem to be the case.'

'The superintendent's wife is very much younger than he,' Indira remarked as they walked home through the night roads of Newbury, their way lit by streetlamps.

'She's not his wife,' Deepak said. 'She's his daughter-in-law.'

'Oh! I thought they were a couple.'

'They are.'

She digested this. 'This does not seem right. And his son?'

'Dead, of leukaemia. Three years ago.'

'Poor man, and yet, this does not seem right to me.'

'Live and let live,' her husband said, 'unless you're Liam Sullivan, of course. He can die and rot in hell for eternity.'

'He's quite a good-looking bloke,' Angie mused as they headed for home. 'Sullivan. Lots of charm.'

Greg, who was driving, concentrated grimly on the road ahead and did not bother to reply. It was all very well talking about the banality of evil but the truth was that evil was glamorous.

Chapter Two

George Nicolaides, known to his colleagues at Newbury CID as Nick, opened one eye, grunted and closed it again. Then he opened both eyes and swore with a startling lack of originality. He jerked upright, naked and hairy and picked up his alarm clock, shaking it as if it might tell a different tale if subjected to sufficient abuse.

'Wassamatter?' His recently acquired girlfriend, Nadia Polycarpou, yawned and stretched, her hand reaching automatically to rub the tattoo on her thigh, which she did every morning, for luck.

'I forgot to set the alarm.' Nick sprang to his feet and regretted it as his head began to throb. He gritted his teeth and gathered up his clothes from the floor. 'I'm due at the station in five minutes.'

'Plenty of time.' Nadia grinned. 'And me, I'm not on duty till six this evening.'

'You nurses have it easy.' She snorted contempt and he leaned over to kiss her on the forehead. 'Make yourself some breakfast, love, and let yourself out. I'll call you tomorrow.' He winced. 'Whose stupid idea was it to open that second bottle of wine?'

'Yours,' she replied serenely.

'Oh, that rings a bell.'

She watched as he stumbled about, pulling on the same clothes he'd worn yesterday, short of time for a much-needed shower. She approved of his hirsute body but it was a fact that you had to keep hairy men clean in summer, just like her mum always said, otherwise they got whiffy.

'Coffee,' Nick exclaimed. 'Can't go out without a cuppa coffee, at least. You want?'

'Later.' Nadia had a strong head for drink and, anyway, Nick had put away most of the second bottle. She purloined his pillow and piled both cushions behind her, dozing in a semi-recumbent position as she heard him banging about downstairs in the kitchen. Fifteen minutes later, the front door slammed.

Nadia picked up the remote and flicked on the portable TV that stood on the chest of drawers against the far wall. She changed stations rapidly but found nothing that kept her attention. News and cartoons: she was equally indifferent to both. She got up, opened a window to let out the smell of hot bodies and sex and stood for ten minutes under a long, cool shower.

Then she set out to examine the accommodation. She'd known Nick for six months now but he'd completed the purchase of this house only a few weeks ago and this was the first time she'd been left alone in it. Usually he came to her flat in Isleworth, an hour's drive away in West London.

The biggest bedroom, where Nick slept, looked over a quiet road at the front and, once she'd put her contacts in, she could see a canal in the distance. There was room for a double bed and the chest but not much else. The small stack of glossy magazines under the bed held no surprises; she'd have been more surprised by their absence.

Two wardrobes had been built into the alcoves either side of what had once been the fireplace. She opened the door of the one on the left. She'd seen most of the clothes in it over the past few months: not an extensive wardrobe and what there was inclined to the cheap and flashy. Didn't matter: it was the easiest thing in the world to take a man like Nick in hand. She'd already changed that aftershave of his that sucked the oxygen out of a room and weaned him off the clunky gold bracelet he was so fond of.

She was surprised and amused to find two police uniforms hanging in the second cupboard; she'd had no idea that Nick possessed such things. One was the normal, scratchy, blue serge you saw men and women wearing in the street; the other seemed more dressy. She tried the first one on and paraded up and down in front of the mirror, swamped in it. She giggled. She might get him to wear it one night and she'd wear her nurse's uniform.

Her friends said you had to reel a bloke in slowly, but Nadia reckoned you could just as easily sweep one off his feet.

The back bedroom was tiny, since the bathroom had been carved out of it at some point in the second half of the twentieth century. It held nothing but a few boxes. It would make a decent enough nursery, she thought, what with babies being so little. She envisaged yellow wallpaper – suitable both for boy and girl – enlivened with teddy bears.

A casement window overlooked the square of parched grass the estate agent had optimistically called a garden. Pave it over, she thought, or – better still – decking, make a barbecue.

On the landing a wooden hatch gave access to the loft. Always a chance for a third bedroom there.

That seemed to exhaust the upper storey, since there was really nothing to say about the bathroom. You wouldn't be able to charge much for a guided tour of the place, she thought with a grin, not like those stately homes her mum and gran loved to visit, with whole rooms used only to store suitcases and trunks.

She walked down the narrow stairs and into the kitchen at the back. This would need refitting, the units shabby and dated. She had an image of what she'd like, all pale wood and

stainless steel like in those property programmes on the telly. That would make the
perfect wedding present from her mum and
dad.

Marriage was definitely the goal: her
parents would hate it if she just shacked up
with a man and she was shrewd enough to
know that live-in girlfriends had no legal
rights. Besides, Greek families knew to be
generous with the presents, not only her
parents, but Nick's too.

A rummage in the kitchen drawers soon
located what she was looking for: a spare set
of keys. She let herself out of the front door
and walked, following the canal, towards the
town centre.

She was surprised to find herself there in
little more than five minutes. She got a cap-
puccino and Danish to go from the Costa
Coffee on the bridge and walked slowly
along the main shopping street, examining
her surroundings as she went while sipping
coffee through the hole in the lid of her
cardboard cup.

There were no surprises, the usual high
street names – Marks and Smiths and Boots
and Waterstones; Next and Gap – and she
soon retraced her route.

Nadia had lived in London all her life,
initially with her parents in Green Lanes,
later in Isleworth, sharing a flat opposite the
West Middlesex Hospital with an Irish girl

called Oonagh. She looked down on the provinces, despising market towns like Newbury as insular and narrow.

But if Nick, also a North Londoner, could take it, then so could she. She'd be thirty next birthday and couldn't afford to be choosy any longer. Oonagh was getting married in the autumn and she was only twenty-three. Catholic, mind, so that might account for it, not that Oonagh was noticeably reticent in the bedroom department.

Not quiet either.

'Tick, tock,' she murmured under her breath. 'Tick, tock.'

Nick's house was in a nice location, Nadia thought, handy for the town. She knew from those same TV programmes that they could add a lot of value if they did it right. She was glad Nick hadn't had time to make rookie errors.

She let herself back into the house and replaced the keys where she'd found them. Nick would surely give her a set in his own good time and it wouldn't do to spook him. She slumped in an armchair in the sitting room – two rooms thrown into one – and ate her Danish in a few large mouthfuls, swilling them down with the last of the coffee.

She didn't like the decor in the room but that was what DIY shops were for. Her dad and brothers would lend a hand with the painting. The carpet was arsenic green, with darker swirls, nothing that a trip to the tip and an afternoon with a rented sander wouldn't cure.

They could open up one of the fireplaces – not for some nasty, messy, real fire but a nice tasteful log effect.

There were no books but that didn't bother Nadia; she was no reader either. Who had the time or the concentration? The collection of CDs was predictable, as were the DVDs: Terminators one and two, all three Die Hards, some softish porn.

Too far to commute to the West Middlesex from here but Newbury had its own hospitals and she knew she could pick and choose – a nurse with ten years' post-qualification experience, a geriatric specialist. Or there was the Royal Berkshire in Reading, easily accessible by train; or maybe some nice private nursing home – the sort of place where rich, old men left their life savings to the angels who cared for them.

She didn't love Nick but she liked him and they were comfortable together. She might come to love him in the end. Who knew? The sex was average to good which was good enough. He would make a fine father in his rough-and-ready way, playing boisterously with the kids and leaving the important decisions to her.

They came from the same Greek-immigrant background which would make both sets of parents happy. He had a steady job: you never heard of policemen being made redundant, nor sacked so long as they kept their noses clean, and the pension scheme was good.

Nadia Nicolaides. She said it aloud. It was whotsit – there was a special name for it, when words all began with the same letter – but it sounded all right.

Some might call her mercenary, she knew. She called it practical. Women were the business-like sex, men the romantics. It wasn't hard to get a man to marry you, not once you'd made your mind up.

And she would be thirty next birthday, or had she already factored that in?

Tick, tock.

'Nice of you to stop by,' Barbara Carey said as Nicolaides rushed into the CID room looking dishevelled.

'Sorry, Sarge. My alarm clock didn't go off. I think there's something wrong with it.' Since detail gave verisimilitude to lies, he added, 'Might nip round to Argos later and get a new one.'

Barbara snorted. 'Alarm clock! Hanging around for a quickie with Nadia more like.'

'If only,' Nick said. 'Where do you want me?'

'You've volunteered,' Barbara said.

'For what?' he asked warily.

'Give a talk to a group of children with learning difficulties.'

Nick sighed. 'Is that "learning difficulties" as in "mentally handicapped"?'

'I guess so.'

'Only I don't see that you do a handicapped kid any favours by making out it's just a bit slow,' he said.

'You may have a point and you can discuss it with Mrs Robyn Marchant. She and her husband Stephen run the home and school for the kids in Inkpen.'

'And what am I supposed to talk about, for God's sake?'

'Seems they had an open day at Easter – fund raising – and Mr Summers went along. Mrs Marchant was telling him how she worries that her kids are vulnerable to predators, especially the teenage girls. The guv'nor offered to get a uniform along to talk to them about personal safety but then he forgot all about it and there's no one available.'

'Why doesn't he do it himself then?' Nick grumbled.

'He's delegated it to me, and I'm delegating it to you.'

'You're not on holiday yet, you know.'

Barbara was due to fly off to Corfu in a couple of weeks, with DCI Trevor Faber of the National Crime Squad.

'But I soon shall be.' Barbara made a lame attempt at a Greek dance. 'Sun, sea, sand

and retsina.'

'They don't make retsina the way they used to,' he grumbled. 'Not enough resin.'

'So, off you go. It'll make a nice change for you.'

Nicolaides made one last attempt. 'Andy'd be much better at that sort of thing than me.'

'Andy's gone to hospital.'

'What! Why?'

'You know his brother, Derek – works in the fire service in Reading?' Nick nodded. 'Well, he was injured at work earlier today.'

'God! What happened? Is he burnt? Will he need plastic surgery?'

'He was sliding down the pole, answering an emergency, and his hand slipped and he fell off. Broke his ankle.'

Nick sniggered. 'Sorry! I know it isn't funny.'

'Actually, it is *quite* funny. Anyway, Andy's gone to fetch him home and he'll be all morning, so suck it up.' She handed him a piece of paper with an address on it. 'They're expecting you at ten, so you'd better get a shift on.'

As he headed for the door she called after him, 'And for God's sake smarten yourself up a bit. You look like you've just rolled out of bed.'

'I'm not putting a uniform on,' he warned her.

'I'd like to make you but there isn't time.'

Nicolaides drove rather faster than was prudent up to Inkpen, high on the Berkshire downs. By the time he'd deployed the deodorant, fresh shirt and electric razor he kept in his desk for emergencies, he was running late.

Inkpen confused Nicolaides, since it was not what he thought of as a village, having no definable centre. True, there was a church and a pub, a primary school, even a village hall, but they were not grouped picturesquely around a green, the way a Londoner thought they ought to be, but sprawled out across a great distance. The roads in and out were narrow, winding and dappled by overhanging trees, and Nick felt as if he was negotiating the labyrinth of Minos.

And why did they call them downs, when they were so clearly ups?

He came to a halt at the top of the hill, uncertain as to his direction, but then he saw a board on the gatepost of the house opposite which had 'Hilltop House' written on it in large black letters. Grunting with relief, he drove through and inserted his car into a gap between half a dozen others on the gravel drive.

He got out, running his hands through his hair in a final attempt to tame it, and surveyed the place. It was a manor house, little short of a mansion. Victorian, he thought, once the home of a single family and all their servants. Must be worth a couple of million.

He switched his mobile off. If Barbara wanted him doing community work then she wasn't having the option of dragging him back for an emergency too.

He took a deep breath, straightened his back and walked to the front door to ring the bell.

It was answered almost immediately by a girl he judged to be fifteen, and there'd been a time when he was pretty good at estimating whether teenage girls were above or below the age of consent. She was tall and loose-limbed, showing a yard of tanned leg in tailored white shorts. Red hair fell long and loose around an open and friendly face. Her unruly fringe shaded candid blue eyes which matched her T-shirt.

She didn't look handicapped, he thought, but maybe it wasn't obvious.

'You the policeman?' she asked. 'I thought you'd be in uniform.'

'CID,' he said. 'DC Nicolaides.'

'Cool name.' She held out her hand for him to shake. 'I'm Charlotte Marchant. Charlie.'

The daughter of the house. That made sense: she had the confidence he associated with people who lived in places like this, a self-belief that came from the core.

'People call me Nick,' he offered.

'Oh, I shall call you DC Nicolaides. Mum's in the assembly hall with the kids. This way.'

Nick braced himself. He understood, in theory, that it was the hallmark of civilisation that the strong protected the weak, rather than preying on them or killing them, but he still felt uncomfortable around too obvious reminders that nature could get things horribly wrong.

What if his and Nadia's kids turned out wrong somehow? It didn't bear thinking about. His and Nadia's kids; where had that come from? He was thirty-two and since the age of fifteen his only interest in reproduction had been in the manufacturing process.

The assembly hall might once have been a ballroom, he thought. About twenty children faced front on hard chairs, ranging in age from six to sixteen or seventeen. Several were clearly Down's syndrome; others harder to categorise. Two were in wheelchairs.

An older version of Charlie, with the same red hair and blue eyes, sat on a dais at the front of the room, smiling benignly as the children chattered and laughed among themselves. She was shorter than her daughter and had the sort of figure described as comfortable of which Nick approved. He didn't like skinny women, whatever the fashion was; he wanted something to get hold of.

'DC Nicolaides,' Charlie announced and, giving a theatrical flourish, ushered him forward.

Her mother rose and said, 'Children. Let's sing the school song to welcome our visitor.'

At the rear of the hall, a grey-haired woman struck up on a piano. Such of the children as were able got to their feet and began to sing. Nick stood uncertainly in the doorway, not hearing a word that they sang, but Mrs Marchant gestured to him to join her and he got up on the raised platform, taking the chair she indicated at her side.

'We are so grateful,' she murmured and placed a small hand on his sleeve. Nick felt his heart pounding. He wasn't a shy man and could hold his own in the pub, but public speaking was another matter and he wished for a moment that he'd throttled Barbara and made a run for it.

As the singing came to a slightly ragged end, the children sat down, seeming pleased with themselves.

As Nick plopped back into his chair over an hour later, weak with relief that it was over, a girl of about fifteen approached him. He saw that she had the flat features and wide face of the child born with Down's syndrome, but her golden hair fell down her back like a cascade of light.

41

'Thank you very much, sir,' she lisped and smiled confidently up at him.

'My pleasure,' he replied.

Her almond-shaped eyes were looking at him coyly under thick dark lashes in a way that made him uncomfortable. Somehow, he didn't expect the mentally handicapped to have normal, healthy urges. Mrs Marchant came forward, took her by the elbow and turned her gently away.

'Time for art class now, Marie.'

'Yes, Mrs Marchant.' She went obediently away, but not before giving Nick a big wink.

Jail bait, he thought.

'You see the trouble?' Mrs Marchant said. 'She's just as keen on boys as any girl her age – more so, if anything, since she has little else to occupy her brain – but without having the nous to deal with the consequences. Let's go and get you some coffee, DC Nicolaides. You must be parched.'

'I thought that went rather well,' Robyn Marchant said a few minutes later. 'The children really took to you, and they listened to your excellent advice.'

'I didn't know I had it in me,' Nick confessed. He added, almost puzzled, 'I enjoyed it.'

She had led him off to the family's private quarters which were at the back of the house. Charlie had gone to the kitchen to make coffee while a young man, introduced as 'My son, Dominic', joined them in the sitting room. He looked about the same age as his sister and Nick wondered if they were twins; only people usually mentioned that, like they'd done something clever.

While Charlie epitomised a happy, healthy teenager, the boy had a more nervous demeanour. He wore his hair cropped very short as if he hoped to make it less ginger that way and, as he fidgeted with his hands, Nick noticed that the nails were bitten right down, a tell-tale streak of red down the side of each indicating that he gnawed his flesh when he ran out of nail.

It was a fine summer's day and french windows stood open to a terrace, beyond which Nick could see the trees and shrubs of a large garden.

It was a moment before he realised that the pianist was also there, sitting modestly on an upright chair in the far corner. She was not a woman men noticed, he thought, a veritable mouse. Scrutinising her now, he saw that she was younger than her wholly white hair suggested, not yet menopausal. He gave her a friendly nod and she looked deliberately away.

He shrugged mentally and, turning back to his hostess, said, 'I do admire what you do here, Mrs Marchant.'

'Robyn, please. And you are?'

'George,' he said, 'but my friends call me Nick.'

'We owe most of it to my husband,' she said. 'He provided the house and his income subsidises us.'

'Is he here?'

'He works in London,' she explained. 'Marchants' Marine Insurance. He gives us his time at the weekends, taking the kids on outings and so forth.'

Nick might be a public servant but he couldn't imagine that degree of self-sacrifice. Charlie came with mugs and biscuits and he accepted refreshment gratefully. His throat was dry from all that talking.

'Do you have a big staff?' he asked.

'We manage with four full timers, although there are people who come in from the village part time to clean the schoolrooms and help with meals. Siobhan, here—' indicating the mousy woman '—is my right hand, our matron. She's the only one who lives in.'

Dominic said rather aggressively, 'What sort of sick bastard preys on a Down's syndrome girl like Marie anyway?'

'But we know that it happens, darling,' his mother said gently. To Nick, she added, 'I have been known to take a girl to the doctor and get her a coil. It's better than the alternative. I may be taking Marie very soon.'

'Were those all the children you have here?' he asked.

'That's all we have room for. You probably know that it's been government policy for some years to educate less able children in mainstream schools wherever possible.'

'Inclusiveness,' Dominic said, as if it were a dirty word.

'Yes, one of those buzzwords the present government is so fond of. But we still have quite a waiting list – children who can't seem to fit in anywhere else. Places don't fall vacant very often.'

Nick said, 'I can imagine.'

She relaxed into her armchair, pulling her legs in grey slacks up under her. 'The happiest moments of my life are when a child we thought was destined for a lifetime in an institution heads off to a job and a hostel, some semblance of independence.'

She picked up a packet of menthol cigarettes from the table and offered him one. 'Do you?'

'I'll smoke my own, if you don't mind.' He reached into his pocket.

'Not everyone likes menthol,' she agreed. 'Actually, I don't myself, but I thought they might help me cut down. I know I shouldn't.'

'Me too!'

She flickered a gold lighter and they lit up in the amicable collusion of two people breaking one of the twenty-first century's strictest laws: thou shalt not smoke. Charlie made a moue of disapproval and flapped her hand. Dominic grinned and said, 'Can I have one?'

'No and, yes, I am a hypocrite. It's an addiction and one I don't want you picking up.' She appealed to Nicolaides. 'If you had your life again, Nick, would you start?'

He looked at his cigarette with affection. 'Terrible waste of money,' he said, 'but if you lead a stressful life...'

'Of course,' Robyn went on, 'there are sad moments too, when a place becomes vacant because a child has died.'

'Down's children are usually born with heart defects.' Siobhan spoke for the first time. Her strong Irish accent took Nick by surprise, although the name should have tipped him off. 'It's part of the syndrome.'

He glanced at her and she flushed as if embarrassed to be drawing attention to herself.

'There was a time when they rarely made it to thirty,' Robyn added. 'Things have improved. The affliction is better understood and it's normal for them to survive into their sixties now ... which creates fresh problems for ageing parents attempting to care for them, of course, not to mention dying and leaving them to cope alone.'

'What happens to them when they grow up if they can't live independently?' Nick asked.

'We have to pass them on to other

institutions, I'm afraid. Hilltop House is first and foremost a school. Those are sad days too, when they leave like that.'

Dominic drained his mug and jumped to his feet, full of restless energy. 'Give you a game of mixed singles, sis.'

Charlie got to her feet. 'If you enjoy being humiliated, bro. Please excuse us, DC Nicolaides.'

'You must be very proud of them,' Nick said when they had left. 'And they have such nice manners.'

'Oh, I am. And thank you.'

'Isn't it hard for them growing up here?'

'They're usually at boarding school,' she explained. 'It's half term this week. It does them good to spend holidays with children who don't have their advantages, anyway, makes them less selfish. Dom'll be back at school on Monday, which won't please Marie. She has a little crush and he's very protective of her, as you heard.'

Through the open window Nick heard the young Marchants erupt on to the adjacent tennis court. It was grass and they were soon pushing each other over and rolling on the ground, shrieking with mirth.

'Charlie plays for Berkshire,' Robyn explained. 'Under sixteens. We're hoping she's going to qualify for a wildcard into Wimbledon juniors this year, hence the humiliation for Dominic.'

'He's not so good?'

'He enjoys it, but he's inherited his father's asthma, which doesn't help. Charlie wants to leave school next year and go to a tennis academy but her father and I are keen for her to do her A levels before she concentrates full time on sport.'

George Nicolaides had a bit of a chip on his shoulder, although he'd have denied it, if pressed. Usually he resented the rich and privileged, but he was prepared to make an exception for Robyn Marchant and her charming children, who gave so much to the community.

He noticed that she wore a silver cross on a chain round her neck. Not a cross, in fact, but a full-blown crucifix with a tiny Christ in agony. Roman Catholic, he thought, with the distrust of one who'd been raised in the Eastern tradition, but she had nothing of the do-gooder about her. He guessed she went quietly about her good works, never letting the left hand know what the right was doing.

He finished his coffee but found himself reluctant to take his leave. He was enjoying himself. He turned over a book that lay face down on the coffee table in front of him.

'*Rebecca*,' he read, 'Daphne du Maurier.'

'My favourite book,' Robyn said. 'Have you read it?'

'Seen the film,' he offered.

'Oh, that's no good! They gave it a botched-up happy ending because they couldn't have good old Laurence Olivier committing murder. In the novel, Maxim de Winter did kill Rebecca – well of course he did!'

'He thought she was expecting another man's baby,' Siobhan put in, 'and passing it off as his so it could inherit his beloved Manderley. So he strangled her.'

'So he got away with murder,' Nick said, interested. 'Scot free.'

Robyn was shaking her head impatiently. 'He gets away with *nothing*. He carries his own punishment within him. After the inquest returns its verdict of accidental death, he and his second wife spend the rest of their lives trailing round Europe.'

'That doesn't sound like much of a punishment to me,' Nick protested, 'especially compared with being hanged.'

'It's a living hell,' Siobhan explained. 'They never go anywhere where they might meet anyone they know and they're bored out of their minds – waiting for the English papers to turn up three days late so they can read the cricket scores and do the crossword.'

She paused to consider then added, 'Perhaps more of a living purgatory.'

'It's a living death,' Robyn said.

Chapter Three

It was several days before Greg picked up Angie's copy of *Behind the Wire*, stealthily waiting till she was out one evening. He supposed that the man had used a ghost writer, this breed being in the back of his mind since the murder of one of their number on his ground six months earlier.

He checked the copyright page but this mentioned only Sullivan. Nor did the acknowledgements thank anyone who had 'helped in the preparation of this book'. It looked as if the Irishman had written it himself. Interesting. Maybe he'd done a creative writing course in jail.

He'd had nineteen years of free time to fill.

He flicked through the early chapters, not wanting to get bogged down in the IRA man's self-justification for his crimes. *I was five years old when I first learned that I was living in an occupied country.* What distorted rubbish. He noted that Sullivan had been christened William by his respectable parents but had adopted the Irish version at thirteen, although his mother still called him Billy.

The prose was plain but fluent, not intruding on the story he had to tell, and Greg was soon absorbed.

What interested him most was the infiltration of Sullivan's terrorist cell by Special Branch, since he'd always been fascinated by colleagues who worked under deep cover, isolated, sometimes for years, from friends and family. They were forced almost to *become* the adversary they fought and there had been cases of operatives going native as they absorbed the values of their targets. They might go by the name of policeman, like himself, but their job was a world away and it was one he did not believe himself capable of.

It wasn't until chapter ten that the man Sullivan knew as Francis Mahoney appeared on the scene: a lorry driver, to all appearances, in his mid-thirties, Belfast born but returning only after many years working in England.

Nondescript, with mousy hair, ruddy cheeks and blue eyes, he faded perfectly into the background. His job made him useful, the border guards growing accustomed to watching his truck trundle back and forth between the Republic and the six counties of the North.

He had references, in that people claimed to remember him from his childhood, to have been at school with him, and Greg marvelled at the planning that went into this sort of operation, the attention to detail.

Sullivan recounted his arrival without emotion, evincing no hatred for the 'friend' who had denounced him.

They didn't trust him with anything important at first, but Mahoney proved himself by running small errands, taking messages and, on one occasion, sheltering a man on the run from the RUC in his flat in the Falls.

For the first six months he had been under almost constant surveillance and Greg, doing a rough calculation, saw that he had spent more than two years gaining the confidence of his targets. He shook his head in disbelief at the dedication of this lonely man.

Meanwhile Sullivan was planning his major bombing and Greg read with interest the details of the chaos at the Angel pub in Windsor on that warm afternoon in late May. Sullivan listed the names of the dead, including Sangita Gupta, and claimed to feel compassion for these collateral casualties of his unilateral war; but Greg had no sense that he saw them as people, as living, breathing human beings with small brothers at home who adored them.

He read with interest that the bomb had actually been planted by the sole female member of the unit, a girl named Aoife Cusack, left in a handbag under a corner table when she went to the Ladies, and thence out of the back door into the street.

The Irishman boasted that Aoife was a

fine actress, mimicking an English accent so perfectly that no one dreamed she was Belfast born and bred. She and Sullivan sat outside the castle, a safe distance away, watching the results of their actions, the terror and the panic.

The bomb blast lasted less than a second but the aftermath made it seem longer: windows shattered, not all at once but in waves over a distance of two or three hundred yards as the percussive sound rippled outwards in circles; then the alarms went off, burglar and fire. Eye-witnesses invariably said, 'It went on for ages, the noise of the bomb. Simply ages.'

Did they feed on the fear, these two monsters, on the screams of pain and terror? Had they been lovers, Greg wondered, the cell leader and the girl? Was it love or conviction that had made her a death-dealer?

He dimly remembered Sullivan's trial at the Old Bailey. There had been four men in the bulletproof dock that day, he was sure, but no woman. He thought he might look that up and, tracking Angie's laptop down to the study, went online in search of the details.

He'd never really got to grips with the refinements of search engines and his first attempt yielded hundreds of hits. After fifteen minutes spent sifting through them, he found a newspaper archive which gave an account of the trial. He saved it to the hard drive, went offline and settled down to read it at leisure.

As he had thought, four men: John Dolan, Mickey Brown, James Finnegan and Liam Sullivan. No woman, no Aoife, and what sort of name was that, anyway, and how did you pronounce it? And yet she'd been a major player in the Windsor bombing a few months earlier, so it looked as if she'd got out just in time.

'Francis Mahoney', actually Sergeant Malcolm Fraser, a Londoner, gave evidence against the four men. With his job done, he had no fear of blowing his cover. There were others ready to take his place and he'd earned an honourable retirement from front-line duty. He, too, made no mention of Aoife Cusack.

Sullivan, having been handed six life sentences for conspiracy to murder, had been dragged back down to the cells, spitting vows of revenge at Malcolm Fraser.

He went back online to search for Aoife's name and found a handful of articles. He saw that she had been seventeen at the time of the Windsor bombing. Little more than a stroppy adolescent, he thought, but old enough to be held accountable for what she had done.

She seemed to have disappeared without trace.

A window popped up unbidden to tell him that dozens of hot, lonely women were anxious to date him. He was surprised they were hot, given how little they were wearing. He clicked it shut. He looked for Francis Mahoney and Malcolm Fraser, both names common enough to bring up a frustratingly large number of hits.

'What you up to then?'

'Agh! I didn't hear you come in.'

'No, you were very absorbed. But in what, and does it involve naked women?' Angie leaned over his shoulder and pressed a few keys. 'I see that it does: hot, lonely women.'

'What? I thought I'd closed that! That's not mine!'

'I can see it's a pop-up,' she said, amused. 'Don't panic.' She dropped a kiss on his brow. 'You're a strange little man, but you're *my* strange little man.' She flipped open another window. 'Aha. Got the bug now, have we? I know what you're like when you get a bee in your bonnet.'

'I don't know what you mean,' he said stiffly.

She laughed and, leaning across him, added a few inverted commas to his search parameters. 'That'll get you up only the web pages that mention first name and surname together,' she explained kindly, 'not all the ones that mention either.'

He said humbly, 'Thank you, darling.'

'Cuppa tea?'

'Why not.' As she went off to the kitchen,

he began to work his way through the new batch of hits and soon came across a newspaper profile of the detective. Sergeant Malcolm Fraser had been born in Aberdeen but moved to Croydon in south London at the age of fifteen.

Probably easy enough to convert a Scottish accent into a convincing Ulster one, he thought. He had a job telling the difference himself. Still, Sullivan would have spotted any discrepancy immediately. If the man was a psychopath then he was probably of above average intelligence. Did you have to be a psychopath to be a terrorist? Or did psychopaths seek out causes as an outlet for their perverse pleasures?

Discuss.

Fraser had joined the Metropolitan Police straight out of school, transferring to a crime squad two years later then, on promotion, to Special Branch. Greg had some idea of the sort of selection process that officers under deep cover had to go through: physical, psychological, emotional.

He had worked for years infiltrating drug and vice gangs in London and had the scars to show for it. Then, in 1979, had come the big test, the one he'd been moving towards all his life: he was to penetrate an IRA terrorist cell. If they rumbled him it would mean certain death, probably prolonged and painful, designed to send a horrible warning to others like him.

The profile ended with the statement that Fraser would be assuming a new identity following his major coup of rounding up four top IRA killers.

Angie called that his tea was ready and he closed her laptop with a sigh. Part of him envied Malcolm Fraser the fear, the adrenaline, and the Queen's Police Medal; but then he remembered the last time he'd thought he was going to die, as a gypsy boy held him hostage at the point of a shotgun for what seemed like weeks, and he was glad of his comfortable house, his beloved girlfriend and the cup of tea that was waiting for him in front of *Newsnight*.

'Morning, sir.'

'Morning.' He paused as Sergeant Doyle swept past him, a regular ball of energy, and called her back. 'Veronica?'

She halted. 'Sir?'

'You're Irish, aren't you?'

'No,' she said patiently, 'I was born in High Wycombe.'

'But your people are Irish.'

'Okay, I confess, but whatever you're trying to pin on me, I have an alibi for it.'

'Very funny.' He pulled out a sheet of paper and a pencil and wrote 'Aoife Cusack' on it. 'Do you know how this name is pronounced?'

She squinted at it. 'That's pronounced Cusack, Guv.' Greg mimed a man whose sides were splitting with mirth. 'I think it's Eefa,' she said with a grin. 'Irish for Eve, mother of us all.'

'Eefa?' he squawked indignantly. 'How do they get that from Aoife?'

Veronica shrugged. 'My family aren't Irish speakers but I know it's a long way from being a phonetic language. I imagine they do it to annoy the English.'

'Well, they succeed!' he snapped.

Eve, mother of us all; how inappropriate, he thought, for a woman given to blowing people up with nitroglycerine.

Evil Eve.

The Marchant family was at supper on Saturday evening when the door to the dining room opened and a young man came in. Not much over twenty, he was tall and thin with dark hair which he wore long, the curling tendrils tucked behind his ears. He was dressed like a student in jeans and T-shirt, a green sweatshirt knotted round his shoulders. His feet wore only socks, silent on the polished wood floor.

He grinned happily at the assembled diners and said, 'Only me.'

'Daniel!' Robyn rose from her seat at the foot of the table and crossed to kiss him on the cheek. 'I wasn't expecting you.'

'I got so sick of studying that I decided to take an evening off. Hello, Mum.' He bent to kiss Siobhan, who smiled up at him and touched his face briefly in greeting.

'I bet you haven't eaten,' Robyn said.

'I'll make myself some beans on toast.'

'Don't be silly. There's plenty of spaghetti left. I made far too much, as usual.'

'It's as though she's always hoping for unexpected guests,' her husband said, patting his paunch ruefully, 'and I have to finish it up. Waste not, want not.'

'You're just greedy,' Robyn said, 'so Danny will be doing you a favour. Here, take my seat.'

'No, really, Robyn.'

'It's okay. I've finished.' She indicated her empty plate, scooped it up and left the room to preclude further argument.

Daniel shrugged and took the seat next to Charlie. The girl sat up straighter, pushing her straggly hair from her face, and gave him her most animated smile. He was a good-looking lad, his long face and high cheekbones giving him a sensitive look, marred only by lips that were on the thin side. He grinned at her fraternally.

'So, how are the exams going?' Stephen asked, reaching across the table to pour the young man some wine.

'The first paper was a dream.' Robyn slid a plate of spaghetti bolognese in front of him and he thanked her. Charlie passed the dish of parmesan and he sprinkled it liberally. 'Just the questions I'd been hoping for,' he went on. 'I'm dreading the next one. It's bound, by the law of averages, to be a nightmare.'

'Well, you should know about the law of averages, if anyone does,' Dominic said, since Daniel Fahey was studying accountancy at Oxford Brookes.

'So what's with the tennis?' Daniel asked Charlie. 'Shall I be seeing you on telly this year?'

Dominic made a scoffing noise and Charlie said, 'Even if I get a wildcard into Wimbledon, they don't normally televise the junior matches.'

'No reason Dan shouldn't come along and cheer, though,' Stephen added. 'He's practically family, after all. Just like a big brother to you,' he added meaningfully.

Charlie blushed. To cover her confusion, she asked, 'Will you take me for a spin on your bike after supper, Danny?'

'If your parents have no objection.' He glanced from one to the other. Robyn looked doubtful, but Stephen said, 'I suppose there's no harm in it. Daniel's a safe rider.'

'You will be careful?' Robyn said. 'Both of you.'

Charlie put on Daniel's spare crash helmet

and stood looking at herself in the hall mirror as he struggled with the leather boots he had discarded on arrival. It wasn't an aesthetic improvement, hiding, as it did, her chief beauty – her hair – and emphasising the fact that her face still had its childish pudginess.

She wondered if her parents would let her have a motorbike in a couple of years. It'd be brilliant if she could roll up at school on it at the start of every term, though there was probably a rule against it.

'You set?' Daniel asked, grabbing his own helmet from the hall table. 'Let's tear up to Inkpen Beacon.'

'Oh yes. We can watch the sunset.' *That will be romantic.*

They let themselves out of the side door and walked round to the car park where Daniel's Honda sat sleekly on the gravel.

'Danny!'

He was almost knocked over by a blur of blonde hair and a pink dress that left little to the imagination.

'Hello Marie. How are you?'

'Welcome home.' She flung her arms round his neck, her full breasts pushing into his chest. Charlie looked gloomily down at her own flat front.

Daniel laughed, kissed Marie on the top of her head and disentangled himself. 'See you later, kid.'

'You going out on your bike? Can I come?'

'I'm taking Charlie.' The girl pouted and he added, 'Some other time.'

'Anything in trousers,' Charlie muttered as she clambered on to the bike, wrapping her arms round Daniel's waist as he started the engine. She laid her cheek against his back, telling herself that it was to protect her face from the burning wind as they sped along the lanes, taking pleasure in the warmth of his skin through his T-shirt.

'She's just exuberant,' he said kindly. 'She doesn't grasp the rules of social interaction. And,' he added, 'she's just a kid.'

'Same age as me,' Charlie said as they set off, but her words were lost under the roar of the engine.

Charlie stepped off the bike a few minutes later, shaking her ginger locks free of the helmet, running her fingers through. It was one of those perfect evenings that occur at the end of an overly hot day, still and calm and stretching on till almost ten. She wished it could always be like this but it was bound to be raining for Wimbledon.

Daniel pushed the bike on to its stand and took her helmet, locking it with his own in the metal case on the back of the Honda. The two youngsters scampered the last few yards to the peak of the hill.

'So what are you going to do after finals?' she asked.

'I haven't got anything lined up jobwise. Just chill out for the summer, maybe take off on the bike for a few weeks, start looking properly in the autumn.'

'I'm sure Dad knows lots of people in the financial world.'

'I'm sure he does,' he said gently, 'but I shan't ask him. Robyn and Stephen have done so much for me – and don't think I'm not grateful – but it's time for me to stand on my own feet now.'

She nodded understanding. They'd reached the summit of the hill, looking back the way they had come.

'I hate that school,' she said suddenly.

He regarded her with compassion for a moment. 'I take it you don't mean Our Lady of Lourdes Convent.'

'Hilltop. Why do we have to live this way instead of like normal people? Dad makes shedloads of money and we could have a boat and a holiday cottage in France or Italy but Mum just pours it into the drain that is the school. She might as well make a bonfire of twenty-pound notes. And we've no privacy – Marie's always wandering into our part of the house, looking for Dom.'

'Mum and I wouldn't have had a home these twenty years,' he reminded her, 'if it hadn't been for Robyn taking us in after my father died. Or maybe it's us who're invading your privacy.'

'You know I didn't mean you!'

'I admire Robyn more than anyone I've ever met.'

'Oh! So do I. At least I should do. I know I'm a horrible, spoilt person.'

He put his arm round her and squeezed. 'Course you aren't, sausage-face.'

She poked him in the ribs. 'Don't call me that!'

'I've called you that since the day Robyn brought you home from the hospital when I was seven and Stephen asked what I thought of you and I said you looked like a big, pink sausage.'

'That was a long time ago,' she pouted. 'I'm not a kid any more.'

'I don't think you're spoilt, Charlie. Children who grow up in a close and loving family like yours are never spoilt.'

'Can we go to the pub?'

'No. Kid.'

'Please. Please. Please.'

He relented at once. 'All right. We'll go to the Swan. You can sit in the beer garden and drink orange juice. Okay?'

'Okay!'

'You don't remember your father, do you?' she asked, when they were settled in the pub's garden. All the picnic tables were taken on a fine Saturday evening and they sat on the grass under a hedge, white daisies

64

in profusion about them.

'You know I don't. He died before I was born. I'm just grateful Mum didn't call me Postumus.' He smiled affection at her. 'Look, Charlie, I know you want to believe that there's some romantic secret about my parentage but I'm afraid real life isn't like that. I'm just plain old Danny Fahey. How's school?'

She made a face. 'It's all right, but I'd rather be at the Academy in Bath.'

'I know, but your mum's got a point about you finishing your education before you concentrate on tennis.'

'Meaning you don't think I can make a living at it either.'

'I didn't say that,' he protested.

'Dad would let me go if it was up to him.'

'Oh, yeah!' He laughed. 'Daddy's little princess gets everything she wants.'

Dusk was falling and goosebumps were appearing on Charlie's bare arms. He un-hooked his sweatshirt and draped it round her.

'Better get off,' he said. 'It's getting dark.'

'Daniel is a sensible boy, isn't he?' Stephen emerged from their en-suite bathroom, toothbrush in hand.

'Of course.' Robyn turned over another page of her book without looking up. She was propped up against two pillows, her knees bent to support the hardback.

'He wouldn't take advantage of Charlie, for example.'

'Don't be silly.'

He sat down on the end of her bed, his hand falling on her ankle under the duvet, rubbing the bone. 'I mean, he'd have to be blind not to see she has a little crush on him.'

She glanced up at last. 'He has that girl at Oxford. Kate.'

'That's been over since Easter.'

'Really?'

He grinned at her. 'Do try to keep up, Mum, as the kids say. Get with the programme.'

'He thinks of her as a sister.'

'All right.'

Stephen went back into the bathroom and rinsed out his mouth. He shed his dressing gown and climbed into the other bed like a blue and white striped porpoise. 'What're you reading?'

'Nothing.' She closed the book and placed it in the drawer of her bedside table, reaching to switch off her lamp. 'Just some tedious autobiography I picked up at Goodrich's in Newbury.'

Chapter Four

Greg had begun to put Liam Sullivan and his book out of his head until one evening at the beginning of June when he stopped at the village shop in Kintbury on his way home from work. As he stood examining the modest selection of wine, a voice in his left ear said, 'Hello. Weren't you at one of my readings a couple of weeks ago?'

'Mr Sullivan,' he said coldly.

'With the excitable Mr Gupta – since I assume that's who he was – and a rather pretty girl. Your daughter?'

'Girlfriend,' Greg growled.

'Really? Congratulations.' As Greg bristled, he added, 'Copper, aren't you?'

Greg seized up a bottle of Muscadet at random and headed for the till. 'What makes you think that?'

'I can smell them a mile off.'

'Oh, yeah?' Greg felt his face contorting into a smirk. 'So were you standing upwind of Malcolm Fraser for two whole years?'

To his surprise, the Irishman laughed. 'Touché, Inspector.'

'Superintendent, actually. Detective Superintendent.'

'Really?' Sullivan said again, apparently casting doubt on Greg's rank as well as his ability to pull a girl half his age.

'That's £5.99, Mr Summers,' the shop-keeper said.

'Well, it's all water under the bridge now,' Sullivan added, as Greg handed the woman a tenner and scrabbled in his trouser pocket for a pound coin. 'Live round here, do you?'

'I might do.'

'I only ask because I'm staying here myself. Nice little place on the Inkpen Road. Wisteria Cottage. Know it?'

'I know it,' Greg said. It was a beautiful old house and he hated to see it sullied by this man.

'Nice to know the police are handy,' Sullivan said, 'keeping the neighbourhood safe for law-abiding citizens.' His accent switched into stage Ulster. 'See yerz.'

He headed for the door. 'By the way,' Greg called after him as he tucked his bottle of wine under his arm, 'whatever happened to Aoife Cusack?'

'Hah!' Sullivan stopped but did not turn round. 'Isn't that the sixty-four-thousand-dollar question!'

And he left.

Greg remembered an old acquaintance at Special Branch who might be worth a chat. Chief Superintendent Colin Meers had been active during the seventies and eighties and had been retired now for many a long year. He had probably moved, or even died.

But the phone rang only twice before Colin's measured Midlands voice said a neutral, 'Hello.'

'Colin? Gregory Summers from Thames Valley.'

He expected a pause of at least a few seconds while Meers digested this and placed him but he responded at once, with warmth. 'Greg! Good to hear your voice again after all this time.'

They exchanged the ritual enquiries after each other's health and families. Meers was troubled by rheumatism in the cold weather and had lost his wife of forty years to a stroke two winters since. Greg sympathised, making no mention of his own dead son, Frederick, avoiding the obligatory commiseration.

'So what can I do for you?' Colin asked at last, 'since I assume you didn't just ring to see how I was.'

'I wondered how well you remembered an IRA unit run by Liam Sullivan,' Greg said. 'It was more than twenty years ago,' he added.

'What's your interest?' Meers asked automatically. Greg laughed and he said, 'Sorry. Force of habit. Still...'

'Liam Sullivan is living up the hill from me,' Greg explained.

'Nice neighbours you have!'

'Yeah, well. You know he's written his memoirs?'

Colin's voice was sour. 'And made a fortune, by all accounts. If I were his victims' families, I'd be suing for compensation.'

'Interesting idea,' Greg said, filing it away to suggest to Deepak later.

'What sort of person buys a book like that?' Colin Meers demanded.

'I assume you got a copy to see what he has to say.'

'...Yeah, well, that's different. Professional interest.'

'I just wondered how much you knew about the case.'

Meers was silent for a moment, then he said, 'It was all a long time ago, so I guess there's no harm. It was my case.'

'You ran Malcolm Fraser?'

'Indeed I did! The bravest man I ever met. Sometimes I wouldn't hear from him for weeks and on at least two occasions I was certain he was dead, but he'd always resurface, and he came up with the goods in the end.'

'What became of him?' Greg asked.

'Honourable discharge after the trial. He assumed a new identity and went to live in ... a Commonwealth country.'

'Canada?' Greg hazarded, since he thought he had read something about it during his

70

trawl of the Internet.

'I couldn't possibly comment ... but it begins with New and ends in Zealand.'

Greg laughed. 'I really wanted to ask about Aoife Cusack.'

'Ah, the one that got away. What about her?'

'She wasn't working for you?'

Colin snorted. 'Are you serious?'

'I'm presumably meant to infer no from that,' Greg said, 'which makes me suspicious.'

'Greg, mate, she was seventeen. We haven't started recruiting them out of nappies.'

'Good point, but I didn't really mean to imply she was an officer, just that Fraser had maybe turned her.'

'Not to my knowledge.'

'Offered her an amnesty, perhaps.'

Meers's voice was ice now. 'Aoife Cusack planted the bomb in the Angel in Windsor which killed six people, dumping her dinky little deadly handbag under a table and walking out like she hadn't a care in the world. I don't do deals with murderers. If I get my hands on her, then she's going to prison for a very long time.'

'You'll never catch her now, surely,' Greg said. Sometimes you just had to accept that and let it go.

'We still keep an eye on her mother back in Belfast, in case she ever decides to pay a visit. She may be lulled into a false sense of security after all this time.'

'Is there a father?'

'He died six weeks after the arrest, when Aoife's part in the Windsor bombing came out, heart attack. There was a brother and three sisters but the brother blames Aoife for their father's death, reckons the shame and the shock did for him. He claims he wouldn't spit on her if she was on fire and I believe him.'

'Is there a photo of her?'

'No, only Malcolm's description.'

'What was she like?'

Meers thought about it. 'The Cusacks were a poor, working-class family, but respectable. Aspirational, even, wanting the kids to be teachers and nurses, anything to get them out of the bombsite that was Belfast back then.'

'She's made a new life for herself somewhere,' Greg said. It was easier for a woman: people expected her to become someone else when she married, complete with a new name. 'It's been more than twenty years. She may have died.'

'We still have her prints on the system,' Colin said. 'Whatever new identity she's concocted for herself, one day she'll make a mistake – she'll get stopped for drunk-driving or arrested for shoplifting – and her prints will flag up and then I'll have her.'

'Not you personally,' Greg demurred. Special Branch weren't even in charge of terrorist cases any more, having reluctantly handed that responsibility over to MI5 when the cold war ended.

'Oh, I've made them promise to call me in when it happens. Until I'm in my grave, I shall be on her case.'

Greg went back to Sullivan's book, leafing through to find the first mention of Aoife. He found it a little over halfway, placed prominently at the start of a new chapter.

I first saw Aoife Cusack in a coffee bar in central Belfast in the spring of 1980. She was just sixteen and in her school uniform, as sweet as a nut. I knew at once that she was the girl for me.

I bet you did, Greg thought: sweet and pure and innocent, and perfect for you to spoil.

I didn't approach her then as she had one of her sisters with her, ugly old trout standing guard and ready to bite my face off. I asked around, found out who she was and engineered a meeting one day when she wasn't chaperoned.

I was a good-looking feller in them days – ask anyone – and when I fell into conversation with her, casual like, I could see she was interested, fiddling with her hair the way girls do and giving me the glad eye.

I needed to know right off that she supported our cause. Her name told she was a Catholic and that her family were probably patriots, it being less common in those days to give children good ethnic Irish names like Aoife, Roisin – that was one of the sisters – or her brother Nessan.

She was politically naive, of course, but she'd seen what the soldiers were doing on the streets, strutting around as if they owned us, with their guns and their shoot-to-kill policy. Insulting good Irish Catholic girls. Her mind was open to education.

And her brain to being washed, Greg thought.

I could see at once that she would be useful to us and the first time I held her in my arms and kissed her I asked her plainly if she would be a Volunteer. Aoife agreed at once; she knew that there were bigger things at stake than our love. She was a good little actress and could fake an English accent like no one I knew.

He didn't actually describe her, Greg noticed, other than as young and sweet: no mention of what colour the hair was that she fiddled with, or if the glad eye were blue or black; how tall she stood against him the first time he kissed her and how well her figure filled that school uniform.

Could it be that Sullivan was protecting her still with his vagueness?

Indira removed her reading glasses and sighed. She got up to make herself a cup of tea, deliberately turning her back on the kitchen table where her textbooks were

74

spread out like a sprawling reproach.

She was sure it had not been so difficult to qualify as a doctor the first time round. Could intellectual decline really be setting in before her thirtieth birthday?

Now she needed British certificates in order to do the job she'd been doing with perfect competence, and confidence, in Mumbai for the past five years. Hundreds of happy, healthy children were not sufficient testimonial to her skills.

She had a recurring dream that she knew was a classic: the exam for which she had not prepared. But Indira's version had one peculiarity: in her dream she had already passed the exam with top marks but, for some reason, had to take it again.

And rationalists claimed dreams were not prophetic!

And where was Deepak? Out again, as he had been every night since the reading at the bookshop in Newbury which had raised so many long-buried feelings in him. Things had been going so well too.

True, her first sight of him three days before the wedding had been a little disappointing: he was short and plump, nothing like the husband she had dreamed of, an Indian Tom Cruise, but his smile had been sweetness itself and, after all those emails, she felt that she knew him.

Besides, she was twenty-nine and acquaintances of her parents had started to ask directly why she wasn't married yet, in the forthright way that people did in India, deeming one family's business to be that of the community. She knew the Mumbai gossips and it would not be long before they were whispering behind their hands to cast doubt on her virginity.

The flat in Newbury was small – less space and comfort than she was used to – and with not a servant in sight, but Deepak was accustomed to bachelorhood and not afraid to cook or even clean – a welcome surprise.

All things considered, she thought herself lucky. Her children would grow up in England – would *be* English –and have all the advantages of the developed world.

To educated Indians, such as Indira, England was a second home, the source of their justice system and democracy – the largest democracy in the world. Her family spoke English as easily as Hindi, albeit with their own accent and inflections. She had been fed a diet of Shakespeare, Dickens, the Brontës and Mrs Gaskell from her early years.

Jane Austen had been her favourite, with that curious mixture of love and self-interest when it came to marriage which seemed so natural to an Indian girl.

She had longed to come to England and had thought to feel at home here in the land of Pope and Thomas Gray, those rigorous eighteenth-century minds who spoke of reason and intellect.

Her youngest brother had tried to warn her. Arun had taken his chemistry degree to a call centre, to the dismay of their parents. There he worked the night shift, fielding calls from customers of a major British insurance company, answering the phone with 'This is Adrian speaking, how may I help you?' and earning twice as much as a schoolteacher.

His training had steeped him in English culture and, even now, he often spent his afternoons watching BBC World on cable so that when a caller said, 'What about that match last night?' he could reply, 'Yeah, that Wayne Rooney. Amazing!' so they wouldn't suspect he wasn't in Surrey.

As she had babbled happily to him about her forthcoming marriage and her move to Newbury, he had told her kindly, in his newly-acquired English accent, 'Don't expect too much, darling. The old world is dying in the filth of its own decadence; the future is Asian.'

She had thought him foolish and idealistic, as if he was still the mop-headed six-year-old she had walked to school.

The kettle boiled and she brewed her tea. Unable to face any more work, she tidied her books away and went to sit in front of the moving pictures of the television. The programme baffled her. A group of people had been placed in a house where they were monitored day and night by cameras and microphones, even in the bathroom. They talked or, more often, bickered or even fought. They had to perform simple tasks and then, every few days, one of them was voted off.

She wondered how people decided which of the contestants they liked least since they all seemed the same to her: loud, angry, vulgar, stupid and lazy.

Growing up in Mumbai, she had been taught at school how Londoners in the eighteenth century used to visit the insane asylum of Bedlam to point and laugh at the inmates; had human nature made no progress in two hundred years?

She could not phone her mother. Quite apart from the fact that it was the middle of the night at home, she knew what her reaction would be.

Do not question your husband; he knows best.

But did he? The affection that had been welling in her since the wedding swelled into terrified love as she grappled with the fear that Deepak might do something truly stupid.

She would see if there was an email from Arun. She logged on to the computer at the desk in the corner and, sure enough, a message was waiting. She clicked it open. As usual, her brother began without salutation.

Have you been to Bath? It's not far from Newbury, I think, although nowhere in your little island is very far. I hear it's very nice, much history. 'World Heritage Site', no less. Last night, I got a call from a man in Bath who wanted to claim for a flood at his house. I felt like asking if his bath had overflowed, but such levity is not encouraged by Mrs Biswas, our dominatrix – sorry, I meant to say esteemed supervisor.

Indira laughed out loud. Dearest Arun; he always cheered her up. How she missed him.

She logged off without replying. She had not been to Bath although Deepak had been promising to take her for months, so that she could see the place where Catherine Morland had first danced with Henry Tilney and Anne Elliot had come to an understanding, at last, with Frederick Wentworth. Her husband did not seem to know who these people were; it seemed that, in England, if you studied science you did not study literature too.

It was only an hour's drive along the motorway but something always cropped up: her mother-in-law needed his handyman skills, such as they were, or he was called into work for overtime or there was a chess tournament. Now he said it would be too full of tourists and they should wait for the autumn.

Although she could drive, she had not yet found the courage to brave the motorway on her own.

Stephen Marchant, after glancing at his balding head in the mirror in the hall, picked up his favourite straw panama and put it on, tilting it to a jaunty angle.

He had never been handsome and middle age had added flab while stealing hair and muscle. If he was honest with himself, his face was that of a giant, pink baby, but it was a happy, gurgling baby and that was the main thing.

'You're not really wearing that hat to mass,' his wife said, laughing. She was standing leaning against the newel post at the foot of the stairs, in her dressing gown.

'Got to keep this unseasonable sunshine off my shining pate,' Stephen said. 'I'll leave it in the car when we get there.'

'Yes, don't want to frighten Father Moike,' she said, mimicking the priest's Limerick accent, unaffected by having spent most of his life in Berkshire.

'Are the children ready?'

'In theory,' Robyn said.

Stephen called up the stairs. 'Charlie, Dom, if you're not down in two minutes we're going without you... No, wait, that's not much of a threat. Just get down here.'

The teenagers came tumbling down the stairs a moment later and their father gave them mock thwacks on the backside with his walking stick as they rushed, shrieking, to the bus.

'Calm down,' Robyn murmured, following them.

'I thought going to mass was meant to be a joyous thing,' Stephen remarked, 'so a pox on solemnity.'

The minibus stood on the gravel with its engine running. Siobhan Fahey and the teenage Marie were already safely belted in, while a wheelchair in the specially adapted rear compartment held a ten-year-old boy named Antonio who suffered from cerebral palsy and who was singing quietly to himself, his head lolling at a typically oblique angle. Every few minutes he would yell something incomprehensible and look to his co-passengers for response.

Dominic climbed in and Marie reached for his hand which she cradled in both of hers.

'Isn't Daniel coming?' Charlie asked.

'He's having a lie-in,' her father said.

'How come he gets to choose and I don't?' she grumbled.

'Because he's an adult. When you're eighteen, you can decide for yourself too. Meantime, your spiritual wellbeing is my responsibility, just like I pay for your grub and your tennis coach.' Stephen clapped her on the shoulder and opened the front passenger door for her. 'Looks like you're riding shotgun today, Charlie.'

'Fine by me.' She lowered her voice. 'Dad,

why does Mum never come to mass with us?'

'Someone's got to mind the shop, even on a Sunday. Your mother goes to Saturday evening service. You know that.'

'Do I?'

'Well, she goes off every Saturday evening,' her father pointed out.

'Might go to the pictures, for all I know.'

'And where in the world would that be with no cinema for miles around?'

Charlie persisted. 'Why can't Siobhan go to Saturday mass one week so Mum can come with us?'

'You ask too many questions, child,' her father said, with a loving smile. 'Now hop in, or we'll be late.'

She did so but now it was he who was dithering. 'To pee or not to pee, that is the question.'

His wife laughed. 'Honestly, Stephen. Get Dr Blaine to look at your prostate.'

'Dr Blaine is not putting his sticky finger up *there*, thanks very much. Be right back.'

He drove away a minute later, acknowledging his wife's farewell wave with a grin.

Chapter Five

Greg and Angie were watching the news at six o'clock that evening, enjoying the sight of hundreds of elderly men setting off to Normandy for the sixtieth anniversary of D-day.

They looked so smart in their blazers and flannels, these brave conscripts who had risked their lives before Greg was born. They had been young then – heart-rendingly so for the sacrifices demanded of them – now they were stooped and withered. He hoped they wouldn't get confused and try to storm the beaches, especially as the German Chancellor was joining the ceremonies for the first time and had probably already left his towel on a lounger.

The doorbell rang. Bellini, their West Highland Terrier bitch, barked, in case they hadn't heard it. Angie jumped up. 'I'll get it.'

'Don't go,' he advised. 'It's bound to be someone canvassing for the elections.'

'Then we shall engage in intelligent political debate,' she laughed. As she left the room he realised that he didn't know if she was going to vote on Thursday or, if so, how; then he realised that he didn't know if *he* was going to vote on Thursday and, if so, how.

He heard her tug the front door open and emit a small cry of dismay. He was at her side in an instant.

Liam Sullivan stood on the doorstep.

'It's all right, love,' he said, pointing at Greg. 'It's himself I was wanting.'

Angie turned away without a word. Bellini, who had followed Greg out of the sitting room, sniffed at Sullivan's ankles then growled.

'Good dog,' Greg said, as Bellini ran away after her mistress. 'How did you know where I live?' he demanded.

Sullivan regarded him as he were half-witted. 'The woman in the village shop called you by name and I looked you up in the phone book.'

'Now see here,' Greg said, jabbing his finger at the man, 'there are laws–'

'No, *you* see here.' Sullivan jabbed back. 'Your mate Gupta is stalking me, if those are the laws you're talking about.'

'What!'

'Everywhere I go, there he is, somewhere nearby.'

'I hardly think so,' Greg said coldly. 'He does have a full-time job, you know, unlike some.'

'Okay,' the Irishman conceded. 'Not during the day. But he's there everywhere I go in the evenings and at weekends. Now there are two

84

ways we can play this, by my reckoning. I can call up my lawyer and we can make a formal complaint of harassment against him at the police station, maybe get him suspended. Or I can talk to you, off the record, and you can have a quiet word with him.'

Greg grimaced. He was well caught. To protect Deep from a whole world of trouble, he was forced to comply with this man's instructions.

'I prefer to do it the easy way,' Sullivan concluded.

'Figure you owe him a small favour, do you?' Greg asked. 'What with having murdered his only sister.'

'Yeah, well.' Did the man look shame-faced for an instant, or was that wishful thinking? 'All's fair in war.'

'An eighteen-year-old schoolgirl counts as a non-combatant in my book,' Greg said.

'At least I didn't try to claim there'd been a miscarriage of justice,' Sullivan said, 'not like a lot of them. I've taken responsibility for my acts and I've served my time. The slate's wiped clean. So I can leave it with you then?'

'I'll see what I can do.' Greg closed the door in his face.

'Has he gone?' Angie called from the kitchen, where she and Bellini had taken refuge.

Well, I wasn't going to ask him in for a cup of tea.' Greg joined her. 'But if you're serious about this project for Dr Sideburns, maybe you should get him to give you an interview.'

'Not today, thanks.'

So, Greg thought, evil wasn't quite so glamorous when it came knocking at your front door.

Outside, Sullivan cast a furtive look back to see if anyone in the house was watching. Angie's hatchback in the drive sported a St George's flag – a red cross on a white background – in support of the England football team in their latest endeavours.

Sullivan reached across and snapped the aerial off with one flick of his fingers, sending the flag into the nearest flower bed.

'Rule Britannia!' he said, and laughed.

Greg had never been to Deepak Gupta's flat but he had no trouble in finding the block, a raw red-brick, three-storey building on an estate where embryo saplings, regularly spaced along the kerbside, attested to its newness. The Guptas were on the first floor and he rang, announced himself and was buzzed in.

Deep was standing at the flat door when he reached the top of the stairs. 'Superintendent,' he said with a note of apprehension. 'To what do I owe this honour?'

He stood aside to let Greg into the living

room. Indira was stacking the dishwasher in the open-plan kitchen, robed in a plum-coloured sari with jewelled sandals and looking even more beautiful than she had at the bookshop. He found himself wondering if Indian women wore knickers under their saris and dragged his thoughts back from the subject with a sharp mental reprimand.

She pressed her hands together and bowed him a *namaste*. He made an awkward bow back and she said, 'Welcome to our home.'

'Can I have a word in private, Deep?' he asked. Indira stopped what she was doing without comment and disappeared through a door into what he assumed was the bed-room, closing it quietly behind her.

Waiting for her departure, Greg took in the neat square room with its pale walls and laminate-wood flooring, its white and stain-less steel kitchen, almost obligatory fittings for new developments these days and, in his view, a little soulless. On the opposite wall hung something more personal – a framed photo of the Guptas' wedding, Deep a little self-conscious in traditional Indian tunic and trousers but with a big grin on his chubby face. Indira looked more solemn, her natural beauty almost eclipsed by the amount of jewellery she had on and the henna symbols that adorned her face and arms.

'I just had a visit from Liam Sullivan,'

Greg began.

'Nice company you keep!'

'He's complaining that you're harassing him, stalking him.'

Deepak stared at him in disbelief, folding his arms across his chest. 'Whose side are you on?'

Greg rubbed his nose in embarrassment. 'Don't do this to yourself, mate. You don't like the fact that he's walking around free? – well, nor do I, but he's done his time and been released. He's keeping it unofficial at the moment, but if he makes a formal complaint we'll have to take it as seriously as we would with anyone else.'

'Not seriously at all, in other words,' Deepak said.

'We do take harassment seriously, Deep, believe me.'

'He got away with murder,' the younger man muttered.

'But he *didn't*. He was caught and tried and convicted. He got sent to jail for nineteen years, from the ages of twenty-six to forty-five.' It was the prime of life, the time when a man was marrying, building a career and bringing up a family. To lose that might not compare with a life lost but nor was it negligible.

'You have to let this go, Deep.'

'The Irish had no quarrel with my sister.' Deepak was almost shouting now, his face ruddy. 'She had not occupied and oppressed them for four hundred years. On the contrary, we Indians were also on the receiving end of British imperialism.'

'You *are* British,' Greg reminded him.

'Am I? I always thought so. Now...'

'What are you hoping to achieve?' Greg asked, when it became clear that Gupta was not going to finish this thought.

'I just wanted to spook him, let him see me wherever he went, remind him that I haven't forgotten.'

'Promise me you won't give him any more cause for complaint, Deep. You're just playing into the vindictive little sod's hands.'

'You have my word,' Deepak said stiffly. 'Now get out.'

Greg let himself out without further comment. He trusted that time would one day heal this wound.

Gupta crossed to the window and watched as Greg left the block of fiats and got into his car without looking up. Behind him, Indira came out of the bedroom and wrapped her arms round his waist.

'You will do as he says, Deepak?' she begged.

'I'll give Sullivan no more cause for complaint.' He extricated himself from her embrace, pushing her gently away. 'Because I'll make sure he doesn't see me.'

Down below, Greg's car drove away. Deep

picked up his keys and left the flat.

Robyn Marchant took her cup of lemon and ginger tea from the microwave and walked towards the sitting room, fumbling in the pocket of her dressing gown for the last cigarette of the day.

Much as she loved everybody at Hilltop, she cherished these nights when she could be alone for an hour or two. Stephen was working, Dominic at school, Daniel back in Oxford, the pupils sleeping in their dormitories. Charlie, who had a county match tomorrow, was asleep upstairs and Siobhan, who was not a night owl, had also retired to bed.

She stopped, aware of a tapping at the back door. It must be someone she knew since strangers always came to the front. She slid back the single bolt and pulled the door open.

A man stood with his back to her, illuminated by the security spotlight his arrival had triggered. It was not a back that she recognised, narrow in its dark shirt.

'Can I help you?'

He turned round and she saw his face clearly.

'Billy!' she gasped. The mug fell from her hands and clattered without breaking across the parquet floor, spilling its sticky contents and sending up a sweet lemon smell.

'Hello, Aoife.'

The Irishman didn't seem to have a car and Deepak, having left his in a nearby close, waited above Wisteria Cottage, melting into the hedgerow when a rare vehicle went past. If he came out at all, then the most likely thing was that he would head down the hill into the village, probably to the pub. He was just as likely to spend the night indoors, as he had for the past two nights, watching TV or working on his new book. Deep gritted his teeth. What would it be next, he wondered? An account of the life of Riley he was leading since his release?

He caught his breath as he heard the back door of the cottage open and shut. The noise of a key being turned was audible, as from a large and old lock, accompanied by a certain amount of cursing. Then a dark-clad figure came out of the drive and turned up the hill towards him.

Deepak pushed his way silently through the hedge, scratching himself and tearing his clothes in the process. Indira would not be pleased to see the silk shirt she had bought him last week come home with rents in the sleeves. He crouched down, watching as Sullivan, oblivious to his presence, walked up the hill. He was whistling, which hardly suggested subterfuge.

Deep gave him a couple of minutes then slipped out after him. There were not many turnings on this road so it would be hard to lose him, unless he was visiting another house in Kintbury.

Sullivan strode out at a good pace, gaining on his pursuer who did not care much for exercise. He looked fit, Deep thought with resentment, no doubt working out in the prison gym. Soon his whistling gave way to singing and Deep caught the words 'Dublin', 'green' and 'Thompson gun'.

Gupta was not a countryman. He'd spent his childhood in Slough, been educated at the University of Sussex in Brighton and lived in Newbury since joining the Thames Valley forensics team six years earlier. He didn't like the countryside – the sinister way the trees swayed above you, even on a still night, the inexplicable sounds of birds and small mammals going about their nightly business.

At Kintbury Crossways, he thought that he'd lost his quarry. He stood for a moment, glancing in both directions for an idea of his route. A small voice in his head said that it was no bad thing, that he should go home, make love to his beautiful wife, stay out of trouble.

He didn't want to tackle Sullivan, to beat him up. He wouldn't stand a chance against such a man and what physical punishment was adequate revenge for a sister blown to pieces? So what was his purpose? He supposed it was the hope of catching the man in some illegal act and sending him back to jail where he belonged. As he was out on licence, it didn't have to be anything major.

As he stood uncertainly, he heard singing from up the hill to his right, the Inkpen road. On an airless night it floated back to him. *Every man will stand behind the men behind the wire.* So that was where he'd got the title for his book, some terrorist song.

Deep hurried up the hill, holding his trouser pockets against his thighs to still the rattle of loose change and keys. Thank goodness he didn't have to do this for a living as he was no bloody good at it.

He reached the top of the hill short of breath and stopped under an oak to recover. A hundred yards ahead, his quarry came to a halt, reading the name on a gatepost, then glanced back. Deep lost himself in the gnarled trunk of the tree. The singing had stopped.

Sullivan walked without attempt at concealment into the drive. Darting after him, Deep saw a huge house, almost a mansion. Not pausing to discover its name or business, he followed the Irishman in, waiting in the shadow of the wall to see him make his way round to the back of the house, ignoring the imposing front door.

There were lights on in some of the windows and Deep had a sudden dread of having to explain himself to an outraged householder. Asians were rare in Inkpen and he would be viewed with suspicion.

Making himself as small as possible, he ran practically on all fours round the side of the house, dimly aware of lush lawns, even a tennis court.

An oblong of light fell suddenly on to the path as a door opened. Luckily the house was the overwrought, Victorian sort with alcoves, and he found shelter.

He thought he heard a sharp intake of breath, an exclamation, then Sullivan spoke in his distinctive accent.

'Hello, Aoife.'

As the Irishman passed into the house, Deepak reeled away, his brain unable to process what it had heard, telling him only that he must flee before the unthinkable. He ran as fast as his stubby legs would take him out of the grounds. He got half a mile down the road towards Kintbury, when a stitch forced him to rest. Momentum gone, he was violently sick on the grass verge.

He walked more sedately back to his car, the taste of vomit in his mouth. He leaned his forehead against the metal of the car roof to cool it.

He heard a voice say, 'Can I help you?' in that peculiarly English way which means, 'You have no business to be here.' A middle-aged woman with a Pekinese was glaring at him. The dog growled, then snapped and he thought the woman would have liked to do so too.

'Call of nature. Sorry. You know how it is.' He unlocked the car as the woman sniffed disapproval.

He drove down to the A4 and the road back to Newbury. He stopped at the Halfway Inn for a pint of bitter, taking the opportunity to swill his mouth out with water in the Gents. He downed his beer in one gulp and drove home.

He was out of his depth now.

'I heard you were out,' Robyn said, 'but for some reason I didn't expect to see you.' She searched again for the cigarette she now craved, fumbling it out of its packet and lighting it with trembling hands.

'Dirty habit, Aoife. I thought better of you. When did you take that up?' She didn't answer and Sullivan made himself at home in the best armchair, stretching his legs out to the grate, crossing his feet in trainers at the ankles. He watched as she almost dropped her box of matches, a calm smile on his face.

'Didn't think I'd come looking for you, Aoife?'

'Don't keep calling me that. Aoife is dead. I've been Robyn for more than half my life.' She pulled feverishly on the cigarette and wondered why she'd ever switched to menthol when she hated the medicinal taste of it.

'You talk like an Englishwoman. You were always good at passing yourself off as one, I remember, allaying suspicion.'

'I am an Englishwoman.'

'You were always a grand actress.'

'I'm not acting. This is who I am.' She gave up on the cigarette, pinching it out and throwing it into the empty grate. 'How did you find me?'

'You remember Jackie Dolan?' She nodded. 'He saw you in Reading four months back with a handful of spaz kids.' She winced at the adjective but he took no notice. 'Gave him quite a surprise. He followed you back here, asked a few casual questions in the village, gave me a ring. Why d'you think I came to this part of the world, Aoife? Coincidence?'

'I've done nothing to you, Billy.'

'Nothing? You betrayed me, Aoife.'

'I didn't. I never did.'

'I thought you loved me and you skipped out on me three days before I was arrested and you want me to believe you had no part in that betrayal?'

'As God is my witness.' They stared at each other for a moment and neither blinked. He found that he believed her, although he didn't want to.

'Then why did you go?' he asked softly. 'I thought we had something, you and me.'

'I was little more than a child, Billy. You turned my head. You talked about my patriotic duty and I fell for it, because I'd fallen for you, and it cost me everything – my parents, my brother and sisters, my self-respect, my very identity.'

'You know that your father died of shame, that your mother and brother and sisters hate you for it?'

She flinched. 'I know it.'

'You read my book?' She hesitated. 'You have, haven't you? You wouldn't be able to help yourself.'

'I've looked at it.'

'And is it how you remember?'

'Mostly, I try not to remember.'

'And *Mr* Marchant?' he asked, after a pause. 'Where is he tonight?'

'Antwerp,' she said reluctantly, 'on business.'

'Not in the police any more then, or is he Interpol?'

'What?' She blinked uncertainly. 'I don't understand.'

'Am I right in thinking he's our old friend Malcolm Fraser?'

'Francis, you mean!' She was stunned into nervous laughter. 'Where d'you get that idea?' She waved her hand over their surroundings and he heard something of the old Belfast in her voice. 'Where d'you think Francis would've got the money for this place?'

He was disappointed. 'But you were sleeping with him.'

'I was not so, ugly little runt. Not that he wouldn't have fast enough. He could see I was having doubts, after Windsor, after I saw the photos in the paper of those dead people, one of them just a girl, a few months older than myself–'

'A Paki,' he sneered. 'What was she even doing in a pub? I thought it was against their religion.'

Distaste was written on her face. 'She was Indian, not Pakistani, a Hindu.'

'Same difference. Who cares?'

'Her name was Sangita. She was eighteen and about to take her A levels. She wanted to be a doctor.'

'Well, someone's been doing her homework.'

'It was in the papers.' Whenever Robyn thought of that day, which was as seldom as possible, it was Sangita's face she saw, happy and carefree in that bar with her friend.

'It was the way you were laughing, Billy, outside the castle, while people were screaming ... Francis talked to me, persuaded me to take off while...'

'While you had the chance?' Sullivan finished for her. 'While there was still time?

You knew he was *polis* and you bailed out without telling me.'

She shook her head. 'I would have told you he was Special Branch if I'd known. I swear. He said we were living on borrowed time, all of us, that the police were closing in, that it was too late for him and you and the rest of the boys but that I should save myself. I went without a word because I knew you'd never let me go.'

'Isn't that the truth! Does Mr Marchant know?' When she didn't reply, he looked her up and down, insolent, and laughed softly.

'You're still a fine-looking woman, Aoife.'

'Robyn,' she reminded him coldly, pulling the collar of her robe more tightly to her neck, her finger lingering on the ever-present crucifix, but taking no comfort from it tonight. 'I've rebuilt my life and I've done everything within my power to atone for my sins.'

'It looks like a nice enough life to me – big house, manicured gardens, lovely family. Is that your idea of atonement – playing Lady Bountiful with a load of cripples?'

She smiled ruefully. 'That's the irony, I suppose. I love what I do, helping the kids, making a difference to their lives. It's been no sort of punishment. I admit that.'

'So where is Fraser?'

'How on earth should I know? I heard tell he moved to Canada but that was just something I read in the paper so it's probably a red herring.'

He yawned and stretched. 'Shame you don't know where he is, since he's the bastard I'd really like to make pay for the nineteen years I spent in that shithole. I guess I'll have to make do with you...

'Aoife.'

Chapter Six

Robyn was working at the computer in her office the following morning, when she heard the sound of the children being released from class for their morning break. A smile spread involuntarily over her face and, despite the fear she had been nursing through a largely sleepless night, she saved the document she was working on and went out to watch the play, letting herself out of the back door.

She almost collided with an improbably fat man who was coming round the corner, wearing a dark suit. Like many obese people, he had a delicate tread and she hadn't heard his approach. The first thing she saw was his well-polished black lace-ups on size thirteen feet.

She let out a shriek. 'Who are you? What

do you want?'

'I'm sorry. I didn't mean to startle you.' He spoke with a strong Berkshire accent and an unexpectedly high voice, which might have been comical had she been in any mood to be amused. 'I was going to ring the front doorbell when I heard voices round here.'

He glanced nervously at the children whose attention had been caught by Robyn's cry. 'I'm canvassing for Britain Out Now.' He indicated his black lapel badge on which the letters BON were etched in white. In his hand was a sheaf of yellow fliers with bold print and lots of exclamation marks.

'Britain out...' Robyn repeated stupidly. It reminded her of the graffiti at home in Belfast when she was growing up: Brits Out.

'For the European elections,' he added, losing heart at her incomprehension. 'Today. For the European parliament. You *are* registered to vote?'

'Um. Yes. I didn't realise...'

'We're asking you to vote for the BON party,' he went on, 'to work for withdrawing our country from the EU and keeping it free and independent.' His tiny voice swelled with pride. 'The way it has been for a thousand years.'

'Sure, and that makes no sense at all.' Siobhan Fahey's tone was scathing, joining them, casting a worried look at Robyn. 'If you don't hold with the EU, then why would

101

you want to get elected to their parliament?' As he tried to reply, she added, 'Getting on the bloody gravy train, that's all, just like the rest of them. Get out. You're frightening the children.'

In fact, most of the children were watching the scene with considerable interest and, as the fat man glanced at them again, it was obvious that he was a lot more scared of them than they were of him.

Marie grinned at him and crossed her legs, showing an expanse of plump, pink thigh.

'Perhaps I could leave you some of our literature,' he suggested, as he began to retreat. He held out some fliers to the two women but neither of them responded. 'Bye, now,' he said and left as fast as his bulk would allow.

Robyn sank down on the nearest bench and buried her head in her hands. 'I thought he was the police.'

'Him?' Siobhan sat beside her. 'I don't see him chasing criminals or climbing over walls. Not enough puff.'

'Not that sort of policeman. Special Branch, or whoever it is now.'

'Not unless they've got desperate lately. You're very jumpy all of a sudden.'

Robyn raised her head. '...I had a visitor last night.' Siobhan went very still, asking no questions. Robyn said, 'It was Billy Sullivan.'

'Jesus Christ! What did he want?'

She shrugged hopelessly. 'Revenge.'

'On you? Seems to me you're the one should be wanting revenge.'

'That's not how he sees it.'

'When did Billy Sullivan ever see anything straight? Whatever he says, you do the opposite and you can't go far wrong. What's he threatening?'

'The worst thing of all – exposure.'

'Ah, it's just blether!'

'It's like 1981 all over again – I jump out of my skin every time the phone rings, every time there's a knock at the door. I can't live that way again.'

They sat in silence for a moment, then Siobhan asked, 'Any progress on the confession front?'

Robyn shook her head. 'I didn't even make it into the box this time. What's the point in getting Father Moike all worked up?'

'You could try going to London, to somewhere anonymous like Westminster Cathedral or the Brompton Oratory. That might be easier.'

'It's not that,' Robyn said. 'That isn't the problem.'

'You're harder on yourself than anyone else. Harder far than God will be. What's holding you back?'

'I haven't atoned enough yet ... I told Stephen I went. Was that wrong?'

'Not if it sets his mind at rest.'

'The Oratory. I was married there.'

'I know.'

'I wish you could have been there.'

Siobhan reached out a hand and stroked her employer's hair, feeling it fluff out under her fingers as if full of electricity. 'We've held on this long and we'll not give up now, child, not without a fight.'

'Oh, Siobhan.' Robyn let her head relax into the older woman's hand. 'How would I manage without you?'

'You won't have to, my angel.' Siobhan smiled reassurance and uttered the old Irish blessing.

'May you be in heaven an hour before the devil knows you're dead.'

When the break had ended and Siobhan had shooed the children back indoors like a strict dog, Robyn returned to the office. She sat in thought for a while then got up and closed the door, turning the key in the lock. She crossed to the filing cabinet and opened the third drawer down, searching under P until she found a sheet of paper which contained only the words 'Pest control' and a mobile number.

She dialled, fumbling for the numbers with clumsy fingers. It answered after the first ring.

A non-committal voice said, 'Aoife?'

She almost dropped the receiver but managed to stutter, 'How did you know it was me?'

'You're the only person who has this number. This phone is only for you.'

'I need help,' she said. 'I'm in big trouble. I'm so afraid.'

Three minutes later, she slammed the receiver down with a pained cry of, 'No!' The phone call she had deliberated so long, which was to have been her salvation, had left her more upset and confused than before.

Indira drove with care in Deepak's bright blue hatchback, sitting hunched forward over the steering wheel. The traffic jams were not as bad in Newbury as in Mumbai but she was still finding her way around and had more than once got lost on the inner ring road and found herself circling the town twice before she located the right route off.

At least there were no rickshaws, although the cyclists seemed as careless of the rules of the road and as inconsiderate of other road-users as the ones at home.

Today she was heading for the Savemore supermarket which was on an industrial estate on the outskirts of Newbury. She preferred it to the shops in the town centre as it was easy to park. She reached the car park, backed cautiously into a space near the entrance and selected the smallest trolley from the three different types.

A young woman jostled her as she negotiated the revolving door and did not apologise.

She was in no hurry. When she had fetched the groceries, she would spend half an hour cleaning. The flat was so tiny that that was all it took. Then she would do some more studying until it was time to prepare her lunch – Deepak did not come back in the middle of the day – then more study.

At home she would be on the wards now, at the clinic, doing her rounds of the sick children. Younger and less experienced doctors would be hanging on her words, asking her advice. Nurses and orderlies would jump to her commands with a respectful 'Yes, Dr Buhpathi. At once, Dr Buhpathi.'

She sighed as she looked at the displays of fruit and vegetables near the door, everything so pristinely perfect and lacking in flavour or scent, much of it wrapped in plastic so you could hardly tell if it was ripe.

She put two aubergines in her trolley and a mango, then lost heart.

She glanced round the shop. She felt like an alien here. Never, in all her dreams of England, had she imagined finding herself so lost in a sea of white faces, so disturbed. It was not that they were hostile; mostly they were indifferent, their eyes sliding over her and away.

She was beginning to understand why so

many of her countrymen congregated in ghettos.

There was air-conditioning, full blast, making her shiver.

She could see two other Asian women steering trolleys up and down the aisles, one of them deftly manoeuvring a double buggy at the same time, twin boys smiling out in identical t-shirts. But they were both dressed in Western clothes and looked as if they belonged here, like Deepak.

Fifteen minutes later, with her trolley barely a quarter full, she made her way to the checkout. The girl said 'Good morning' to her brightly, then, hearing her accent, began to speak more slowly and – or did she imagine it? – more loudly. 'Do. You. Need. Help. With. Your. Packing?'

She shook her head, reaching for the plastic bags, fumbling to prise them open. 'I am fine, thank you.' As her purchases rolled down the conveyor belt she crammed them at random into the bags, wanting to be out of there. She gave the girl her new credit card, the one that Deepak had added to his own account, and signed her name, remembering that she was now a Gupta and not a Buhpathi.

Buhpathi was a better name, not so common.

The girl told her that she should be sure to have a nice day. Indira tried to smile as she headed for the exit door which opened before her with a swish.

She knew that the feeling of alienation came from inside herself and was not the fault of Newbury, of the checkout girl, of the other shoppers. As a doctor, she suspected that she was sliding into depression, but her training as a paediatrician had left her with scant knowledge of the illness or its remedies and she could not face the GP and his brisk sympathy.

Deepak was thirty-two and had a complete life here. His widowed mother lived half an hour's drive away along the motorway. He had his job, his colleagues, plenty of friends to go to the pub with. His life was now her life, his family hers, but he didn't seem to understand that she had had a life in Mumbai, one she had freely given up to marry him, that it had been a sacrifice.

So many people had been part of her daily life in India. As well as Arun, there had been her two older brothers with their wives and children, then all the aunties and uncles and cousins. Okay, so they sometimes drove her crazy – especially the aunties – but now she missed their constant interest, the stream of gossip.

All she had were emails to Arun most days and a once-a-week report to her father, her mother refusing to have anything to do with the Internet.

She opened the boot of the car and put

her bags in. She felt slightly faint and could not face getting into the stuffy interior at that moment, negotiating the baffling roads. She locked up and walked out of the car park on to the pavement, glancing to left and right along the concrete expanses of the trading estate before selecting a direction at random. She passed a DIY superstore, an electrical retailer, some office blocks, seeing nothing, her stride steady.

She did not return for more than an hour. The ice cream she had bought – Deepak had an ice cream addiction – had melted all over the boot.

'I love this time of year,' Robyn said, 'when it doesn't get dark till half past nine and the children can run around and play. And the evenings are perfect in this hot weather.'

She sighed and Siobhan glanced at her. They were sitting on a bench in the garden, watching as the younger children played simple ball games and the older ones watered the flower beds. A fourteen-year-old boy named Dylan who suffered from crippling epilepsy was having fun with a hose, spraying as much water over Marie as over the earth, to her squealing delight.

The two women kept a close eye on them, knowing how quickly such boisterousness could turn to tears and, with Dylan, a near-fatal seizure.

'Will Stephen make it over to Chiswick to watch Charlie play on Friday?' Siobhan asked.

'He's sworn he'll be there and I believe him. It'd take the sinking of the Titanic to keep him at his desk when his baby girl's strutting her stuff on the tennis court.'

'You must be so proud of her,' Siobhan said.

'Of both my children. Siobhan ... if I can't go on ... if something happens so I can't continue to run the school, promise me that you will stay and keep it going.'

'Haven't I always done everything you've asked of me, at whatever cost to myself?' There was no sourness in the older woman's voice, only love. 'But it won't come to that. He's playing with you, child, as a cat plays with a mouse, for his own sadistic pleasure. He has no reason to denounce you.'

'Since when does he need a reason?'

'If he was going to turn you in he'd have done it by now.'

Robyn shook her head. 'You don't know Billy like I do. In the old days, when he ordered a punishment beating or a kneecapping, he'd let the victim know days in advance, so they could have the full terror of anticipation. Then, if they tried to run for it, he'd have James and Mickey waiting for them at the airport or the docks or the border and the beating would be twice as bad.'

110

'Why did you ever get involved with such a man?'

The younger woman's eyes filled briefly with tears. 'I thought I was in love... I've been thinking. What if I were to tell him about Daniel?'

Siobhan went very still. 'You can't do that, Robyn.'

'It might make him think twice about turning me in to the authorities. He might feel some sense of responsibility, a recognition that he owes him something.'

'You're assuming that he's a human being with normal human reactions. Haven't you learned better by now?'

'He's an Irishman – he has a sentimental streak a mile wide. I can't go to prison, Orla. I couldn't face it when I was seventeen and I sure as hell can't face it now.'

'It's been years since I heard that name,' Siobhan said. 'It hardly seems to belong to me any more.'

Robyn laughed bitterly. 'There's a lot of things we thought we'd put years behind us.'

'Think what the truth would do to Daniel. Then Stephen would be bound to find out, after all these years.'

'I think there's nothing Stephen wouldn't forgive.'

Chaos erupted at that moment as Dylan turned the hose up to maximum and drenched Marie. This was not, in itself, a

111

problem but Marie's response was to remove all her clothes, causing the younger children to collapse in hysterical laughter, pointing and shrieking as Marie paraded her adolescent body up and down, her substantial breasts a source of pride to her.

By the time Robyn and Siobhan had restored order, the sun was setting and it was the children's bedtime. The two women walked slowly back into the house, but did not resume their conversation.

'I'll see to the children and then I'm for bed myself,' Siobhan said, and started up the stairs.

'Daniel's my trump card.' Robyn looked up at her. 'And I won't play it unless I'm forced to.'

After twenty-three years that dreadful day was still fresh in Deep's nightmares, and that night he was forced to revisit it.

He had come home from his after-school chess club and – anything to put off the evil hour of homework – switched on the early evening news. In the kitchen next door, he could hear his mother preparing supper, smell the gradual merging of spices.

Was he the only person who experienced the sense of smell in dreams? He had tried asking other people but they looked at him so strangely that he soon gave it up.

It had been the top story of the day. A

bomb had exploded in a crowded pub in Windsor, killing six on a fine summer's day. No one had yet claimed responsibility but there seemed little doubt that it was the work of the IRA.

Deepak was young enough to be excited by such events so close to home. He knew that Sangita had gone into Windsor that day with Rachel and he envisaged the stories she would tell over supper. She would claim to have been much closer to the carnage that she truthfully was. She would say she had heard the distant explosion and known it at once for a bomb. His mother would cover her face with her scarf and exclaim in her guttural accent, 'No more, Sangita, no more to speak of such things!'

His father came in from work, calling a cheerful greeting to his wife and son as he went to wash before his meal. Deepak's stomach was rumbling and dinner was ready, but they waited for Sangita.

And waited.

And then the doorbell rang and it was two policemen, or rather a policeman and a policewoman. His mother had been mortified, terrified that the neighbours would see the white and red car outside and assume the worst.

That was before they were told the worst.

That night he slept in his parents' bed – nine years old though he was – curled

113

between them into a tight ball of misery which began in his empty stomach – none of them had been able to eat a bite of the lovingly prepared meal – and radiated out through every organ and every limb.

To live through it once was bad enough. Why did he have to relive it in his dreams? How could nature be so cruel?

'Hello, Aoife.' An Irish voice echoed round his head. Two words that had devastated him anew. A name that aroused so much hate in him that he thought that his skin could not contain it. He had been back to the house on the hill, pausing outside in his car. Some sort of private school, by the look of it.

There would be a number of women there so how could he know which was the right one when he had seen nothing of her the other night? She must be about forty; that was all he knew.

For a long time after losing his sister he had thought that nothing could truly hurt him again. Until tonight, arriving home long after Indira had gone to bed, he'd been idly toying with the computer and had found a copy of an email she'd sent to her brother two days earlier.

You were right, dearest Arun, and I have made a terrible mistake.

Deep knew when he was dreaming – he always had – but that didn't mean that he could wake himself up and end the torment.

'So how did the training go today?' Robyn asked her daughter on the evening of Thursday, the seventeenth of June.

'Not bad. Never as good as I hope.'

'Well, you don't want to peak too soon.' Robyn gathered Charlie in her arms and pressed her close until the girl squirmed – embarrassed, like most adolescents, by too overt a display of parental affection. Robyn would not release her, however. 'Have I ever told you,' she said, 'how much I love you and how proud I am of you?'

'Aw, Mum! Stop it.'

'Whatever happens. I want you to remember that.'

Charlie managed to break away at last, her face pink.

'Well,' she said with an attempt at casual, 'I'm going to get a hot bath and an early night. Tomorrow's the most important day of my life.'

'Yes,' her mother sighed when the child had gone. 'It may well be.'

Siobhan came lightly down the back stairs. Bedtime for the children was the best part of her day, policing the controlled mayhem of the dormitories, hearing their prayers or reading them stories, making sure they were not too hot or too cold and had brushed their teeth.

When it was over and all lights out she felt a sense both of satisfaction and anti-climax. If Stephen or the Marchant children were home then she would retire to her room, watch a little TV or, more likely, read; but when Robyn was alone she would join her for a last cup of tea and they would mull over the doings of the day and the plans for the morrow.

As she reached the bottom of the stairs she heard Robyn speaking and wondered if Stephen had come home unexpectedly as he sometimes did. It warmed her heart to see how that man loved his wife. Then she realised that it was only one voice and that her employer must be on the telephone.

It was late for a parent to ring.

She waited in the hall, not wanting to intrude, but couldn't help but hear.

'I must see you,' Robyn was saying. 'There's something I have to tell you – something important. Can you come up tonight, late, like last time?'

Then, like a splash of cold water on Siobhan's face.

'Please, Billy.'

Chapter Seven

Charlie was too excited to sleep, which annoyed her. An astonishingly rational child – her father liked to tell people she'd been born aged forty-five – she knew that she needed to be rested if she was to play her best tennis tomorrow.

She found herself glancing continually at the digital glow of the clock radio, counting the minutes off one by one.

There was a tickle in her throat which might herald the onset of a cold but was more probably nerves. She tried to do a relaxation exercise her coach had taught her, but her mind kept drifting.

She had two great dreams, both of which depended on her winning her crucial qualifying match: the first saw her holding aloft the winner's trophy for the girls' tournament at Wimbledon in three weeks' time; the second saw her shaking hands with her hero, Martina Navratilova.

She admired Martina for so many reasons: because she had transformed the women's game; because she'd left her mother and stepfather in Czechoslovakia to defect to the West at the age of only nineteen, not knowing if she would ever see them again; because she had been open about her sexuality, even when she feared it might cost her her longed-for American citizenship.

In her fantasies, Martina was telling her that she was the most promising player she'd seen in years. She was offering to take personal charge of her training...

Only her bloody mother would probably put the kibosh on that too.

It was no good. She'd drained the glass of water on her bedside table, but still her throat tickled. The clock read 22:15. That was part of the problem – that she had gone to bed too early. She should have sat up with her mother, exhausted herself.

She slid out from under the duvet and padded barefoot down the stairs. The light was on in their sitting room – hardly surprising since her mother, a famous insomniac, never went to bed before the small hours. She poked her head round the door to report her sore throat, hopefully to receive comfort, reassurance – and lozenges, just in case.

The room was empty.

She stepped inside. Her mother's favourite armchair was placed where it always was, by the fireside, but turned to give a view of the gardens. The standard lamp glowed, the sole light in the room, on to where she should be sitting. Her current book lay face down on the arm, as if abandoned in a hurry. Charlie

118

had a vision for a second of the *Mary Celeste*, deserted in the midst of everyday life, without explanation. Foolish, she knew, since it was obvious that her mother had stepped into the garden to enjoy the night air, fragrant at the end of another hot and humid day.

She had not bothered to put her slippers on but the path from the french windows to the herb garden, her mother's favourite haunt, was grass, just clipped a little shorter than the rest of the lawn. She didn't hesitate to step out, making her way to the gap in the privet hedge that separated the lawn from the herb garden.

At the gap, she turned and looked back at the house, the only home she had ever known. There were lights on here and there – one in Siobhan's room, one in the dormitory where Marie slept with two other girls of similar age.

She coughed, not wanting to startle her mother, and stepped through the hedge, but there was no one there, only the familiar regimented ranks of sweet basil, tarragon, oregano, rosemary, dill, chives, interleaved with rows of jolly marigolds, yellow and orange.

In the centre of the garden stood a sundial, more ornament than use, since the shade of the external wall fell on it for half the day.

The sky was cloudless but there was no moon. Orion, rearing in the sky, his belt glittering, was the brightest thing. As Charlie grew accustomed to the starlight and could see, like a latecomer at the cinema, she realised that a dark shape was lying on the ground beside the sundial.

At first she took it for a bag of garden rubbish left half full but then she remembered that old Rodger, who came to help with the gardening three times a week, had taken all the refuse to the farthest reaches of the grounds that morning and lit one of his massive bonfires, the white smoke swirling out over the downs like a papal election.

She walked across to investigate.

For a moment, she hardly recognised her mother, as she lay on her back. The animation she had known in her face was gone, as was the gentle light of her eyes which stared blankly at the velvet sky.

Gone, too, the restless energy of a woman who spent the day on the move, giving to others.

Charlie didn't scream, although she permitted herself a sharp intake of the night air. Nor did she call out her mother's name in anguish. She knelt beside her and placed a finger against her neck. The absence of a pulse did not surprise her. She'd done first aid at school, but knew from the coolness of her mother's skin that she was beyond help. The soap-scented warmth that had been part of her life since babyhood in frequent hugs and snuggles had fled.

She rose, aware of something wet seeping through the cloth of her pyjama bottom, too sticky for dew. She wiped her knee with her hand and raised her finger to her face, smelling the faintly metallic scent of blood. She could see now that her mother lay in a small puddle on the grass, confined to her top half, below her back.

She stood in shock, her mind waiting for her body to recover and obey its commands, to move her legs back to the house and whatever help was now to be had. It did not occur to her that she might be in danger, that the perpetrator of this evil might be waiting to claim a second victim.

On the other side of the wall, a car accelerated, skidding slightly on the corner as it sped off towards Ham.

It was enough. She spun round, peering into the sinister shadows but seeing nothing. She walked stiffly back through the hedge. Her senses seemed unnaturally alert and she saw that Marie's light had gone off, no doubt at a chiding from the matron.

She went in at the french windows and to the kitchen, picked up the phone and dialled.

It didn't occur to her to seek the help of an adult, of Siobhan. She knew what had to be done.

As she began to speak, she realised that the tickle in her throat had gone. And that she was shaking uncontrollably.

The 999 call came in shortly before ten-thirty that night and was routed to Newbury since Hungerford police station, the nearest, kept office hours.

A teenage girl, the operator realised, reverting to little more than a child in this moment of high drama, struggling for coherence.

'Please help me. My mother ... she's dead.'

The voice tailed off and the operator could hear her struggling not to cry. She said, 'Give me your name and address, dear... In your own time. Take a deep breath.'

'Charlotte ... Marchant. Hilltop House. Inkpen.'

'Is there a street name?... Hello?'

'It's called Folly Road but it's not well marked. When you turn up from Kintbury Crossways, it's a few yards along on your left... She's in the garden.' She gulped. 'There's no pulse and there's blood on the grass.'

'You've done very well,' the operator said. 'I'll send an ambulance too. Please return to your mother and wait. Try not to touch anything and don't let anyone else near. Is there another adult there? Your father?'

Charlie hung up without replying.

A patrol car was there in twelve minutes: two uniformed officers, Tom Reilly and Sharon Moore. They were old hands and one look told them that Robyn Marchant was past medical help. No pulse, no heartbeat, all bleeding ceased. They radioed for CID and closed off the crime scene.

'Some sort of boarding school,' Sharon said, looking at the vast building, its gothic gables looming in the starlight. 'We'll want to keep the kids indoors. They're bound to wake up with all the kerfuffle and they don't need to see this.'

Tom crossed to the teenage girl who was sitting on the back doorstep, looking very young in a pair of blue pyjamas like a tracksuit, her feet bare.

'Are you Charlotte?' he asked gently.

'Charlie. Yes.' She looked up at him. 'You'll forgive me for not getting up. I don't think I can.'

'And that's your mother?'

'Yes. Robyn.'

He sat down next to her. She was shaking and he wished he could put his arm round her but that sort of physical reassurance had been deemed inappropriate for many years.

'Are you cold?' He began to unfasten his jacket for her but she said, 'No. Not cold.'

'You're being very brave,' he said. 'Is your father home?' She shook her head. 'He works in London and he stays up there three nights a week. We have a flat in the Barbican.'

'So who was in charge here?'

'Mum.' She gestured in the direction of

the herb garden. 'I wouldn't normally be here – I'm at boarding school in Bristol – but I have a vital play-off match in Chiswick tomorrow...'

'Match?'

'Tennis. I was hoping for a wildcard for Wimbledon juniors.' She began to cry at last, either because of her dead mother or the lost opportunity. Even she wasn't sure.

Tom gave her his handkerchief. 'What time did you see her last?' he asked.

'About nine.' She rubbed the white cotton across her red eyes. 'We had some herbal tea together and I went to get a bath and an early night. Mum's not a good sleeper. She usually sits up reading till at least midnight, tiring herself out.'

'So what made you come down again?' In the distance Tom could hear sirens, probably the ambulance. Charlie would have to go over it all again with CID but he was curious.

'I was too excited to sleep and my throat was tingly so I came down for a Strepsil.' She was speaking mechanically, almost by rote, the only way she could keep control. 'The light was on in our sitting room so I looked in to say good-night again to Mum but she wasn't there. The french windows were open so I thought she'd stepped out for some air.'

'So you went after her.' Tom looked at her bare feet, dirty from the gravel, a smear of dried blood on one big toe, more on the

124

knee of her pyjamas. Poor kid, he thought, sitting here in her mother's blood. They would need her clothes, but that could wait till Barbara arrived.

She answered him. 'I walked into the herb garden, which she said was her favourite place in all the world. At first I thought she wasn't there and I was about to leave, but then my eyes got accustomed to the dark and ... there she was, on the ground.'

'Did you touch her?'

She shuddered. 'I felt for a pulse. I couldn't see any wound on her, you see. It was as if she was just lying there. I thought she might be playing a game with me, then I saw that there was blood on the grass beneath her.'

Tom had also seen the blood, seeping from under the body, not a great deal of it. He thought that it must have been a quick death and there had been a serene look on her face as if she had died happy. He'd seen many worse corpses.

The ambulance turned in at the gate at that moment, killing its siren as it did so. He saw Sharon walk across to them. There probably wasn't a lot of point in their hanging around: it would be hours before the body could be moved.

'Thing is...' Charlie said.

'What?'

She made to answer him, 'There was a man, late one night...' but a new figure erupted from the house, a thin woman in a paisley dressing gown and slippers who stared at the mayhem around her in disbelief.

'What the hell is going on here?' she snapped.

Tom rose and she shrank back a little at the sight of his uniform. He said, 'And you are?'

'Siobhan Fahey. I'm the matron here.'

Tom glanced at Charlie. 'You didn't think to wake her?' She shrugged. 'I'm sorry to tell you, Miss Fahey–'

'Mrs.'

'–that a body has been found in the garden.' Barbara Carey's car pulled off the road at that moment and he apologised, hurrying over to brief her.

'Body?' Siobhan said weakly.

Charlie answered her. 'It's Mum. She's been murdered.'

Siobhan threw her head back and let out a wail of despair.

'No-o-o-o!'

Chapter Eight

'So who've we got?' Greg asked Barbara, shortly after eleven. As his house was only two miles away, he had been there within five minutes of her call.

'Dr Chubb's certified death and left.'

'Already! What is he, jet-propelled?' Greg demanded.

'He says it's his wedding anniversary and that his wife's waiting at home in a teddy.'

'That's an image I won't get out of my head in a hurry.' Greg remembered Amanda Chubb as a pneumatic woman, to the point where he'd wondered if plastic surgery was the good doctor's hobby and if he practised on his wife. 'Did he estimate a time of death?' he asked.

'Only that she hadn't been dead long, probably less than half an hour before she was found.'

'That's something.'

'SOCO are on their way. Andy's looking after the adolescent daughter. She found her mother's body.'

'Ouch!'

'Yeah, I know. Andy thought it best to call her GP out, just in case.'

'Good thinking.'

'I couldn't get hold of Nick and he's not technically on call tonight. He knew the victim, of course.'

'Did he?'

'That talk you arranged.'

'Didn't I delegate that to you?'

'And I delegated it to Nick.'

'I see ... I feel they deserved better.'

'That's not fair, sir. Mrs Marchant rang

me that afternoon to say what a good job he'd done.'

'Okay.' He held his hands up in surrender. 'My bad.' This was an expression he'd picked up from Angie who'd got it from an American television programme she favoured. In theory, he disapproved of it; in practice, it seemed useful.

'And you knew her too,' Barbara added.

'Not to say *knew*. I'd met her once, at the Easter fund raising. Knew *of* her, of course. She's something of a local celebrity. People say she's virtually a saint.'

'Well, somebody didn't like her,' Barbara said.

'I'll talk to the daughter while you keep an eye on things out here.' He hesitated. 'Aren't you due off on holiday tomorrow?'

'Yes, sir.'

'When's your flight?'

'Saturday morning. I'm meeting Trevor at Gatwick airport at nine o'clock.'

'But you have Friday booked off too?'

'Shopping, washing, packing.'

'Okay,' Greg said, which left her none the wiser.

Detective Constable Andy Whittaker was sitting with Charlie at the kitchen table. He had brewed tea and he and the girl were drinking in comfortable silence. She'd changed into a tracksuit, yielding up the pyjamas she'd been wearing at the crime scene to Barbara. She had a blanket draped round her shoulders, despite the warmth of the night, and her eyes seemed wide with shock under the single fluorescent light, focussing upon her mug as if drinking tea required great concentration.

Andy was a tall, well-built man in his late twenties and his presence was a reassuring one for the girl.

'Is that tea still hot?' Greg asked.

'Yes, sir.' Andy rose to pour him a cup. White, no sugar. 'This is Miss Marchant,' he added.

'Charlie,' she said and glanced up at him.

'How old are you, Charlie?'

'Fifteen.'

'Okay. I need a responsible adult present if I'm to talk to you.' He held up his hands to forestall her inevitable protest. 'I don't make the rules.' To his constable, he said, 'Have we got in touch with Mr Marchant yet?'

'Only the answering machine at his London flat.'

'I think it's his opera night,' Charlie said dully.

Greg and Andy exchanged glances. It was a harsh fact of life that the partner of a murder victim was the first possible culprit they looked to. Greg hoped that the husband had a good alibi, since it pained him when men killed their wives. It seemed sneaky, somehow, unfair, to take advantage

129

of all that trust.

'I left a message for him to call your mobile as soon as he got in,' Andy added. 'Didn't want to be too specific on the phone.'

'Is there anyone else?'

'Siobhan's around somewhere,' Charlie said.

'And she is?'

'Siobhan Fahey. I suppose she's the school matron, although we don't go in much for formal titles.'

'Oh, yes. I think I remember her.' A silent presence at the fund raising, flitting about, never talking to anyone for more than two minutes and with not much to say for herself when she did. A plain woman such as no one noticed.

'She's gone to see to the pupils,' Andy supplied, passing a mug of tea to his superior officer. 'Most of them woke up what with the sirens and all those people milling about in the grounds and she wanted to reassure them and make sure they stayed in their rooms.'

'I suppose she'll have to do if there's no adult member of the family present,' Greg said.

'She's certainly not *family*,' Charlie said dismissively, 'but she's been here for ever.'

'She lives here?'

'Yeah. She doesn't seem to have a home of her own. She claims she's a widow with a son, Daniel. There's a photo in the sitting room that's supposed to be her dead husband but he looks nothing like Danny, so I reckon he was really a little accident and she's too proud to say so.'

'You don't like Mrs Fahey,' Greg hazarded.

'I don't *dislike* her, it's just that she has so much influence over Mum ... Had. Like she has some sort of hold over her. Had! Danny's in his final year at university but he lives here in the holidays.'

As Greg sipped his tea, Andy murmured to him under his breath. 'Tom Reilly told me she was starting to say something about a man when they were interrupted and she clammed up.'

'What man?' Andy shrugged. 'Okay, thanks. Can you go and help Babs outside?'

Dismissed, the constable left. In the doorway, he stood aside to let in a middle-aged woman who was returning. What struck Greg, seeing her close-up, was how *flat* she was, all angles and no curves; she had the figure of a super-model, which only went to show how far removed from a desirable woman's body that was.

Her face was long and narrow into a pointed chin. On a face that thin he expected to see cheekbones like knives, but she displayed none. She wore a knee-length tweed skirt, brown, and a baby-blue cotton sweater with short sleeves, old-fashioned at a time when women her age mostly dressed like their daughters.

'Mrs Fahey?' he asked. She nodded and he introduced himself, brandishing his warrant card. 'Can I ask you to sit in as responsible adult while I talk to Charlie?'

'Of course.' She sat down next to the girl and laid a hand on her shoulder but was shrugged off.

'You said something to PC Reilly about a man,' Greg said.

Charlie screwed up her eyes as if concentrating on the earlier conversation. 'I don't think so.'

'It was just before my sergeant arrived,' Greg prompted her. 'Something about a man you'd seen hanging about the place.'

She shook her head. 'No, he must have misunderstood. It's all ... so confusing.'

Greg looked at her curiously for a moment, then he glanced at Siobhan Fahey. She was staring intently at Charlie, a frown on her lips. He couldn't call the motherless child a liar to her face, nor could he lean on her too hard on this traumatic night. He'd just have to hope that she changed her mind and decided to tell him whatever it was she was hiding.

A middle-aged man arrived at that moment, short and plump and good-humoured, not in the least disconcerted at being dragged out on a home visit so late in the evening. Greg recognised the local GP,

Arthur Blaine. He nodded a greeting to Greg who acknowledged it with a thin smile. Dr Blaine had been the first to suspect Frederick's leukaemia – sending him for urgent tests which confirmed the worst – but Greg couldn't hold that against him for ever.

Charlie hailed him as an old friend and, when he spoke kindly to her, finally burst into tears.

He said, 'Bed for this young lady, I think, Superintendent. Your questions will do just as well in the morning.'

'That's all right, doctor.'

He led her away and Greg sat down again. He wanted to talk to Siobhan Fahey.

'You live here?' he asked.

'Me and my son, only he's away at university now.'

'How long have you known Mrs Marchant?'

'Since she and Stephen started the school about twenty years ago.'

'How did you get the job here?'

'It was advertised and I applied. I was looking for somewhere that I could live in, have my son with me. We didn't have a settled home after my husband died.'

'When did your husband die?' he asked.

She paused before answering. '1981.'

'Who's up for the post-mortem?' Barbara asked. 'Dr Chubb's doing it first thing.'

133

'You'd better go,' Greg said, 'if we can't get hold of Nick by then. Andy banged his head quite badly the last time he passed out. Have you packed your cases yet?'

'Not yet. I was just making a list when the call came in.'

'Okay. Do the post and then get off.'

'Thank you, sir!'

'I'm not about to interfere with people's holiday plans. We'll cope. Now, have we talked to the neighbours yet?'

'I got no reply at the nearest house that way.' Barbara pointed. 'I was about to try the other side when you arrived.'

'Nowhere's exactly close,' Greg grumbled. 'You could probably carry out a massacre without anyone hearing, but we'd better try, make ourselves popular by waking people up. Come on.'

He led the way on foot to the neighbouring property, a much more modest place than Hilltop, only a bungalow, though a sprawling one, set in a large and neglected garden. A tangle of mauve clematis needed cutting back at the front, half obscuring the door with its peeling burgundy paint. No car stood in the drive which suggested that no one was home, even in the middle of the night. There were lights on inside but they were probably to deter burglars.

He rang the bell all the same – a two-tone chime – and was rewarded after a moment

134

by the shuffle of feet in slippers on a parquet floor.

The door opened only a crack and on a chain. They were always telling people to be careful; finally somebody was listening. He held up his warrant card to the aperture and said, 'Police. Could I have a word, sir.'

The door closed again without a reply, but he heard the noise of the chain being removed. When it reopened, a man of about eighty stood there in peach silk pyjamas and a dressing gown in a tartan which no Highland clan was likely to lay claim to. He had perfectly white hair, which fell to his shoulders, and a beard to match.

He might have been Old Father Time.

'You're a policeman,' he said eagerly, his blue eyes sparkling bright. 'At last. I'd given up hope. Come in. Come in.' He stood back and ushered them into the hall. Five doors led off it but all were firmly closed. He peered into the darkness behind them. 'I suppose you have to come at night, for security reasons. I understand.'

Greg, not used to being so welcome, said, 'Er...'

'You've come about my letters.' A grandfather clock behind him struck midnight deafeningly and without warning and, when the echo had died away, he added, 'Rather late but better that than never,' and giggled.

'Letters?' Greg queried.

'About the death of Diana.'

'Diana?' Greg was momentarily baffled. His ex-wife, Diane, now called herself Diana and he was thinking that he hadn't heard that she'd died, since it would have been an occasion for rejoicing and putting out flags.

The man went on, making himself clearer. 'Only was that really Henri Paul driving the car, or an MI6 officer surgically altered to look like him?'

'Huh?' Greg said bovinely.

'I have evidence that the real Henri Paul is living in Algeria but I can't get anyone to take me seriously.'

Greg, aware that Barbara was trying desperately not to laugh, dragged the conversation back to the matter in hand. 'Actually, Mr...?'

'Chapman,' he supplied. 'Desmond Chapman. Surely you know that. I signed them all. I'm not afraid. They can try to intimidate me but as a true-born Englishman–'

'Mr Chapman, I wanted to talk to you about your neighbours, the Marchants.'

'What about them?' Before Greg could answer he went back to his own fixation. 'There's a plastic surgeon in Buenos Aires called Miguel Gonzalez Hernandes. I have a sworn affidavit from him saying that he did the surgery on an Englishman in the spring of 1997.'

Barbara grabbed her mobile phone from

her pocket. 'Excuse me,' she spluttered. 'I'd better take this.' She almost ran back out into the night, her shoulders shaking.

'I didn't hear her phone ring,' Chapman said.

'She has it on vibrate,' Greg said solemnly. 'Now, about the Marchants.'

'And do you know where Dr Gonzalez Hernandez is now?'

'Er, can't say I do, no.'

It was like being run over by a steamroller, he thought. Much as you might try to dodge into the hedge, the sheer immensity and momentum of the oncoming vehicle made avoidance impossible. He might as well lie down in the road and wait to be crushed flat in the hope that he would spring back up again like Wile E Coyote.

'And nor does anyone else!' Chapman exclaimed triumphantly, 'because he disappeared early in 1998.' His voice dropped an octave, portentous. 'Diana the huntress became the prey.'

'Are you aware that Mrs Robyn Marchant was murdered a couple of hours ago?' Greg asked in desperation.

It seemed he had finally penetrated the carapace of Chapman's obsession as the old man sank on to a padded telephone table, his hand reaching for his chest. Greg feared he was having a heart attack, but he spoke again. 'Robyn? Dead? Do you mean next door?'

'Yes, tonight, in the garden.'

'But don't you see?' He leaned forward eagerly. 'It was me they were after. They mistook their target. No one would have a reason to kill Robyn. Goodness! I'm in danger.'

The prospect did not seem to displease him. On the contrary.

'You?' Greg said stupidly.

'They want to get rid of everyone who knows the truth. Come with me.'

He got up with surprising agility and led the way through a door to his right. Greg saw no option but to follow him. He found himself in what must once have been the dining room but, as his host flicked on the light, he saw that it had been transformed into a shrine.

A Welsh dresser filled the far wall like an altar, festooned with photographs of the late Princess of Wales peering, with her trademark, heavily-mascara-ed coyness, at the camera. A table and sideboard were similarly laden. Three virgin white candles stood in silver candlesticks.

'I light them on the anniversary,' Chapman whispered. 'It is not long now.'

'Yes, it's, um, very nice.'

Greg wanted desperately to get out of this madhouse. He walked back into the hall and the old man followed him, closing the door of the shrine behind him after one last respectful glance.

'Mr Chapman,' he said firmly. 'I need you to concentrate. Mrs Robyn Marchant was murdered this evening–'

'Just like *her.*' He jerked his head back to the shrine.

'...Perhaps, but Mrs Marchant is my case and I'd like to focus on that, if you don't mind. Have you been in all evening?'

'Oh, yes. I seldom go out. Just in case. I patrol the perimeter occasionally.'

Greg said, 'I know it's some distance to Hilltop House but did you see or hear anything out of the ordinary around ten o'clock this evening?' He heard Barbara come back into the bungalow behind him, having presumably got control of her hysteria. They both waited expectantly as the old man focused his mind on the question.

'No,' he said finally. 'I heard nothing. Not tonight. There have been men hanging around lately.'

'Men?'

'All sorts of men. Big, small, black, white, old, young. Surveillance. There's no escape from them.'

It was increasingly clear that they were wasting their time. As Greg thanked Mr Chapman courteously and turned to leave, he asked, 'Am I to have police protection?'

What?' Greg said in exasperation.

'I shall surely be next, when they realise their mistake.'

'Do you think that's wise?' Greg said.

'…I see. You mean that I couldn't trust a policeman? That he might be in league with … the forces working against *her*?'

'I wouldn't risk it myself.'

'Mrs Gandhi!' he hissed.

'Sorry?'

'Assassinated by her own bodyguards.'

'Brilliant!' Greg said.

The old man drew back nervously, pulling his dressing gown closer around him as if it were bulletproof. 'I'll patrol no more to-night to be on the safe side.'

'Perhaps that's best, sir.'

'Thank you!' He seized Greg's hand, pumping it up and down. 'You, at least, are an honest man.'

'My pleasure,' Greg said, and left. He heard bolts being drawn behind him. 'Perhaps that's just want I want you to think,' he muttered and tried a manic laugh under his breath. 'Well, that was a big help,' he added as they stood together in the balmy night air, balmy being a word that sprang into his mind for some reason.

'I'm sorry about earlier, boss. I don't know what came over me.'

'Don't blame yourself, Babs. He was disconcerting. It was all I could do to keep a straight face myself. I'm amazed he isn't wearing a tinfoil helmet so we can't read his thoughts.'

'I saw on the Internet that Diana was killed because she was about to reveal that the royal family are really giant lizards from Alpha Centauri.'

'That's ridiculous,' Greg said. 'Since everyone knows that already, why would they need to kill her?'

They both giggled. 'Seriously,' Barbara said. 'If I ever get that bonkers, promise you'll shoot me.'

'So long as it's reciprocal.'

'Deal!'

They shook hands on it.

Chapter Nine

As they walked back to Hilltop they came upon an altercation between a young man on a motorbike and one of the uniformed constables who were securing the scene.

'Sir!' Sharon Moore appealed to Greg in relief.

'What's going on?'

'That's what I'd like to know,' the boy said belligerently. 'This woman says I can't go into my own home.'

'You live here?' Greg asked. He could see the youth more clearly now: early twenties, he thought, dark hair, dishevelled by the crash helmet he'd taken off, pale blue eyes, slim build. By his feet stood a backpack, the enormous sort people carried if they were walking round the world.

'My mother's the matron here.'

'May I ask your name, sir?'

'Daniel Fahey... See here. What's going on?'

'There's been a sudden death,' Greg said, 'a suspicious death. Naturally my constable is being careful about who enters or leaves the scene.'

'Sudden–! Who?'

'Mrs Robyn Marchant.'

'Robyn! That's impossible. How...? What...?'

'It might be helpful, sir,' Greg said, 'if you could find somewhere else to stay tonight.'

'Like where? It's the middle of the night. Anyway, I need to see my mother. If something awful's happened to Robyn, then she's going to be very upset.'

'Daniel? Is that you? I thought I heard your voice.' Far from being upset, Siobhan Fahey seemed unnaturally calm as she embraced her son. 'I wasn't expecting you till next week.'

'Well, with finals over there didn't seem much point in hanging about in Oxford, so I thought I'd surprise you. But what's this nonsense about Robyn? It can't be true.'

'I'm afraid it is.' She picked up his backpack without apparent effort. 'But let's get you indoors.'

Sharon glanced at Greg for instructions. He nodded to let the boy pass.

The Scene-of-Crime team arrived in their van, the head SOC officer, Martha Childs, in her usual place in the front passenger seat. They pulled over, out of the way of the police officers and their vehicles, and all alighted, eerie in their white suits, due to get eerier as they pulled the hoods over their heads, covering any hair that might contaminate the scene.

Greg said heartily, 'Evening, all.'

Martha dragged her heavy kit out of the van and replied through tight lips. 'Superintendent.' She was a short, slightly-built woman in her early thirties, her features delicate inside the shiny overall, her mouth unsmiling.

'Sorry to drag you out so late, Mrs Childs.'

'No problem.' She looked at him coolly. 'That's what I'm paid for. Where's the body?'

'Barbara will show you,' Greg said. 'I'll be with you in a minute.'

The sergeant led them off, throwing a puzzled glance back at her boss as she went.

Greg took out his mobile phone and made another attempt to contact Stephen Marchant. Once again, he got the answering machine and he hung up without speaking and followed the others.

In the herb garden, a tent had been set up around the crime scene to preserve it from curious eyes. In the darkness beyond, Greg could see the glimmer of white suits as SOC officers searched the garden for evidence. He wondered what Desmond Chapman would make of them if he spotted them; alien invaders, probably, come to carry out unspeakable experiments on him.

Inside, the tent was lit by arc lights for the photographer to work by and the man was still snapping away. Until he had finished, the body would not be moved. Greg had never worked on a murder case where the exact position of the victim proved crucial in court but that didn't mean he never would.

Martha Childs had already put her hood up and stood looking austere. He thought that she had aged visibly in the past six months. She was little more than thirty but fine lines were appearing round her mouth and eyes and she wore the look of a woman who had stopped caring about herself.

He avoided her eye and joined Barbara and Andy who were standing well back, getting his first glimpse of the dead woman. It struck him that her body looked arranged, as if the killer had laid her down carefully on the ground, making sure she was comfortable. Her legs were neatly together, the flowered silk of a summer dress falling chastely below her knees.

The post-mortem would tell him if she had been sexually assaulted but his first instinct was that she had not. He hoped not; although an intimate assault left more forensic evidence than any other, it was that much more traumatic for the family.

One white sandal had fallen from her foot and lay a few inches to her left. She had painted her well-cared-for toenails a baby pink.

'Okay,' the photographer announced. 'I'm done here.'

'So, what do we have outside?' Greg asked Martha Childs.

'No mud,' she said, 'as it's been unseasonably dry, but we may pick up some usable footprints on the flowerbeds. If he kept to the grass then I think we've had it.'

'No dew?' he asked.

'It was barely dark, only four days to the solstice. No dew had formed as yet.' Her voice was businesslike, almost a monotone. He realised that she was depressed and felt a surge of pity for her, but she had a job to do and so did he.

'Tyre tracks?' he asked.

'Any number. It's not Piccadilly Circus but most of the cars going in and out of Inkpen go along that road. I've got Simon and Janie out there but we can't just close the road off so don't hold your breath.'

'The blood appears to be all beneath her,'

he remarked. 'Shall we turn her over?' She nodded and came to help him, rolling the body over on to its right side, bending one knee to support her, rigor not yet begun. The dress had a white background with a pattern of forget-me-nots, but on the back the blue petals were stained the colour of rust.

He thought she had been wearing the same dress when they'd met at Easter but with a jacket over it against the spring cool. He tried to visualise the scene. They had spent perhaps ten minutes talking about the school and the joys and problems inherent in running such an establishment. He thought in retrospect that Mr Marchant had not been there, that he had never met him.

'I can't see a wound,' he said. Barbara, staring down from above him, shook her head in agreement. 'What about you, Mrs Childs?'

'Not my area of expertise, Superintendent,' she said crisply. 'Leave that to the pathologist.'

He traced his fingers up her cool forearms. 'No defensive wounds,' he remarked to Barbara. If a victim saw the attack coming then she would put up her arms to ward it off but Robyn had made no attempt to protect herself.

'Struck down from behind,' Barbara agreed. 'Never saw it coming.'

'Is the mortuary van here?' Greg asked of no one in particular.

'Came a few minutes ago,' Andy replied.

'Then they'd better take her away,' Greg said.

They all stood to one side as two efficient men zipped the dead woman into a body bag and lifted her on to a stretcher.

'Okay,' Greg said to Martha. 'With that blood and no visible wound I assume we're looking for a knife of some kind.' She curled her lip as if he were stating the obvious and he added quickly, 'Well, I don't need to teach you your job, Mrs Childs. Barbara...' He walked away and she followed him. 'You'd better get home if you're to be up for the PM in the morning. I'll wait around to see if the husband calls back.'

'So what's the deal with you and Martha?' she asked when they were out of earshot of the crime scene.

'I don't know what you mean,' he said, realising as he spoke that he had answered too quickly.

'A few months ago you were Gregory and Martha, lately it's "Mrs Childs" and "Super-intendent". What gives?'

'All right.' Greg sighed and opened his car door for her. 'Get in and I'll tell you exactly what happened so you don't go imagining something much more. Okay?'

'Okay.' Barbara snuggled down in the passenger seat as he got in at the driver's door. 'I'm sitting comfortably so you may begin.'

'It happened when her marriage collapsed so suddenly last November. She was in my office one morning, giving me a report, when she broke down and started crying. Naturally, I comforted her but it got out of hand and she tried to kiss me. I shoved her away and then you came in.'

'I remember! I noticed she'd been crying but thought it best not to say anything.'

'So both of us have been thoroughly embarrassed ever since. And there's nothing more to it than that.'

'I believe you,' Barbara said, 'but it's making people suspicious, all that formality.'

'What people?' Greg yelped.

'Well, Nick asked me recently if you and Martha were having an affair.'

'Did he indeed!'

'It's like a few years ago – don't you remember? – when Jean Cooper and Sam Arthurs were having a fling and suddenly it was all "Constable Arthurs" and "Sarge!" where they'd been on first-name terms before. No one was in the least surprised to find out they were at it like rabbits. It's a dead giveaway.'

'You make a good point,' said Greg, who'd seldom been so astonished as the day Sergeant Cooper's husband had stormed in and punched PC Arthurs plumb on the nose in front of half the station.

His mobile rang, a London number displaying on the screen. He answered it, thankful to change the subject. It was Stephen Marchant, returning Andy's call at last. This was one of the hardest parts of the job: it was bad enough breaking tragic news face to face; doing it on the telephone was intolerable, but he could hardly demand that the man return home without giving at least some detail.

He identified himself to the puzzled caller. 'I'm afraid there's been an incident at Hilltop House, sir,' he said carefully.

'Is it one of the children, the pupils?'

'Nothing like that. The incident concerns your wife. Can I ask you to return home as soon as possible?'

'Robyn? But is she all right? Can I speak to her?'

'I'm afraid that won't be possible,' Greg said. 'Your wife...'

Marchant sounded almost angry. 'Spit it out, man, for God's sake.'

'Your wife died this evening, sir.'

'Oh God! Oh Jesus Christ! ... I'll be there in an hour.'

'Sir–' Greg began, since, even in the middle of the night, he would have to drive at a hundred miles an hour to get from the Barbican to Inkpen so quickly, but he'd hung up.

'Go home,' he said to Barbara. 'I'll handle Mr Marchant.'

Stephen Marchant must have averaged very nearly a hundred on his journey, since he pulled into the drive at Hilltop only an hour and a quarter later.

Greg liked him at once; a homely man in his mid-fifties, Stephen could never have been handsome and was now flabby and balding. Although his car was shiny and new and his casual clothes expensive and well cut, he was still Everyman.

'Are you Mr Summers?' he said, as Greg opened his car door for him. 'Can I see her?'

'Not just now,' Greg said. 'We've taken the body to the mortuary. I'm afraid we have to hold a post-mortem, in the circumstances.'

'I have to see her, or I'll never really believe...'

'You shall,' Greg said. 'We'll need a formal identification from you as next of kin. I am so very sorry.'

Marchant slumped against the front wing of his Jaguar, as if the news was only now registering. 'What happened?'

'All we know at the moment is that your wife was found dead in the herb garden shortly before ten-thirty. It looks as if she walked out there herself and met her assailant.'

'Dead how?'

'That's not immediately apparent so we shall have to wait for the results of the post-mortem.'

'Who found her?'

'Your daughter.'

'Charlie! I clean forgot she was sleeping here tonight. The damned tennis. My poor little girl.' He jerked upright and turned towards the house. 'I must see her.'

Greg laid a hand on his arm. 'The doctor's given her a sedative and put her to bed.' Apart from anything else, he didn't want the two to talk until he'd interviewed the husband to his satisfaction. 'Let her sleep. It's very late.'

'Of course. You're right. And my son? Does he know?'

'We thought it best left till morning. He's at boarding school, I understand.'

'Yes, in Sussex. I'll call his housemaster first thing. No. I'll go myself ... I don't know what to do.' He looked at Greg with mute appeal, wanting the decision taken from him. 'I can't think straight.'

'What's best is if you come indoors,' Greg said kindly, 'maybe have a cup of tea and tell me all you can about your wife, about any enemies she might have had.'

'Tea. Yes. Good.' Marchant let himself be led away. 'I'll help in any way I can.'

'When were you here last, sir?' Greg asked when Marchant was furnished with a soothing hot beverage. He pushed his own cup away, fearing that tea would start to pour out of his orifices if he drank any more.

'Tuesday, first thing. I work in London

151

Tuesday to Friday, sleep over three nights a week.'

'Have you spoken to your wife since then?'

'We speak every day.' His face filled with wistful affection. 'I don't let a day go by without hearing her voice.'

'So you spoke last night?'

'About six o'clock.' He glanced at the digital timer on the oven which read 2:20. 'Barely eight hours ago ... I can't believe I shall never hear her voice again.' His speech became muffled as he struggled not to cry.

'Was there anything unusual about your conversation?' Greg asked when he had collected himself.

'Nothing. We talked about the school, about the kids, about Charlie's tennis match tomorrow... Today.'

'Had she seemed worried lately?'

'No. She was as always. She was Robyn, the ... the best and kindest person I ever met.'

'You don't keep a dog?'

'No, we have enough to do. There are hamsters and ornamental fish, even some stick insects for the school but none of them is much good when it comes to intruders.'

'You weren't at your flat when my constable rang earlier. Opera night, Charlie said.'

'Opera is Wednesday. No, there was nothing on TV – I'm not a football fan – so I went down to the theatre.'

'Which theatre?'

'Downstairs.'

'The Barbican? What did you see?'

'Weird, musical thing. Not something I'd normally have gone for but it had Marianne Faithfull in it and somehow that reminded me of my youth.'

'Mmm!' Greg too associated Marianne Faithfull with a time when anything had seemed possible, an era of freedom that had been all too short, sandwiched between the dreary conformity and hypocrisy of the fifties and things like terrorism and AIDS. 'You went alone?'

'Yes.' He looked apologetic. 'And I didn't see anyone I know and I paid cash at the box office so I doubt they'll remember me ... I do understand, you see, Superintendent, that I'm your number-one suspect.'

'I wouldn't say that, sir. We just have to eliminate you from our enquiries. I don't suppose you have a ticket stub.'

'Maybe. Probably.' Marchant felt in his pockets – trousers and the sports jacket which he had flung over the back of his chair – producing a variety of till receipts and odd scraps of paper, even a bus ticket. 'I'm a hoarder. Robyn ... used to laugh at me for it, went through my pockets once a week and chucked everything out. Here it is.' He handed over half a theatre ticket on which Greg could make out the previous evening's date. Which proved nothing.

'What time did the musical finish?' he asked.

'Say, quarter to eleven. Then I had a drink in the bar. The flat can seem a bit lonely sometimes and the complex doesn't really empty till about midnight, so I walked around a bit, then went back upstairs and got the message on my Ansaphone.'

'Had your wife made a will?'

He nodded. 'We had those mirror wills. You know? Where we leave everything to each other – barring a few small legacies – and then to the kids.'

'Did she have a mobile phone?' Greg asked.

'Actually, no. She essentially worked at home and didn't see why people should pester her at Tesco.'

'I shall need to check calls made to and from your land line over the past few weeks,' Greg said.

'Whatever you want,' Stephen said. 'Whatever will help. We have two lines – school and private.'

'I take it there's an email account.'

'Several, including a private one for Robyn.'

'One of my men will take a look at your computer first thing in the morning. Meantime, I'd like to ask you not to touch it. I'll have the room locked.'

'I do all my computer work at the office.'

'Have you been wearing those clothes all

day?' Greg asked.

'No. Suit at the office, alas. I changed when I got to the flat.'

'I'd like to take those clothes.' Greg got up. 'Can we do that now?'

He knew it was a waste of time. If Marchant had killed his wife then he'd had plenty of time to change and dispose of the clothes he'd been wearing. But maybe he'd just cleaned himself up; maybe he didn't know that they could find the minutest traces of blood, even after washing. Maybe he'd never watched a cop show on TV.

What were the odds?

Greg went upstairs with Stephen and waited while he changed, bagging up his clothes and shoes.

'You should probably get some sleep,' he said kindly, as the bereaved man stood before him in a grey flannel dressing gown, old and paunchy. 'I know I should. We'll talk some more when we're rested.'

Chapter Ten

When Charlie awoke, her father was sitting at her bedside, keeping vigil, just as he had when she was younger and had the flu or a stomach bug. She didn't know at first why her head felt so heavy. It occurred to her that her father looked older – more wrinkled, more grey both in hair and face, as if she was seeing him after a long time apart, rather than a routine few days.

Then she remembered.

'Dad!'

'My darling!' He grasped her tight in a bear hug, pressing her suddenly wet face into his shoulder. 'My poor darling. Why did it have to be you who found her?'

'If not me then somebody else,' she sniffed.

'So let it be somebody else. Siobhan. She'd have known what to do.'

Charlie was indignant. 'I knew what to do! I checked for a pulse and there wasn't one and I didn't touch anything so as not to disturb evidence and I dialled 999.'

'Sorry!' He held her away from him and kissed her hot forehead. 'I'm sure you were splendid, as always.'

'It would have been worse if it was one of the children,' she said, 'and Siobhan's taken it very hard.'

They looked at one another for a moment, each wanting to reassure the other, unable to find the right lies, both certain that they would never be happy again.

'Remind me what time you have to be in Chiswick,' he said eventually.

'Oh, Dad! I can't think about tennis at a time like this. I'll have to scratch.'

'That's such a shame, such bad timing.'

'Like there would have been a good time to have Mum murdered. Dad...'

'What, my lamb?'

'There was a man. I almost told the policeman but then I thought I'd better not, not till I'd talked to you.'

'A man?'

'It was a few nights ago. I dunno. Last week some time. While you were in Antwerp.' Stephen went very still. 'He came late,' she went on, 'after I was in bed. I went down for a glass of water and he was in the sitting room with Mum and they were talking.'

'What were they saying?'

'I couldn't hear. I didn't want them to see me, to think I was eavesdropping, but she was in her dressing gown and it seemed odd.'

'Did you know him, this man?'

She shook her head. 'I didn't recognise his voice.'

'Would you know him again?'

'I didn't see him, only the back of his head.' Her tone became indignant again. 'Sitting in *your* favourite armchair.'

'And why didn't you tell the police this?'

'I thought if Mum was...' She gulped for air then forced out the words. 'Having an affair...'

'I know she wasn't.'

'And if you'd found out...'

'Then I might have killed her, out of jealousy?' Charlie nodded dumbly, her eyes darting away, not meeting his, ashamed that she could think such a thing. 'I swear to you, darling, on my immortal soul, that your mother didn't have another man and that I didn't kill her in a fit of jealousy.'

'Thank God. I never really thought ... but still.'

'All the same, Charlotte, I wouldn't mention it to the policeman if I were you.'

'But why not? He might be the man who killed her.'

'But you can't describe him, or identify him. You and I know that he wasn't your mother's lover, but you know what filthy minds policemen have, like sewers. They'll decide that he was and they already suspect me without that.'

'Suspect you!'

He smiled ruefully. 'Just routine. It's what they're paid for – to think the worst of everybody.'

Charlie was still uncertain. 'You know what Mum would say – tell the truth and shame the devil.'

He looked deep into her eyes for several seconds. She was so much her mother's daughter. He loved her so completely and it made his heart ache that he couldn't protect her from everything life might throw at her.

'You must do as you think best, my love.'

Normally, Charlie showered and dressed in five minutes. Today she took her time. So long as she stayed upstairs, she could convince herself that her mother was still alive down there, that she had only to descend and she would see her. The noise and bustle she could hear all over the house was the start of a regular school day and not the upheaval of a murder enquiry.

Her father had left to drive to Dominic's school and tell him the awful news. He would bring her brother back with him and the sorrow would redouble. Who was it said that a trouble shared was a trouble halved? Whoever they were, they could not have known much trouble in their lives.

Finally, she could put it off no longer and slipped down the stairs into the kitchen. She could hear the voice of the man in charge, whose name she couldn't remember, in the hall. She hadn't expected him to be there so early. She wasn't ready for him; she had yet to make her decision.

She poured cereal into a bowl and added milk from the fridge. She sat at the breakfast bar, looking at it for a few minutes as the brown wheat absorbed the white liquid, then swept it all into the bin. Taking an apple from the fruit bowl, she bit into it, munching her way round the core in even bites, tasting nothing.

Then she washed the apple down with cold

159

coffee and went in search of The Policeman.

Tell the truth and shame the devil.

The policeman stood with his back to her, talking to the handsome young constable who'd been so kind to her the night before. The constable was handing him a book. She realised that she didn't know his rank but supposed he was an inspector, like the ones on TV.

He was about fifty, she thought, a little younger than her father but the same vintage. Not overly tall and, unlike her father, devoid of middle-aged spread. His hair was greying but not receding.

He noticed her at that moment and came towards her.

'Charlotte, isn't it?'

'I prefer Charlie.' She was grateful that he hadn't asked her how she was in that pointless way strangers so often did, as if they couldn't guess.

'Charlie it is, and I'm Gregory Summers. Superintendent.' He stood looking at her with a smile of genuine empathy and she found his eyes intelligent and kind.

'There's something I'd like to tell you,' she blurted out.

'I thought there might be.' He put his hand on her shoulder. 'Shall we go into the office?'

In there, he offered her a seat and put the book down on the table while he went in search of Siobhan. She glanced at it, recognising it as the biography her mother had been absorbed in these past few days. He was back in a few minutes with her chaperone – not Siobhan, as it turned out, but Daniel.

'Is it all right if Mr Fahey acts as your responsible adult, Charlie?' he asked.

'Oh, yes! I didn't even know you were here, Dan.'

'Dearest Charlie, I am so sorry. I can't tell you.' He took a seat to one side. 'I got here late last night, after you'd gone to bed. Are you still going to Chiswick today?'

She shook her head. 'It seemed so important yesterday.' She spoke more to the policeman that to Daniel who, she was sure, understood. 'Now...'

'Have you called them?' Daniel persevered, 'let them know you're not coming?'

'No.'

'Would you like me to do that for you?'

'...Yes.' She managed a watery smile. 'Thank you, Dan. I don't think I'd have been up to explaining without...'

'I know.' And he did; he knew how much store this strange little girl set by her self-possession, how it would pain her to sob to an LTA official on the phone.

'So,' Greg said. 'You have something to tell me, Charlie.' He added disingenuously, 'Something you've remembered since last night.'

He listened to her story without interrupting, his fingers playing over the shiny jacket of the book in front of him. She noticed that his hands were small for a man's and that he wasn't wearing a wedding ring. When she'd finished he said, 'And you'd never seen this man before.'

'He didn't look at all familiar.'

'Do you think you would be able to work with a police artist to make a likeness?'

'Nuh-huh. I only saw him from behind. He had dark hair, quite short. Oh, wait! He had an accent.' She hesitated then added doubtfully, 'Irish or Scottish.'

Greg glanced at Daniel. 'Would you have any idea who he might be, Mr Fahey?'

'Because he's Irish?'

'Not necessarily. Just in general.'

'Not the slightest.'

Greg said, 'I know this is a hard question to answer, Charlie, and I'd like you to believe that it's a hard one for me to ask. Was your parents' marriage happy?'

She didn't answer for a moment as her cheeks bloomed crimson in anger; then she swallowed the emotion and said, 'I knew you would think that. That's why I hesitated to tell you. Yes, they were happy. Whoever this man was, he was not her lover.'

'They were the happiest couple I know,' Daniel put in, earning a grateful smile from the girl.

162

'Your brother,' Greg said. 'Dominic?'

'Yes. Dom.'

'Was he here that night? Could he have seen the man?'

'He was at school. I was only here because I had a county match the next day.'

Greg picked up the book. *'Behind the Wire,'* he said, 'by Liam Sullivan. Any idea why your mother was reading this?' Charlie shrugged. 'Was she fond of autobiography?'

'Not really. Mostly she read novels.'

'Romance, fantasy, crime?'

'Classics. Nineteenth century, early twentieth. She liked Mrs Gaskell, Hardy, Orwell, Huxley, Virginia Woolf.'

Greg looked at the author's photo inside the back cover. Sullivan grinned cheekily back at him. A man with an Irish accent, he thought and, although his dark hair was long here, it had been shorter at the book store the evening of the reading.

But what sense did that make?

Barbara didn't mind post-mortems. In her early days in CID her male colleagues would send her to witness them, expecting her to come back green of face and jittery of stomach, but she had disappointed them and been briefly nicknamed The Ghoul.

To her the corpse was just a lump of flesh, mostly water, its essence gone. She did not fear death, not because she believed in a soul or an afterlife – she was agnostic on that point – but because she believed that death was the right true end of a life well lived.

And the planet was crowded enough without people living for ever.

An autopsy meant, almost by definition, that a life had been cut short by violence – be it accident, suicide or murder – but the principle was still the same.

To live for ever, to Barbara, would be intolerable, eternity a yawn and, from what she had seen and heard at Hilltop, Robyn Marchant had lived the best of lives, the one spent helping others. Not that that gave anyone to right to cut that life short – on the contrary – and she would move heaven and earth to bring the killer to justice ... just as soon as she got back from Corfu.

And, contrary to the way pathologists were usually depicted in the media, in Barbara's experience they treated their corpses with great respect.

As she was glancing at her watch, which told her that Dr Chubb was ten minutes late, the man in question arrived, breezing into the room without apology.

'Hello, Babs. You drew the short straw then.'

'Hello, Aidan. How did the anniversary go?'

He grinned. 'Amanda's been reading a book called *"How to keep your marriage fresh"* and I'm reaping the benefit.'

'Good for you,' Barbara said sincerely. She respected couples who could make a long-term relationship work; she just didn't think she could. She got bored easily. Ten solid days alone with Trevor in Corfu was a daunting enough prospect for her.

'Thought you were off on your hols,' Aidan said.

'First thing tomorrow.'

He whistled. 'Bad timing. I know how you like a good murder.'

'I wouldn't put it quite like that,' she protested.

Dr Chubb took his jacket off and started preparing for the autopsy, donning his surgeon's green overalls, whistling something classical. 'You know where the throwing-up sink is,' he commented, knowing full well that she would have no need of it. 'We have a woman, aged around forty, one metre sixty-three, and of normal weight...'

Nicolaides arrived at Hilltop in a flurry of gravel shortly after nine. Greg went out to see what all the noise was.

'Sorry, sir.' Nick almost stumbled out of his Vauxhall Astra in his haste. 'I stayed the night at Nadia's and I'd let my mobile run down.'

'Well, you're entitled to the odd night off,' Greg said.

'Is it true Robyn Marchant's been murdered?'

'I'm afraid so.'

'Dammit!' Nick slammed the roof of his car hard with his fist. 'She was such a nice lady. What can I do?'

'Andy's taking statements from everyone who lives or works here,' Greg said. 'I want you to make a start on the phone calls. There are two lines, personal and business. Start with personal.'

'Well, no doubt about your cause of death.' Dr Chubb had turned the body over and was running his hands carefully over the torso. 'She's been stabbed. Look.'

Barbara leaned forward and examined what looked like a tear in the dead woman's skin. 'It's tiny,' she said. 'Hardly more than a nick.'

'Outside, yes.' He spread the whitening flesh back carefully. '"'Tis not so deep as a well, nor so wide as a church door, but 'tis enough, 'twill serve."'

'You what?' Barbara said.

'Shakespeare. *Romeo and Juliet.* Didn't they teach you anything at that comprehensive of yours? See how it penetrated straight into the heart. Death would have been almost instantaneous – very little blood as the heart stopped pumping right away, which is what we saw at the scene. I doubt if she had time to say "What the hell…?"'

He fired up his saw and began to cut the

body open, reaching in to scoop out the shattered heart, letting it nestle in the palm of his right hand.

'So what would the weapon be,' Barbara asked, '–something like a stiletto?'

'As thin as that but broader and– Oh! That's odd.' Barbara peered where he indicated, screwing up her eyes in concentration. 'Look at the shape of the wound. Usually, the tip of a knife is in the centre, as with a letter opener. If not, then it's to one side, with the slanted edge tapering up right from the bottom, like most kitchen knives. But this one has two straight edges, then tapers acutely to a side point just two centimetres from the top.'

'Can you draw me a sketch?' Barbara asked.

'I'll do my best. I don't think I've ever seen a wound quite like it. I'd say this was a knife designed for killing –like something belonging to a warrior – but like nothing I know of in European culture.'

'Wouldn't you need a knowledge of anatomy to strike so accurately?'

'Hard to say. The killer might just have been lucky. Oddly enough, the ribs almost guide you in. Someone didn't put enough thought into that design.'

'Is there anything lying around a house that could have made this wound?' Barbara asked. 'I dunno – a skewer?'

Chubb shook his head. 'Not sharp enough and entirely the wrong shape.'

'Only normal people don't have *warrior* knives lying around.'

'No, so your killer came armed and ready. Here's another thing: the angle of the wound suggests that the blow was struck from the left and slightly below.'

'So if someone crept up behind her in the garden, they were striking up and left-handed.'

'Let's see.' He stepped back, drawing his right hand across his body and making a stabbing motion upwards, his arm fully extended. 'It's not impossible for a right-handed person to pull it off but why would they do it that way?'

He scooped out some more of the offal that lay hidden beneath Robyn's skin. 'Let's get some samples off to the lab along with her fingerprints.'

Barbara had her mobile out almost before he had finished speaking. Now that they knew what weapon they were looking for, it would allow SOCO to focus their search.

'A professional killer's knife?' Greg said, when she'd explained. 'Of – what? – Asian or African provenance. Is he sure? All right, I'll get ... Martha on to it.'

'Aidan's doing a sketch of what it looks like which I'll get over to you soonest. Also, the angle of the cut suggests that our killer

168

may be left-handed.'

'Okay. I'll read the report later today. Now you go, Babs. I don't want to see you again for a fortnight and then with a terrific tan.'

'You don't have to tell me twice, boss.'

'Bonnes vacances.'

Chapter Eleven

Stephen knew every twist and turn of the cool stone passageways of St Aloysius's, since it had been his school too and had changed very little in forty years. The cold showers had gone, by all accounts, and there was a lavish computer lab, but here was the caretaker's cupboard where he had hidden to avoid Latin; there the cellar where he had sneaked off for an illicit smoke; in the main hall, more creditably, the cup he had won in the senior squash tournament.

He had been thinner then and lighter on his feet, his asthma less troubling. At least he'd had a little hand-eye coordination to pass on to Charlie.

He was too preoccupied to remember his schooldays this morning, making his way purposefully to the headmaster's study in the oldest part of the building, overlooking perfect lawns and – another innovation since his time – the outdoor swimming pool.

The Head's secretary greeted him by name and with enthusiasm since he was a major benefactor. She examined her diary in vain for an appointment, as if it were her fault that his name wasn't listed. He explained the urgency but not the precise nature of his visit and she was sure that Dr O'Brien would see him.

Stephen asked her to wait five minutes and then have someone fetch Dominic from his class.

Patrick O'Brien, who had the build and the ruddy face of a navvy and looked incongruous in his scholar's gown, greeted him with a warm smile which turned rapidly to dismay as Stephen told him why he was there.

'I'd like to take Dominic home with me,' he concluded, 'for a few days at least. The family should be together at this time.'

'Of course. My dear Stephen, I can't tell you how sorry I am.' O'Brien's accent was improbably fruity, sitting as ill with his features as his gown did. 'It's inconceivable. Murder! Robyn, of all people ... I don't know what to say.'

'No.'

The man's face was fierce. 'Whoever did this must be very wicked.'

There was a tap at the door and Dominic came in looking mildly guilty, which suggested that he could think of a few good reasons why the Head might have sent for him. 'You wanted to see me, sir – Dad!' His broad, open face was all smiles. 'What are you doing here? Do I get to go to Chiswick and see Charlie play after all?' He faltered at his father's sombre face. '...Dad?'

'I'll leave the two of you alone together,' O'Brien said. As he left the room, his hand gripped Dominic's shoulder briefly in pity.

The boy stared at his father with terror in his eyes.

'Dad?'

'I am so glad you came to see me,' Mrs Arathi Gupta said.

She sat her daughter-in-law down and poured her the inevitable cup of tea. She spoke in Hindi, still her favoured language, although odd English words and phrases crept in where no Hindi equivalent existed or the English alternative sprang first into her mind. These phrases were pronounced carefully, as if in inverted commas.

'You don't have to tell me about homesickness,' she added. 'Nitin and I came here in 1964, when Sangita was a "babe in arms" and Deepak not yet thought of, and still there are days when I long for home. Back then, things were harder too. "Bed and breakfast" places had signs that said "No Pakis" and that included us, even though we are not from Pakistan!'

'Really?'

'"No Pakis, no blacks, no Irish, no dogs",' she quoted. 'And that first winter! I thought I should die with the cold and the damp. They seeped into my bones. I can feel them still some days when the wind is wrong.'

'I just feel like I'm being feeble,' Indira said.

'Not at all,' Mrs Gupta said, switching to her sing-song English. 'It is hard to have so much new at once – not just new husband but new country too.' Back to Hindi. 'At least I had been married already two years when I came to Slough.'

She stood behind Indira, released the younger woman's hair from its careful knot and began to run her fingers through it, loosening the tangles and massaging her scalp. Indira thought that she had never known anything so soothing. Tears of nostalgia started in her eyes. It took her back to childhood when her nanny would perform the same ritual at bedtime, singing little songs to her as she did so.

Mrs Gupta was not singing, but her hands were gentle. Indira knew that she was lucky to get on so well with her husband's mother. Indian mothers-in-law were often far beyond a joke.

'Things are all right with Deepak?' she asked.

'Oh, yes. We are getting on very well. Very

happy.' She couldn't tell Arathi about her fears regarding Liam Sullivan and his effect on her husband. The photo of Sangita still had pride of place on the teak-effect mantelpiece above the fake electric fire and she would not stir up ancient agonies in this withered old lady.

'Things ... in the bedroom, for instance?'

'Oh, yes.' Indira flushed. 'That is not the problem at all.'

'That's my boy!' Mrs Gupta said in English.

'I just feel so lost, Mummy.'

'I know.' Her fingers circled rhythmically on the young woman's head. 'Home is home and "There is no place like it", as the English say. Forty years I am here, two-thirds of my life, and still I long to watch the moon rise over the sea of Arabia.'

'Still?'

'In a few years, Newbury will seem a little like home.' She glanced out of the window and added mischievously, 'At least it's better than Slough!'

Stephen's Jaguar drew up outside Hilltop again shortly after eleven. He got out and went to open the passenger door for Dominic, who was sitting there, staring into the distance without seeing. The boy didn't move.

'Dom,' his father said, with infinite gentleness, 'we're home.'

The boy's mouth moved to make the word 'Home' but no sound came out.

Greg came out of the front door at that moment and stopped to look at the tableau. He had considered sending a constable with Marchant to fetch his son but the man had been adamant that he was fit to drive and, given that the boy had been miles away at the time of the murder, there seemed no harm in leaving father and son alone together.

He walked over to the car and raised his eyebrows at Stephen who said in a low voice, 'I thought he was all right by the time we left the school but he seems to have gone into shock.'

'It's probably the worst thing that can happen to a child,' Greg said with sympathy. 'You stay here and I'll find your daughter, see if she can help.'

'Thank you.' Stephen hesitated. 'You're a good man.'

Greg returned in five minutes with Charlie. The girl took her brother's hand and led him into the house. He followed her like a docile animal.

Greg was sitting in the kitchen an hour later, lost in thought, when Charlie poked her head round the door. He waved for her to come in.

'How's your brother?' he asked.

'Resting.' She sat down opposite him. 'As

far as he can with your people rampaging over the house and grounds.'

He chose not to apologise. 'It's necessary. It's vital that we find the murder weapon.'

'I understand.'

'How are you doing?' he asked.

'It's not real yet. I mean, I'm at boarding school and I don't come home every weekend so sometimes I don't see her for a fortnight. You know? So the fact that she's not here today ... that I haven't seen her all morning... You know?'

'Yeah, I know.' It was a classic coping mechanism, a way of easing the bereaved into full acceptance of their loss.

'Anyway...' She shook herself as if physically pulling herself together. 'I was wondering if you'd spoken to Mr Chapman next door, only he wanders about a lot at night – *patrolling.*'

'I've interviewed him,' Greg said. 'He's ... eccentric.'

'He's always been eccentric,' Charlie agreed, 'but since his only grandson was killed in the invasion of Iraq last year, he's been plain barking.'

'Poor soul,' Greg said soberly. 'How old was he?'

'Twenty-two. Can you imagine?'

'Only someone who's been through it could know what it's like,' Greg said carefully.

'Of course, he's convinced Josh's death

was engineered by Diana's enemies to get at him.'

'He would be.'

'Actually, he's okay so long as he takes his medication, but every so often he decides that the medical profession is trying to poison him and stops taking the pills for a few days. Mum used to drop in on him several times a week, for a cup of tea and a chat. She said he was lonely and only wanted someone to listen to him. She...' She came to a halt and he saw that she was struggling with tears.

'Your mother was a wonderful woman,' he said. He passed her a handkerchief. 'Here, have a good cry.'

'Thanks, but I'll be okay.' She took the handkerchief anyway, dabbed her eyes and pocketed it. 'Mum used to get his groceries for him, make sure he ate properly. He'll probably end up in a home now.'

'Do you have any idea what he did,' Greg asked, 'before he...?'

'Went potty?'

'Retired.'

She thought about it. 'No. He's been there as long as I can remember, just shuffling about, always some obsession.'

'What did he obsess about before Diana?' Greg asked.

'Hmm. There was something about Harold Wilson being a Russian agent. He was Prime Minister back in the sixties,' she added, in case Greg might not know that. The ludicrous rumours that the decent bluff Yorkshireman had been a KGB plant had been current even in his boyhood. Charlie got up. 'Is the herb garden open again now?'

'No, I'm afraid it'll be a day or two yet.'

'I shall go and sit among the roses for a while then, think about Mum.'

He smiled at her. 'That's a very good idea.'

The Victorians understood about grieving, he thought, doing it properly: dressing in black clothes and refusing invitations for a year. Now people were expected to pull themselves together and look to the future; genuine mourning was seen as morbid.

When his mother had died he had been, as a young DI, in the thick of a series of armed robberies, which had been escalating in violence to the point where it seemed inevitable that somebody would be shot dead if they didn't catch the perpetrators soon.

He had barely had time to organise and attend her funeral and it had been several weeks – and a good arrest – later before he'd been able to spend a day at her bungalow, pack up her clothes for Oxfam, sort out a couple of mementoes for himself and book a house-clearance firm to do the rest.

Waiting for them to arrive in her old-fashioned sitting room, amidst the chintz and the china ornaments, he had found himself helpless with tears and had barely been able to calm himself when, twenty minutes later, he heard the van pull up outside.

Greg waited until the afternoon to seek out Stephen again. He found him in the sitting room, sprawling in an armchair in front of the empty fireplace. The *Financial Times* was open on his lap but he wasn't reading it. He glanced up as Greg came in.

'I was wondering if we could talk a little more, sir.'

'Of course.' Stephen gestured at the chair opposite and half his paper slid pinkly to the floor.

Greg sat. 'I can't help noticing,' he said, 'that you and your wife have separate beds.'

'And you draw a conclusion from that?'

'Not necessarily.'

Stephen laid the remains of his paper on the floor and looked at Greg for a moment, his hands folded in his lap. 'When Robyn and I married we decided to start a family as soon as possible, but three years went by and nothing happened, which wasn't a major problem as she was still only in her early twenties and the school was taking a lot of our time and energy. We told ourselves it was God's will and tried not to panic about it. Then, suddenly, she was pregnant with Dominic and Charlie came along only eleven months later – what they call Irish twins.'

'I've heard that expression,' Greg said. 'I

just wasn't sure what it meant.'

'Common enough in Catholic families. Well, we had our hands full and we decided that our family was complete.'

'You both decided?'

'I suppose the decision was ultimately Robyn's,' Stephen conceded. 'She was the one doing most of the work at Hilltop and she was the one who had to have them, after all. She felt that she couldn't give true commitment to Hilltop and to more than two children of our own. We had a boy and a girl, which you might call the perfect family.'

'And you've had separate beds since,' Greg guessed.

"Which doesn't mean that our marriage wasn't perfectly happy. I know many people these days think that sex is the be-all and end-all, but I grew up in an earlier era and ... it was never that important to me. I once thought briefly about becoming a priest, you see, which would have meant a vow of celibacy, and I felt myself quite equal to that challenge.'

'Thank you for being so frank with me,' Greg said.

'I gather Charlie told you about the man she saw here one evening when I was away.'

Greg nodded. 'Talking to your wife, who was in her dressing gown.'

'I wouldn't want you to jump to any conclusions.'

179

'Do you know who the man was, sir?'

'I have no idea, but I'm certain he wasn't some illicit lover. Robyn had other priorities in life.'

Greg was thoughtful for a moment. 'Would it bother you, sir, if I were to talk to some of the staff at your office, perhaps your secretary or personal assistant?'

'To see if I keep a mistress in town?' Stephen smiled at the idea. 'Go ahead. I don't suppose I could stop you if I wanted to.'

'Perhaps you could let me have a name and phone number.'

Marchant tore off a corner of his newspaper and scribbled down a number for him. 'Cynthia Thorley, my PA. That's her direct line.'

'And if I might have a key to your flat...'

Chapter Twelve

As it was three o'clock on Friday afternoon, Greg realised that he was going to have to move fast. Retiring to his car he rang the number Stephen had given him and arranged to meet Cynthia Thorley as she left work that day at six. She seemed a little hesitant and he suggested that she ring her boss to confirm that he had no objection to their speaking.

Normally, he would have dispatched Barbara on a job like this, let her bond with another woman, gain her confidence. Nick and Andy were both hard pressed at the house and, besides, he didn't trust either of them enough for such a delicate mission. Andy hadn't the experience and Nick was too rough and ready.

Why had he let her go? He'd had his leave cancelled often enough as a young DS. It had probably contributed to the break-up of his marriage.

Question asked; question answered.

He was still without a chief inspector; the most promising candidate to offer himself recently had decided to take up a vacant post in Kent instead.

He rang the station and told them to arrange to pay the congestion charge for his car and to make a courtesy call to the City of London police to warn them that he would be trespassing on their ground. Then he called home, leaving a message on the answering machine to say he'd be back late. He headed through Hungerford, up to the M4 and east to London.

He was going against the weekend traffic and had an easy enough run until he came off the motorway at Chiswick, after which it was stop-start all the way with frequent consultations of the A–Z.

He pulled up outside Marchant House in Charterhouse Street near Holborn at a quarter to six, desperate for a pee. He parked on a meter, ran into the nearest pub, used the facilities and was in reception by five to the hour.

Cynthia Thorley was already waiting for him.

She was thirty and attractive in a girl-next-door sort of way. Her oval face peeked out from a swinging cap of black hair in a page-boy style and he guessed from the shape of her dark eyes and the pallor of her skin beneath careful make-up that she was part Chinese.

She wasn't wearing what he thought of as the uniform of a City PA – dark suit and white blouse – but had on a vivid summer dress topped with a plain linen jacket in cream to match her sandals. He remembered that it was Friday and many firms had a dress-down policy to ease the transition to the weekend.

'Superintendent Summers?' Her voice betrayed her as a Londoner, perhaps with an overlay of elocution lessons. Her hand-shake was firm as she transferred her calfskin briefcase from right to left hand to greet him formally. 'I don't know what help I can be but Stephen says I'm to answer all your questions.'

'Just getting background,' he said. 'There's a pub over the road which wasn't too busy a minute ago. Let me buy you a drink.'

'I'd rather have coffee,' she said. 'I have to be at a dinner party in two hours and there'll be enough booze there to sink a battleship – preferably not one insured by us. There's a place round the corner.'

'As you wish.' He let her lead the way and the security man at the front desk called out, 'Night, Mrs Thorley,' as they left, receiving a smile in reply.

Greg had already noticed the wedding band on her third finger but she might be divorced or separated.

The café she had chosen was quiet but not so quiet that he feared to be overheard. She asked for an almond latte and he decided to have one himself, fetching them from the counter. It wasn't part of a chain, or not one he'd heard of, and the man who served him sounded authentically Italian.

'I couldn't believe the awful news when Stephen rang me this morning,' she said when they were settled.

'What time was that?'

'About nine-thirty, just as I got in. He said he was calling from Dom's school on the Sussex Weald. I was just thinking that it was odd that he wasn't already at his desk when he rang through. Robyn.' She shook her head. 'Who could do such a thing?'

He assumed the question was rhetorical and asked, 'How long have you worked for Mr Marchant?'

'Eight years. I came as a temp when his old secretary was on maternity leave and we got on well together. When Marcia decided not to come back, he offered me a permanent job on the spot. It was less money than temping but I liked the work so I accepted and I've always been glad I did.' She smiled, a small moustache of milk forming on her upper lip. 'I met my husband Ashton at Marchants.'

'As his PA, I bet you know Mr Marchant better than anyone outside his immediate family.'

She thought about it. 'I imagine so.'

'What sort of man is he?'

She treated the question with great seriousness, her beautifully manicured finger tracing circles in a small spill of cane sugar on the table. 'He was quiet, but funny. Is, I mean! Why am I talking as if it's him who's dead? Perhaps because it's so hard to imagine him going on without Robyn.' Her eyes took on a glazed look as she fought back tears.

'They were that close?'

'That thing they say about finding your other half? Robyn and Stephen made me think of that. When Ashton asked me to marry him, I wasn't sure what to do. I mean, I loved him an' all but it's such a big step. I asked Stephen's advice and he told me that marriage to the right person was the best thing in the world.' The glazed look went and she smiled happily. 'And it is.'

He smiled back at her, touched by her simple contentment. She had cast off her glossy veneer of efficiency with her working week and he liked her the better for it. 'You were telling me what sort of person your boss is.'

'Right. He's generous and considerate, never moans if people want to take time off for personal stuff. And the School – Hilltop – he puts so much into that place. And now it's like he's just half a person. Please, Mr Summers–' She turned anxious eyes on him. 'Who killed Robyn?'

'It's too soon for me to say.'

'But you have some idea?'

'Truthfully, Mrs Thorley, I don't. We weigh up the evidence, interview people like yourself, try to get the full picture. Eventually, things start to fall into place.'

'But you will find him?'

'Yes. We will find him. Or her.'

'Can I ask you a question?'

'You can ask.'

'Have you ever failed to solve a murder?'

'Not so far.' His hand reached automatically to touch wood and they both laughed since the table was made of glass and chrome. After a moment, he said, 'Would it be indelicate to ask how much he's worth?'

She shrugged. 'He said I should answer all your questions and the information is in the public domain. Marchants Marine Insurance has a market capitalisation of two hundred and sixty-two million, as of this morning's share price, and Stephen owns fifteen per cent of it.'

'Phew!' Greg puffed out his cheeks. That made Marchant easily the richest person he'd ever met. If Robyn *had* had a lover, *had* been contemplating divorce, it would surely have been bad news for Stephen financially.

'Of course,' she went on, 'that money is tied up in the business. He can't start selling shares without people thinking there's something wrong.'

'So the money isn't accessible – it's a paper fortune.'

'He pays himself a good salary. Then there's Hilltop. You'd know better than me how much that's worth.'

Greg had a pretty good idea what a house that size sold for in Inkpen and it had a lot of noughts on the end. 'Has he enemies – business enemies?' he asked.

She shook her head. 'Insurance is a pretty cut-throat trade, but even so...'

Greg had to agree. It seemed ridiculous that even the most desperate businessman would stab his rival's wife in the back. He tried another tack.

'And he sleeps three nights a week in town.'

'Sure, but lots of City men do that... Okay, a lot of them take the opportunity to play around but not Stephen.'

'How can you be so sure?'

'I'd just ... know. I saw enough of it when I was temping; there were always signs: personal phone calls, being asked to buy presents, send flowers and not to the home address. Most of them don't even try to be discreet – it was like I was some android whose opinion didn't count. I know those men and Stephen is different. He's a Roman Catholic too – the real thing, not just lip service.'

Her voice rose in indignation. 'The very idea is risible and I can't believe you're wasting your time on it.'

He waited for her anger to subside through lack of response. After a moment, she grew embarrassed and took a lipstick and compact out of her bag, fussing with them. He asked, 'Have you been to his flat in the Barbican?'

'Once, to help him prepare a drinks party he was holding.' She squeezed her lips together, compressing the fresh waxy brown layer she had applied, and put her compact away. 'It isn't very homely but it's not what you'd call a bachelor pad either. He stays at the office till seven or eight most nights, then he picks something up at Simply Food – he doesn't like to eat alone in restaurants, says he finds it depressing. Zaps it in the microwave and watches television. Except for his opera nights.'

'Wednesday?'

'That's right.'

Greg drained his latte, enjoying the last concentration of almond syrup at the bottom. 'To sum up, Mr and Mrs Marchant were a happy and united couple, not a whiff of gossip about either of them. Is that right, Mrs Thorley?'

She looked him straight in the eye. 'They were the happiest couple I ever met.'

Greg had never fancied living in London and it got no better with the passage of years. He was sure that there was more litter in the streets than there used to be. As a child, he'd been fascinated on a rare visit to the panto-mime one Christmas to see the gutters being washed down at dusk with streams of water from a hydrant; no council did that now.

Twenty years ago the idea of beggars on the streets of the capital had been unthink-able, now they sat in doorways and on pave-ments, often with mangy dogs, uttering their unvarying litany: 'Spare some change?'

He'd worked out his route to the Barbican in advance. Even so, he was thwarted by some one-way streets and unexpected road-works. He almost wished he'd got Nicolaides to chauffeur him – the constable had been born in London and knew its secrets well – but that would have meant listening to his tedious attempts at conversation.

Finally he found the huge complex and followed the signs for short-term visitor parking. The car park was full with the glossy vehicles of patrons of the arts and he had to drive round twice in search of a space, until he spotted a 4X4 backing out and raced a Porsche for the gap. The other driver made a sign with his fist and his forehead which Greg had no trouble interpreting as 'dickhead', as if his more expensive car came with parking priority.

'I got the space,' he said under his breath. 'So who's the dickhead now?'

The flats of the Barbican rose above the theatres and concert halls like grim blocks of social housing, except that their owners saw little change from half a million, even for a one-bedder.

Stephen Marchant had not indulged in a penthouse or paid for a panoramic view. His flat on the fifth floor overlooked the roof of the theatre. There was no concierge and Greg let himself into the block with one key and the flat with two more – a mortise and a latch.

It had the feel of a hotel room – or rather a suite, since doors stood open to reveal a bedroom and kitchen beyond the character-less sitting room.

He crossed first to the answering machine. A steady red light showed that the messages had been retrieved but not erased. He pressed the play button and heard Andy's voice asking Marchant to ring Greg's mobile as soon as possible, however late the hour.

He tried last-number redial and his mobile chirped in his pocket. He hung up. They would have to get Telecom to trace the calls on this line too. He walked round the flat, which didn't take long. There was no sign of a home computer and a plasma television was the only luxury, suggesting an important role in Stephen's entertainment on bachelor nights.

He checked the bathroom cupboard but found no female toiletries, no women's garments in the wardrobe, just a collection of suits, like his own in their blue/grey dullness, only more expensive. It seemed that even Robyn didn't visit here, let alone any other woman.

The fridge held milk, a bottle of white wine with two glasses drunk, a microwave spaghetti carbonara and three eggs: no caviar, smoked salmon or champagne for the reception of lady friends. In the freezer compartment were ice cubes and a pair of cufflinks with a family crest, which he thought were solid gold; because no burglar would think of looking there. Right?

The place made him sad and he tried to

analyse why. He realised that if he had been Stephen he would now be regretting the many nights spent alone here instead of in the bosom of his family, the affection of his wife, however sexless that affection might have become.

How much did sex matter in a long marriage? He loved Angie and their relationship was still new enough to remain passionate, yet there had been so many single years after his divorce when he hadn't held a woman's body against his and it hadn't seemed to matter. If there'd been anything he'd missed, it was someone to come home to, someone who cared if he lived or died.

If he'd stayed married to Diane, they would have celebrated their silver wedding by now, probably not with a night of non-stop lovemaking.

On which scary thought, it was time to go home, to his own happy nest.

'Dad?'

'Huh?'

Dominic laid a hand on his father's shoulder. 'It's the middle of the night, Dad. You need to come to bed.' He picked up the empty whisky bottle from the kitchen table and dropped it into the recycling bin in the larder. The dirty tumbler went in the sink.

He helped his father to his feet, pulling the man's right arm round his shoulder, winding his own left arm as far round Stephen's substantial waist as it would reach. 'Right foot forward,' he suggested. 'Good. Now the left.' It was a bit like the three-legged race from primary school, only with four legs, two of them shaky.

The stairs were the hardest but they made it up in one piece and he thankfully let his father collapse on to the nearest of the twin beds in his parents' room. It was his mother's bed, but she wouldn't be needing it.

'Let's get you undressed,' he said. 'Or you'll feel like crap in the morning.' He unlaced his shoes, dropping them to the floor by the bed. He unzipped Stephen's trousers and began to slide the shiny material over his ample buttocks.

'What's going on?'

He glanced round to see his sister standing in the doorway. She was in her pyjamas, her arms wrapped around her chest as a defence against a world that had turned so suddenly hostile.

'Dad's been drowning his sorrows.'

'That's not like him.'

'Which is why he's practically comatose,' Dominic said. 'I'm just going to undress him and get him into bed.' He finally succeeded in removing the trousers and began to un-button his shirt.

'Are you okay?' Charlie asked in a whisper. 'You've been asleep all day.'

'I feel rested.' He turned tired eyes on her, eyes that gave the lie to his words. 'Realised I hadn't eaten since breakfast, at school, feels like days ago. Went down to raid the fridge. Found him like this. Still can't quite...'

'Manage pronouns? Sorry! I know.'

'It's worse for Dad,' he said.

'He can always get another wife,' Charlie pointed out. 'We can't get another mother.'

'Can you really imagine that – Dad with another woman?'

'Here, let me give you a hand.' Charlie laid a firm hand on the waistband of her father's boxer shorts but Dominic stopped her.

'I can manage. He'd be ashamed, like Noah with his daughters uncovering his nakedness.'

'Bro,' she said, shaking her head. 'You spend way too much time in scripture class.'

But she left him to it. He completed his task and pulled the sheet and duvet over the man's fat, pale body, turning him on one side in case he was sick later.

He fetched a chair to the bedside and sat for a few minutes with his head bowed, praying. He asked for God's mercy on the soul of his mother and His help that they might all get through this time of unbearable grief.

To thee do we cry, poor banished children of Eve; to thee do we send up our sighs, mourning and weeping in this valley of tears.

Before leaving the room, he bent to smell

the pillow, to get a last whiff of his mother's scent, but the stench of sour whisky masked it and made him gag.

Chapter Thirteen

Although it was Saturday, Greg went into the office the following morning. Chief Superintendent Jim Barkiss was off at a conference of senior police officers, which left Greg in charge of the station, and if he spent all his time at the crime scene there was no knowing what the Uniform mice would get up to while the cats were away.

It also gave him a chance to review the case in peace. He read the post-mortem report with care and went through the preliminary notes from SOCO which Martha Childs had left for him at the front desk, rather than bringing them to him in person as she would have done not long ago. This meant that he had not had the chance to talk to her, to suggest that they both stop being childish and rebuild their former cordial relationship.

The constable who'd brought the report up had given him a knowing look, or had he imagined that?

He was going to miss Barbara – the person he most bounced ideas off.

It had turned humid and a fly was driving him crazy by buzzing lazily round his office, although never quite lazy enough to be thwacked into oblivion with a rolled-up copy of *The Times*.

Martha's report said that nothing they had found in the house, garden or surrounding area could conceivably have been the murder weapon. Unfortunately, this didn't mean that no one in the household had killed her. Most killers knew by now that getting safely rid of the murder weapon was crucial, although that suggested a certain amount of calculation too, and a cool head.

But then the murder had not struck him as a spur-of-the-moment thing: to be stabbed in your own garden at night might be the stuff of women's nightmares, but Robyn Marchant had not been the prey of some passing madman, not in his opinion.

An enemy had planned this crime and had the cunning to keep it simple.

He was surprised to receive a phone call at nine-thirty from Stephen Marchant, saying that he wanted to come to the station with his solicitor.

He agreed to meet them at ten-thirty and hung up thoughtfully. Usually when someone volunteered to come in all lawyered up, it meant that they had a confession to make and that the case was over bar the paperwork.

Which would be almost disappointing.

'You look half asleep.' Dr Pat Armstrong, head of forensics at Newbury police station, looked at her junior colleague with interest and sympathy, her head tilted back, the better to read his face.

Deepak tried to tough it out. 'You know how it is – Friday night down the pub. Didn't think I'd be working on a Saturday.'

Pat was not fooled. 'Not sleeping well?'

Deep threw in the towel. 'Do you ever have nightmares you can't wake up from, Pat?'

'I used to. Of the day I ended up in this.' She gestured at her wheelchair. 'I'm driving along, minding my own business, not knowing that round the corner is a drunken driver on the wrong side of the road. If only I could stop, or pull over, until he was safely past ... but then he might have maimed or killed someone else.'

Pat paused to think this through with her habitual sharp logic. Was she really saying that she wouldn't rather it had happened to someone else? Not anyone she knew, naturally, but a random stranger. She gave up the conundrum and asked, 'Is it Sangita?'

'You say you used to?'

'I developed a mechanism over the years, a trigger.'

'A trigger?'

'In my case it's rain. Rain starts to fall steadily on the windscreen of my car and I

196

have to switch my wipers on. That's my cue to wake up.'

'Does it work?'

'About three-quarters of the time.'

'I'll give it a try.'

'Okay, but get your own trigger! Now, this murder in Inkpen. Can you run the victim's DNA against the database while I deal with her fingerprints?'

They did not expect to find a match in either case and Pat soon got confirmation that the prints were negative.

'No go,' she said. 'Oh, bollocks!'

'What?'

'Nothing. I thought the system had frozen for a minute, but it was just having one of its little rests.'

DNA matching took longer but Deep confirmed that the dead woman's genes were not on the national database.

Pat fired off an email to Gregory Summers and they turned their attention to the rest of the evidence.

'Who was the victim?' Deep asked idly.

'Woman named Robyn Marchant. Haven't you heard of her?' He shrugged a negative. 'She's something of a local legend, runs a school for disabled children on the downs.'

Deep paused at his computer screen. 'Whereabouts?'

'Inkpen. It's called Hilltop... Deep? You okay?'

'It's a bit close today.' He got up, sucking in a long breath. 'I'll just step outside for some air.'

You have mail.

Greg poked at the computer keyboard and read Pat's email. It came as no surprise that Robyn Marchant was not known to the police.

The front desk called two minutes later to say that her husband had arrived for their meeting, so Greg put on his jacket and slipped down the stairs.

Stephen Marchant had not come to confess to his wife's murder.

He was accompanied by a man in his eighties who seemed to embody the expression 'old stick', skinny and dry. He introduced him as Guy Marchant and added, 'My uncle.'

'I'm retired, of course,' the old man said, 'but I still deal with legal matters where it concerns the family.'

Greg thought that Stephen looked hungover, but who could blame him? He'd cut himself shaving and there was a patch of dried blood on his chin. He wore a suit but it looked crumpled and his shirt was open at the neck, in sharp contrast to the old man who was dapper in a Prince of Wales check over a silk shirt with pink and green bow-tie, a tight new rosebud in his buttonhole.

Greg ushered them both into an interview room and the older Marchant came straight to the point. 'Stephen rang me yesterday morning and asked me to get probate underway on Robyn's will.'

He hadn't wasted any time, Greg thought.

'Now call me a bit of an old stickler, but the first thing I do before proving a will is to contact the Probate Office to make sure they don't have a will registered for that person. I know the youngsters don't bother because they think it so unlikely, but it saves time in the end.'

He fixed Greg with his sharp eyes. 'You know about that, of course – man in your position. It's possible to register a will at Somerset House and that will can then only be superseded by another will so registered.'

'I know about it,' Greg said, 'I've just never been quite sure what the point of it is.'

'I struggled with that myself,' Stephen said.

Guy glared at them both as if they were two exceptionally dim schoolboys who could not grasp Pythagoras's theorem despite repeated explanations.

'I am Mr Lear,' he snapped, surprisingly. 'I want to leave my estate equally between my three daughters – Goneril, Regan and Cordelia – but I'm going to live with Regan in the granny flat above the garage in her lovely house in Weybridge and I know that her husband–'

'Cornwall!' Greg said triumphantly since, luckily, he had 'done' *King Lear* for A level.

'Quite so. I know that my son-in-law is a nasty bit of work who will put pressure on me to change my will in his wife's favour.'

'So you register a will giving your true wishes with the Probate Office,' Greg said.

'And when Cornwall and his two thuggish witnesses come to get me to make a new will, I meekly comply, knowing that on my death, he will be sorely disappointed.' He grinned skeletally. 'I will have the last laugh.'

'And if we can cut to the chase,' Stephen said patiently. 'It turns out that Robyn registered a will five years ago.'

'Ah!' Greg said.

Guy drew a document from his inside pocket. 'Since this might be germane to your enquiry, Superintendent, I sent a courier round to Somerset House for a copy yesterday afternoon. I think you will find the contents of interest.'

Greg took the sheet of paper from him and glanced down it. The will was short and left everything Robyn Marchant possessed to Daniel Fahey.

'Christ!' he said.

'Indeed,' Stephen said. 'Daniel is the sole heir to her estate, such as it is.'

'Such as it is?' Greg queried.

'Robyn had few possessions.'

'But the house, the school?'

'Belong to me,' Stephen said. 'That was the way Robyn wanted it. When we bought the place–'

'With *your* money,' his uncle put in.

'That's neither here nor there,' Stephen snapped, looking at his uncle with active dislike. 'Everything was put in my name because Robyn said she didn't want to own property. She wanted to go through life ... unencumbered.'

'So what does her estate consist of?' Greg asked. 'Did she have an income? Savings?'

'She was paid a modest salary as director of the school but she made frequent donations to charity.' Stephen shrugged. 'She may have a couple of thousand in the building society – rainy-day money – but that's all. The bequest seems more of a ... a *gesture* than anything else.'

'Plus her personal possessions, naturally,' Guy said.

'That's what hurts,' Stephen said quietly. 'Not that she wanted to provide for Daniel at the expense of her own children – he's been like part of the family and they will have all the Marchant money – but that she should deny me even her most private mementoes.'

Guy handed over a sheet of headed vellum paper with a name, address and telephone number etched on it in his psychotically neat handwriting. 'The solicitor who wrote and registered the will,' he explained. 'I looked him up and he's a sole practitioner. Still,' he sniffed snootily, 'he seems to have drawn it up and had it witnessed correctly – more's the pity.'

Greg felt like employing another of Angie's favourite phrases – *It's not brain surgery* – but thought better of it. He thanked Guy and put the paper in his pocket. He scanned the will quickly again.

'She made you her executor, though, Mr Marchant.'

'Daniel was seventeen at the date of that will,' Stephen said, 'technically a minor. Besides, I'm sure she trusted me to carry out her wishes.'

The old man reclaimed the will and read aloud the names of the witnesses.

'Johnny Yip and Albert Wing. I ask you.'

'Have you spoken to Fahey about this?' Greg gestured at the document. 'Does he know about it?'

'No, we came straight to you,' Stephen said, 'and I don't think he has any idea.'

'You have no means of knowing,' Guy said. 'If she could conceal this from you...'

'Even if he did know,' Stephen protested, 'the idea that Daniel would harm Robyn for a couple of thousand pounds is just–'

'What if he didn't know it was only a couple of thousand?' his uncle persisted. 'What if he thought, like the superintendent, that it was half the marital assets?'

Greg felt like saying that a couple of thousand might not be much to a man who owned the best part of forty million pounds' worth of insurance business, but it was a fortune to some people. 'I think I'd better ask him,' he said, getting up. 'Is he still at Hilltop?'

'Yes.' Stephen rose with him. 'Come with us, Uncle Guy. Daniel should have someone to represent him.'

Guy Marchant grunted and hauled himself reluctantly out of his chair.

Chapter Fourteen

Greg drove through Kintbury and up into Inkpen. A cricket match was unfolding on the recreation ground in Post Office Lane, as though in slow motion. That was how the game should be played, he thought: thirteen men, all amateurs, any age from twelve to seventy, in varying shades of white flannel, not the pastel tracksuits favoured by the professionals these days.

The away team would arrive two men short and the home team would lend them the Clutterbuck twins, who had never scored more than ten runs between them but who would try their best for the opposition.

The English summer incarnate.

Every other car he passed had a St George's cross flying from roof or wing, often two. He began to sing to himself under his breath: *'There'll always be an England, where there's a country lane, wherever there's a cottage, small, beside a field of grain.'*

He somehow made it out to Hilltop before the two Marchants. A pile of floral tributes had appeared at the gateposts over the past twenty-four hours, mostly roses and carnations of garish hues, wrapped in cellophane, but he spotted a posy of wild flowers. One or two bystanders were hanging around in the lane, looking a little disappointed at the lack of visible excitement.

Letting himself in through the open front door into the hall, Greg came upon Nicolaides.

'Is Daniel Fahey about?' he asked abruptly.

Nick looked round doubtfully. 'He's here somewhere.'

'What do you want with my son?' Siobhan Fahey glided out of the shadows like a ghost, making Nick start visibly. There was something intimidating about her thin presence.

'I need to ask him a couple of questions,' Greg said.

She stood looking at him for a moment, very erect, as if she had a pile of books on her head. 'Daniel wasn't here the night of the murder. You know that. You saw him arrive.'

Ah, but did I? Greg wondered, *or had he been there all along?* 'If you could just tell me where to find him,' he said.

'He's in the library.' Seeing that Greg was at a loss, she added, 'This way.'

He followed her along a corridor and into a room at the back of the house. The wood-panelled walls with their dark patina suggested that it had once been a smoking room and the boarded-up fireplace was a magnificent confection of green and cream marble.

The bookshelves might always have been there except that instead of rows of matching sets of hardbacks – obscure travel books, philosophy, dry as dust – there were volumes of colourful modern children's stories, their jackets showing witches, talking animals, cheeky-looking kids in bright clothes against primary backgrounds.

The tables were like the ones he remembered from his own school – plain pine, serviceable, a little too small for adolescent knees. At one of these, by the window, he saw Daniel Fahey. He was reading aloud to a teenage girl who seemed to Greg to be sitting uncomfortably close to him.

'We're trying to keep things as normal as possible,' Siobhan said. 'Routine is very important to the children.'

'But they know that Mrs Marchant's dead?'

She nodded. 'Those who can understand the concept of death.'

Greg walked over to Daniel. 'Hello again, Mr Fahey,' he said. 'I was wondering if I could have a quick word. In private.'

Daniel handed the book to the girl saying, 'Why don't you see how you get on by yourself, Marie. I'll hear you read when I get back.'

'Okay.'

He could see now that the girl had Down's syndrome. As Daniel got up, she peeked round him at Greg, eyeing him up and down. As he followed the young man out of the room, he found himself glancing back at her in disquiet.

'Marie has a mental age of eight,' Daniel said in an undertone, 'allied to the body of a grown woman. It's disturbing for her.'

Not just for her, Greg thought.

'So what can I do for you ... is it Superintendent?'

'Yes, sir. Actually, I think Mr Marchant wanted his uncle to sit in on our talk, so we'd better wait for him.'

'Old Guy?' Daniel laughed. 'What on earth for?'

The man in question arrived at that moment, puffing along the hall towards them with quick little steps like a geisha. 'Superintendent, I must protest.'

'I haven't started the interview yet, Mr Marchant.'

'I should think not.' He took Daniel by the arm and steered him away. 'I shall have a word with my client first.'

'What do you mean, client?' Daniel queried.

'If you'd like to wait in the office.' Marchant indicated a door to Greg's right without answering the boy's question.

Greg shrugged and let himself into the room. It was functional, cold and spare, with racks of filing cabinets and a deal table which served as a desk. A cork noticeboard overflowed with papers pinned higgledy-piggledy. He sat down at the desk behind a computer-shaped space, the machine having been removed by his own men.

Ten minutes went by and he was getting bored. If the computer had been there he could have had a game of patience. Free cell was the best patience since it could always be got out, however many attempts it took. There was nothing like the automatic moves of solitaire to set the mind roving free on a problem.

The door opened and Fahey came in with Guy Marchant. The boy looked stunned. 'I had no idea.' He sank down on to a chair opposite Greg and Guy pulled one up beside him.

'I gather Mr Marchant has broken the

news to you,' Greg said.

'I can't take it in. Why would Robyn leave me her estate?'

'That's what I'd like to know.' Greg watched the younger man closely. His pale eyes looked watery. 'Did Mrs Marchant ever say anything to you about her intentions?'

'No, it's come completely out of the blue.'

Greg leaned forward. 'I'm sure you've already given a statement to one of my constables about the night of the murder, but you'll understand why I'd like to go over it again.'

'...I suppose you think this gives me a motive.'

'Can you just tell me your movements on Thursday evening?'

'Yes, I had–'

Outside, in the front drive, a girl began to scream, not once but continuously, like a soul tormented in the flames of hell. Greg jumped to his feet and shot out of the room, Daniel, who was nearer the door, a few yards ahead of him.

The onlookers had something to watch at last. A middle-aged woman in expensive clothes was attempting to force Marie into the passenger seat of a shiny red sports car while Siobhan harangued her at the top of her voice. It was Marie who was screaming and, as Greg and Daniel arrived, she broke free of the woman's grasp and hurled herself face down on the gravel, thrashing her hands and feet in the air, still shrieking like a tribe of banshees.

'What's going on here?' Greg demanded.

Siobhan ignored him. 'You see what you've done,' she yelled at the woman. 'You're ruining years of painstaking work with this child.'

'She's my daughter,' the woman snapped, 'and I won't leave her in a house with a murderer.'

'Oh, please! You've taken no interest in Marie in the ten years she's been here. She's an embarrassment and you just dumped her here and tried to forget her existence.'

'Mum!' Daniel protested.

'Now, you feel guilty and you're trying to throw your weight about. She's made it clear that she doesn't want to leave and I won't let you take her.'

Daniel was helping Marie to her feet. She seemed calmer for his presence and wrapped her arms round his waist, burying her head in his shirt front and sobbing, her shoulders shaking, bare in their skimpy sundress.

Greg cleared his throat. 'Mrs Fahey, if this lady is the little girl's mother–'

'Who the hell are you?' the woman demanded rudely.

He showed her his warrant card. 'I'm a police officer, madam.'

'Good! Then tell her she can't stop me taking my own daughter away.'

'I fear that may be the case,' Greg said to Siobhan, who snorted, 'but shall we all go indoors and talk about this calmly?' He glanced at the avid spectators, who had now grown into quite a crowd and were discussing the rights and wrongs of the case freely.

'Can't you get rid of those ghouls?' Siobhan hissed. She jerked her head. 'And *him* especially.'

Greg realised that Liam Sullivan was the 'him' referred to, standing in the group, his arms folded, a look of quiet amusement on his face.

'Please go inside, Mrs Fahey,' he said, 'and take Mrs...?'

'Honeyman-Jones,' the expensive woman supplied.

'Mrs Honeyman-Jones with you. I'll join you in a moment.'

As the two women departed with Daniel and Marie, Greg walked over to Sullivan.

'Just taking my morning constitutional,' Sullivan said.

'Never volunteer information,' Greg said.

The Irishman laughed. 'Who was that woman you were just talking to?'

'Mother of one of the pupils.'

'Not her, the other one, the shapeless woman.'

'Why do you want to know?'

Sullivan shrugged and walked away without a backward glance. Greg went back indoors. He passed Andy Whittaker in the hall.

'What's all the row?' Andy asked.

'I'm dealing with it. See if you can get those people to disperse.'

'Right on it, sir.'

He found the two women in the library, sitting in murderous silence. Daniel was still tending to Marie who had calmed down and was drinking a bottle of red liquid through a straw.

'Now, Mrs Honeyman-Jones,' he said. 'I gather you want to take your daughter home.'

'There's been a murder,' she said. 'What would people say if I left my child in a place where such things happen?'

'Yes, what would people say at the bridge club?' Siobhan sneered. 'You used to be more concerned about what people would say about you having a handicapped child.'

'I don't think this is getting us anywhere,' Greg said firmly. 'Mrs Honeyman-Jones, no one can stop you taking your daughter home if that's really what you want. However, you saw how she reacted to the idea. Now, I have a number of police officers here and there is no reason to suppose that Marie is in any danger.'

The woman looked from him to the girl and back again. Her eyes, as they fell on her daughter, were not benign. As Marie let some of the red liquid dribble down her front, her face twisted in disgust. She made no move towards her and it was Daniel who took out a handkerchief to dab at her chin and neck.

'Why don't you just leave her here?' Greg said gently. 'You can tell people she's being well looked after.'

'...All right.' Mrs Honeyman-Jones rose, gave Siobhan a last glare and walked out with her head held high. Marie gave no sign that she had even noticed her mother's departure.

Greg had never understood why someone with a perfectly good name like Honeyman would want to tack the prosaic Jones on the end, just for the sake of having a double barrel. He'd met a lot of Mrs Honeyman-Joneses in his life and not liked any of them.

'Mr Fahey,' he said. 'Perhaps we can continue.'

'What's going on?' Siobhan asked, but got no reply.

They went back to the office, where Guy Marchant was sitting exactly where they'd left him, with his eyes closed and his head lolling forward.

'I'm not asleep,' he said, opening his eyes without haste.

'Now where were we?' Greg resumed his seat and gestured to Daniel to do the same.

'My client was recounting his movements on Thursday evening,' Guy supplied.

Both older men looked expectantly at Daniel.

'I'd finished my last exam that day,' he said, 'and I was supposed to spend the evening carousing with my mates, but somehow I wasn't in the mood. I haven't been much of a party animal since I split up with my girlfriend at Easter. I went to the pub with them but I only had one pint and when they wanted to go on to a club, I decided to bail. I suddenly wanted to be here, with Mum and my extended family, so I got on my bike and rode out here. You saw me as I arrived.'

'So your friends will be able to confirm that you were in Oxford until ... what? Closing time?'

'Yes. Eleven – eleven-fifteen.'

'Do you know much about how the school is organised?' Greg asked.

'I'm not sure I follow you.'

'Who owns the building, the equity and so on.'

'I've never given it a moment's thought.'

'But if you had, you might have assumed that Mr and Mrs Marchant owned the school jointly.'

Fahey frowned. 'I suppose. It's the normal thing.'

'Making Mrs Marchant's estate rather valuable.'

The boy flushed. 'Now see here–'

'All right,' Greg interrupted. 'Can you give

me a list of names – the people you were with on Thursday night, contact numbers for them – soon as possible. Mr Marchant – a word, if I may.'

Daniel got up to leave but in the doorway he turned. 'I'm an accountant. At least, I will be, assuming I've passed my exams. If I thought Stephen and Robyn owned the house and school together then I'd have assumed that it was as joint tenants, which means Robyn's half would pass automatically to Stephen and could not be willed away. So there.'

He left and Greg turned to the old man. 'That's a good point, isn't it?'

'It's *a* point,' Guy conceded. 'Now, how can I help you, Superintendent?'

'I get the distinct impression that you didn't approve of your nephew's choice of wife, sir.'

'Oh, I wouldn't say that. I suppose we had some reservations at first since no one seemed to know who her people were, but she worked out all right in the end. At least she was a Roman Catholic. The Marchants are one of the oldest recusant families in England, you know,' he added with pride.

'Er, no. I didn't know.'

'For over a hundred years, under Elizabeth and the Stuarts, we were tortured and killed for our beliefs – what were perceived as our traitorous loyalties. Then came a couple of centuries of petty persecution –

214

couldn't stand for parliament, couldn't join the army or be a lawyer – but still we kept the faith of our fathers.'

Pig-headed was the expression that sprang into Greg's mind.

'Things are different now, of course.' Guy sounded wistful. 'We can do what we like, assuming little Charlotte doesn't want to marry Prince William. Where was I? Yes. We were starting to give up hope of Stephen's marrying and settling down. He was thirty-six and he'd been a bit of a drifter in his youth – tried his hand at a couple of possible careers before he gave in and joined the family firm.'

He chuckled. 'Still, I can't talk. I rattled around a bit myself as a young man, mostly in the colonies – the white man's burden, so to speak – and I never did marry. We're not thrilled to see so much family money disappearing into this place but, when all's said and done, it's charity and *noblesse oblige.*'

No sooner had the old man left the office than Siobhan came in, shutting the door firmly behind her. She leaned forward, her hands in fists, on the desk and said in a low but vehement voice, 'I want to know what is going on.'

'Sit down, Mrs Fahey.'

'I'll stand, thank you.'

'As you wish.'

Greg folded his arms and looked up at her. He had thought her a plain woman, but now it seemed to him merely that she made no effort with her appearance. Her eyes were a luminous blue – as unlike her son's as the summer sky is to the sea – and there were still strands of ginger in her white hair, giving it a strawberry sheen in the light from the window.

'Can you think of any reason,' he said, 'why Mrs Marchant would make a will leaving her entire estate to your son?'

Siobhan gasped. He gestured to the chair and, without further protest, she sat. 'I see that this news is as much of a surprise to you as to Stephen and Daniel.'

When she got her breath back, she said, 'But she and Stephen made wills a few years ago, leaving everything to each other. I was one of the witnesses.'

'She made another will – one her husband knew nothing about – that overrides that.'

After a pause for thought she said, 'But it can't amount to much – her estate. Everything is in Stephen's name.'

'You knew that?'

She looked puzzled. 'Of course. It wasn't a secret.'

'But your son didn't know.'

'What? Of course he did.'

'I asked him.'

She faltered. 'I suppose it never came up.'

Chapter Fifteen

'Can I help you?' The mortuary attendant glanced up from his book and gave the young Asian man a suspicious look.

'Newbury police. Forensics.' Deepak Gupta produced his ID card and the attendant relaxed visibly. 'You have a body here – Mrs Robyn Marchant.'

'Yeah, I know the one.'

'I need to take some more samples.'

The man shrugged and got up. 'Thought they did all that sort of thing at the autopsy.'

'Usually, but my boss wants some extra hair and skin to do additional tests.' Deep felt a tremble within himself. Was he explaining too much, acting suspiciously? 'Can I see her?'

'Sure. This way.'

The attendant led him into the cold room and pulled open a refrigerated tray, twitching back the sheet that covered her face with one deft movement.

Deepak stood staring at the woman he was sure was Aoife Cusack. He didn't know what he'd been expecting; not this, anyway, not a tranquil woman of forty who looked as if she'd died peacefully in her sleep.

He felt in his pockets for his paraphernalia since he would have to take some samples while the attendant watched. He scraped a few skin cells from the inside of her mouth, wincing at the cold feel of it. He plucked a couple of hairs, checking for the roots which would contain her DNA.

'Okay?' The attendant had a note of impatience in his voice as Deep continued to stare at the dead woman. In a more kindly tone, he asked, 'Did you know her, mate?'

What? No.' Deepak collected himself. 'I never met her. Thanks. I'm done here.'

So long as no one in CID suspected her true identity, then he was safe.

As Greg got back to the police station, he encountered two women constables – Jill Christie and Emily Foster – who were starting their shift. They stood aside to let him pass with due deference to his rank.

'You two on late relief this week?' he asked.

It was Jill who answered. 'Yes, sir.'

'How do you fancy doing a bit of overtime for CID tomorrow morning?' The late relief worked from two till ten which gave them the morning free. With Barbara away, he could do with some extra bodies and, young as they were, he thought the two women were shaping up well.

Jill and Emily looked at each other and

Emily said, 'Yes please, sir.'

'Guv!' Jill corrected her.

'Yes please, Guv.'

'Sir will do fine. Okay. Unless you hear different in the meantime come to my office at nine tomorrow.'

Greg didn't think that Robyn's secret solicitor would be at work on a Saturday but he rang the number Guy Marchant had given him out of habit. He got an irate woman.

'I'm sick of telling people he's not on this number any more,' she snapped.

'Do you happen to know–' She had hung up. He tried the telephone directory and found the man, John Fountain, at a different address. He dialled the number and a voice said, 'John Fountain.' Greg, expecting an answering machine at best, hung up without speaking.

As the office wasn't far from the police station, he preferred to drop in on him unannounced. He liked to see the faces and body language of the people he was interviewing wherever possible.

He found a scruffy office above a bookie's, the door open at the top of a steep flight of stairs. It was one room with a table which served as a desk, half a dozen gunmetal filing cabinets and two moth-eaten chairs.

Nor was Fountain what he expected of a solicitor: he was a skinny man of about thirty, with dirty blond hair curling over his collar and intelligent grey eyes. He wore jeans and a polo shirt and was eating a prawn and mayo sandwich washed down with Coke from a two-litre bottle.

He had his feet up on the desk and they were bare and not especially clean. Laid-back was the description that sprang to mind and lawyers were usually uptight.

'Come in,' he said, when Greg knocked on the door frame, his feet swinging down to the linoleum floor. 'Take a pew. Have some Coke.' He wiped the neck of the bottle with his finger and offered it across the desk.

'I was thinking of making a will,' Greg began, declining the tempting offer of somebody else's germs.

'Then you've come to the right place.' As Greg looked round doubtfully, he added, 'I'm cheap and, you may be surprised to hear, I'm a bloody good lawyer.'

'Then how come...?' Greg waved his hand over his surroundings.

'I love the law,' Fountain explained, 'the subtle beauty of it, like a rapier. What I hate are its trappings – the leather offices with deep pile carpet and the bespoke suits, deliberately designed to intimidate the lower orders and keep them in their place, the brown-nosing to the boss to get a partnership. So I set up as a sole practitioner and I keep my head above water, mostly by word of mouth. Who recommended me to you?'

Greg didn't answer. 'But you've moved offices lately.'

'Yeah.' Fountain's friendly eyes clouded. 'I was nice and comfy down by the canal and then suddenly I couldn't afford the rent any more because they'd tarted the place up. Urban regeneration, they call it. I ask you. What's wrong with slums?'

Greg laughed, liking the man. 'What I wanted to ask about was registering the will at Somerset House. You can do that?'

'Sure thing, though not many people want it. Not many people even know about it.'

'So when did you last do one?'

Fountain narrowed his eyes. 'It's been years,' he said vaguely. 'Who did you say recommended me?'

'Mrs Robyn Marchant,' Greg lied. 'Was she the last person you registered a will for?'

'I'm afraid that's confidential.'

Greg produced his warrant card. The lawyer reached over to examine it, pinching it between thumb and forefinger, comparing the photograph with the man in front of him.

'I may have misled you slightly, Mr Fountain,' Greg said. 'I don't want to make a will. Are you aware that Robyn Marchant was murdered in Inkpen the night before last?'

'I heard something about a murder on the downs Thursday night,' Fountain said slowly, 'but no details. Too late for this week's *New-*

bury Weekly News, of course.'

'Indeed.' The *News* came out on a Thursday; the editor must be swearing at the timing. 'Mrs Marchant was your client?'

'Yes.'

'Can you tell me how that came about?'

'Not really. She came to the office – the old one. Not my usual sort of client, frankly – looked like she'd a few bob and could afford the leather and the deep pile – but she was businesslike. Told me she wanted to make a will and register it at the Probate Office.'

'Did she say why?'

'I didn't ask – none of my business – but she said something vague about living alone and wanting to be sure the will was found after her death.'

'She didn't live alone.'

'I kinda figured that since the executor was at the same address – I guess she wasn't used to lying.'

'You didn't know who she was?'

'No. Should I? Was she famous?'

'She was pretty famous in Inkpen.'

'Not so much my patch. Anyway, I drew up the will pretty much on the spot. She signed it and the two blokes from the Chinese chippy next door witnessed it. They often did if the testator didn't have witnesses of his or her own. They seemed to get a kick out of it, felt important.'

He frowned. 'Have to drag punters up

from the bookie's now and they're always suspicious, like I'm trying to put one over on them, or they want paying.'

'And then?'

'And then nothing. I registered it like she asked. Bit of a palaver but mine is not to reason why.'

'And you sent her a copy?'

'Nope. Didn't want one. She was very specific about that – that I shouldn't write to her at her home address under any circumstances. Mine is not to reason why.' He glanced at the filing cabinets. 'I still have a copy if you want.'

'I've seen the original, thanks.'

'Of course you have, or you wouldn't be here.' Fountain slapped himself on the forehead with the heel of his hand. 'Earth to John!'

Greg got up. 'Well, thanks for your time, Mr Fountain.'

'No problem.' The younger man didn't rise to see him out but picked up his bottle of Coke again. 'If you ever want a will or some conveyancing, you know where to come.' He handed Greg a card in which the old address and phone number had been scored out and replaced in biro.

Classy.

'I have a will,' Greg said, pocketing the card, 'and no intention of moving, but thanks anyway.'

'Sir.' Nicolaides was holding a sheaf of papers. 'I've been working through the phone calls made from the Marchants' personal line. Trouble is there's just masses of them.'

'Even more on the business line,' Andy put in glumly.

'Found anything so far?'

'I'm working my way back from the time of the murder and there are two calls I thought you ought to see.' Nicolaides pointed to the same number highlighted twice in yellow. 'This call was made six days ago and this one on the day she died. It's local, to a house just down the hill called Wisteria Cottage.'

Greg snatched the paper out of his hand. 'Are you sure?'

'Yes, sir. Telecom says the line's recently been taken over by a tenant, a Liam Sullivan. Only he's got form, sir, serious form. IRA terrorist.'

'I know.'

'He's out on a life licence and had to report his current address to the parole board.'

'Yes,' Greg said patiently. 'I know.'

This was the last thing he'd expected. What possible business could a respectable women like Robyn Marchant have with low-life like Liam Sullivan?

'Of course, we can't be sure Mrs Marchant made the calls,' Nick pointed out. 'Most of the staff have access to the phone and the matron here is Irish.'

'Not technically illegal,' Greg said. A connection between Liam Sullivan and Siobhan Fahey? It seemed unlikely. Siobhan had a disapproving air about her which sat ill with an IRA sympathiser. Could she be a relative of the ex-con – a sister or cousin, a girlfriend who had waited for him – and, if so, what were the implications of that?

Unless she'd aged very badly, Siobhan was too old to be Aoife Cusack.

Now, what had put that thought into his head?

He fetched Robyn's copy of *Behind the Wire* from where he'd left it in the office and went in search of Charlie. He found her reading in her room and this time he didn't wait to get her a chaperone.

'The man who called on your mother on the ninth,' he said without preamble.

'What about him?' She blinked up at him.

He opened the book at the back, showing her the author's photo on the dust jacket. 'Is that him?'

She took the book from him and studied the picture. 'It might be,' she said at length. 'As I told you, I saw him only from the back but the hair's the right colour and he looks about the right build.'

She turned the book over to study the front, then leafed over to the blurb on the inside front cover. 'I don't understand,' she said. 'Why was Mum reading this – it's not her sort of thing at all, and what could she possibly have to do with this man?'

'That's what I'd like to know,' Greg murmured. 'So I think I'll go and ask him. Speak to you later.'

As he went out by the front door, Barbara's car drew up in the drive and the sergeant got out, looking sheepish.

'What the hell are you doing here?' Greg demanded.

'I couldn't run out on a murder enquiry, boss. Just couldn't do it.'

'You want your bloody head examined. You know that?'

'I know.'

'What does Trevor say?'

She shrugged. 'One of the advantages of dating somebody in the Job. They understand the demands.'

'You told him I'd cancelled your leave, in other words.' She grinned. 'Thanks for making me out to be an ogre.'

'He was muttering something about Shrek as he went through the departure gate,' she conceded.

'So he's gone alone?'

'Oh, yes. I'm sure he'll find some companionship when he gets there.'

'Have you considered talking to someone about your commitment phobia?'

'I don't have commitment phobia!'

'Hmm. Denial.'

'I was going,' she protested, 'right up to the last minute. I have my suitcase in the boot to prove it.'

'Okay, you'd better come with me.'

'Where to?'

'Just down the hill in Kintbury. I'll fill you in on the way.' He held the passenger door open for her then got into the driving seat. He reached into the back and picked up a brown paper bag.

'Nectarine?' he said.

'Don't mind if I do.'

They each took one and bit into them. The fruits were ripe and they were soon wiping the orange juice from their chins with the backs of their hands.

'I'm trying to eat more healthy snacks,' he explained.

'Good thinking, especially at...'

'My age? Is that what you were going to say?'

'No! At your time of life, was what I was going to say.'

'Yes, because that's completely different,' he said sarcastically. 'Still, you're not wrong.' He put the nectarine stone in the bag, licked his fingers and fastened his seatbelt. 'Let's go.'

Chapter Sixteen

Sullivan answered the door promptly and looked at them without speaking. Barbara, seeing the mass murderer for the first time, examined him with open interest.

'Can we come in?' Greg said.

'For what?'

'To ask you a few questions about the murder in Inkpen.'

'Have you got a warrant?'

'No.'

'Then you're about as welcome as Ian Paisley.' Sullivan leaned against the door post and folded his arms.

'Very well,' Greg said. 'We'll do it here. I want to know what your connection was with the dead woman.'

'Didn't have one.'

'Then why did she telephone you less than two hours before she died, the second call she'd made to this number in less than a week?'

Sullivan considered this. 'Who says?'

'British Telecom. She rang you at 8:37 on Thursday, to be precise, a call lasting less than a minute. She also rang three evenings earlier and the two of you talked for over five minutes on that occasion.' Seeing the Irishman now at a disadvantage, he cautioned him and Barbara took out her notepad and pen.

Sullivan said, 'Perhaps you'd better come in after all. Just don't steal anything.'

He walked away, leaving them to follow. Greg found himself in a small sitting room with an inglenook fireplace and beams. That its picture-book perfection was, even temporarily, the property of a man like Sullivan infuriated him. He didn't wait to be asked but took an armchair by the fireplace. Barbara sat opposite him.

Sullivan perched on the window seat with the sunlight behind him, making his expression hard to read.

'I do know what you're talking about now,' he said easily. 'There was a middle-aged woman bought a copy of my book at a signing I did in Marlborough about ten days ago. She hung around till the end and we got talking. She happened to mention she lived in Inkpen and I told her I was down the hill in Kintbury.'

'So you gave her your phone number?' Greg said sceptically.

'Of course not, but there is such a thing as directory enquiries. I was astonished when she rang up to tell me how much she enjoyed my book.'

'In less than a minute?'

'That was the first time. I thanked her and we chatted vaguely for a couple of minutes.'

'And the second time?'

'Same sort of thing.' He shrugged. 'I cut her short. I figured she was one of these bored housewives who fancy a bit of rough and she wasn't my type. It's not like I can't get a woman when I want one.'

He looked Barbara up and down with an insolence that made Greg want to hit him. The sergeant could take care of herself, however. 'Yeah,' she said. 'It's not like there aren't brothels.'

'It didn't occur to me that the woman who rang me was the one who was murdered,' Sullivan went on. 'Same night, you say? Now, there's a thing. Maybe she'd already had a few bits of rough and the old man found out.'

'Glad you accept you're as rough as a sow's arse,' Greg said crudely. 'So you've never been to Hilltop?'

'Where's that?'

'Her house. It's...' Greg gestured, 'as its name suggests.'

'Nope.'

'So what would you say if I told you that one of her family identifies you as a man seen visiting her ten days ago?'

'I'd say they can't have got a very good look.'

'Because you were careful?'

'Because it wasn't me.'

There was a bowl of fruit on the coffee table next to Greg. He picked up a green apple and looked at it.

'I told you not to steal anything,' his host said.

'I don't want it. Catch.'

He tossed the apple above Sullivan's head. Left in its trajectory, it could easily have broken the window behind him and the Irishman reached up and caught it, looking puzzled. He rose and stood in the doorway.

'Now, unless you're arresting me, Super-intendent, I think our business is done.'

Greg rose without haste. 'This isn't over.' He walked to the door and thrust his face very close to the other man's, gazing deep into his weak eyes. 'You're scum, Sullivan,' he said softly. 'They should never have let you out of prison and the sooner you go back there, the better.'

He bristled out with Barbara following. Sullivan shouted after them, 'And have a nice day yourself.'

Greg got into the car and fastened his seat belt. As he reached for the ignition key he found that his hand was trembling. 'Are you all right, boss?' Barbara asked. 'I've never seen you lose it like that.'

'I've never dealt with anyone so evil before.'

'He swallows insults easily enough.'

231

'You grow a thick skin in nineteen years behind bars.'

'Do you believe his story?'

'Not a word.' He started the engine.

'So why don't we arrest him, shake him up a bit?'

'He's too tough to break and he'll have a lawyer that makes Dee Washowski look like a pussy cat. We'll end up releasing him after a few hours with no progress made. I prefer to keep my powder dry.' Deirdre Washowski was Newbury's fiercest criminal lawyer and the mention of her name made hardened police officers groan.

'Besides,' he added, 'Charlie wasn't able to identify Sullivan as the man she saw, only to say that she didn't rule it out. I was bluffing there. Also, he caught that apple right-handed and the blow was struck from the left.' He let out the clutch and drove up the hill, back towards Inkpen.

'I don't suppose he does his own dirty work,' Barbara commented. 'From what I read in the paper, he let his underlings do that.'

'But he doesn't have a gang any more, a cell, an "Active Service Unit" to do his errands. And what's his motive?'

'What if he makes a run for it?' Barbara said.

'He can run but he can't hide.'

'I figure he can do both, boss.'

As they reached Kintbury Crossways, he told her about his visit to London the previous day. She said, 'Are we treating the husband as the prime suspect?'

'Not really. If he isn't totally devastated then he's the world's best actor.'

'And the PA was adamant that there's no other woman?'

'That's right.'

'But she would say that – if *she* were the other woman.'

'She isn't.' As she opened her mouth to speak again he added, 'Trust me on this. And there was no sign of another woman at his flat.'

She shrugged. 'So he went to her place.'

He told her about the Marchants' sexless marriage, wanting her opinion, although he was fairly sure he knew it already. To his surprise, however, she deemed it unimportant.

'People have different sex drives. Some men think of almost nothing else. Everything they achieve in life – wealth, fame, power – is in the pursuit of getting more women to sleep with them. But I've known plenty of blokes who'd just as soon have a nice cup of tea. It's only a problem if the couple aren't compatible. Are we sure he isn't a closet gay?'

'...Can't say it had crossed my mind.'

'Why – because he doesn't have a collection of Judy Garland CDs? They're practising Catholics, right?'

'Right, serious about it according to Cynthia Thorley.'

'So he's repressed it. He married late, nice Catholic girl, had the requisite two kids, then retired happily to the twin beds, duty done.'

'Then why would he want to kill her?'

His mobile rang before she could reply. He pulled the car over to the side of the road and took it out of his pocket. The display told him it was the front desk at Newbury police station. He answered it. 'Summers.'

The voice was that of Sergeant Dickie Barnes. 'Bloke rang for you just now, sir. A CS Meers from Special Branch. Asked for you to call him back urgent.'

'Did he leave a number?'

'Said you had it.'

'Okay.' Greg hung up and did a five-point turn on the narrow road, heading back down the hill. 'I have to go home,' he told Barbara, 'and return a call from a retired Special Branch officer, although I'm starting to have an inkling of what he's going to say.'

He called Meers back from his study ten minutes later.

Sure enough:

'You know that fingerprint flag we were talking about,' Meers said without preamble. 'Well, it's just flipped up.'

'This changes everything,' Barbara said, when Greg explained to her. 'We're not looking at a domestic murder any more, or a burglary gone wrong, or any of the usual things.' Her eyes were shining; this had a holiday in the sun beaten hands down. 'This is...'

'Bigger,' Greg supplied. 'It's huge. And we start again from the beginning.'

'With all the people who had cause to hate Aoife Cusack,' his sergeant said.

'Which is any decent person, in my book. If I'd known who she was, I'd have hated her myself.' He had detected no apprehension in her during their conversation at Easter, he realised; even talking to a policeman of his seniority, she had believed herself safe in her new identity.

'I've asked Meers to email Cusack's prints straight to forensics,' he added. 'I'd like Dr Armstrong to verify the match before we start running round like headless chickens.'

'Or Deep,' Barbara remarked.

'No, not Deep.' Seeing her puzzlement, he explained Gupta's connection with the Windsor bombing.

'Blimey,' she said. 'I had no idea. Poor Deep.'

Dr Pat Armstrong had already received the email by the time they reached her. She'd uploaded the prints on to her software and was examining them minutely against the ones the pathologist had taken during the autopsy.

'Odd we didn't have these prints on our

system,' she remarked. 'I ran a check this morning but got no matches.'

'Special Branch,' Greg said curtly. 'Probably with MI5 by now. You know how they don't like to share.'

'Like only children,' Pat said with a grin.

'So what's your verdict?'

'The match is exact.' Pat wheeled her wheelchair away from the work station with an air of finality. 'There's no doubt. So who is this woman – Olga the glamorous Russian spy?'

Greg pretended he hadn't heard. 'Let's go,' he said to Barbara. 'Meers in on his way to Inkpen.'

'He's not going to muscle in on our case, is he?'

'Certainly not. He's retired so he has no official standing, but Aoife Cusack's been something of an obsession of his all these years, from what I can gather. When he asked if he could come I hadn't the heart to say no and we can always use an extra pair of hands, not to mention an extra brain.'

'Just so long as he doesn't chuck his weight about,' Barbara muttered.

'Now I find myself wondering who knew Aoife's secret,' Greg said, as they headed back to his car. 'We have a husband, children, the Fahey woman who's lived with the Marchants for donkeys' years.'

'And that son of hers,' Barbara reminded

him, 'who also gets to inherit what he might have thought was a small fortune.'

'Let's start with the obvious one – the husband.'

'What about Sullivan? Because now we have a humdinger of a motive for him.'

'So long as he thinks we haven't found out her real identity, he'll keep.'

'This is going to sound like an odd question,' Greg said, 'but how well did you know your wife?'

Stephen thought about it. 'You're right. It does sound like an odd question.'

'When and where did you meet?'

'It was about twenty years ago. I had a weekend cottage in those days, in Whitstable in Kent. There was a café where I used to take my breakfast Sunday mornings and one day she was there, serving me. It was out of season and not so busy and we got chatting. The next weekend I ran into her on the beach early Saturday morning.'

He paused and swallowed, moved by his own memories. 'She was much younger than me and I didn't really fancy my chances but faint heart never won fair lady so I asked her out to dinner and she accepted. By the time we got to the coffee, I felt like I had come home. We were married six months later.'

'Did she know then the extent of your wealth?'

'Ah, yes. Cynthia told me you'd asked about that.' A faint smile played across his lips. 'Sometimes it impresses even me. Robyn had no interest in my money, except insofar as it allowed us to set up this place.'

'And what was her name then?' Greg asked.

'Robyn Simpson.'

'And you had no reason to doubt that?'

'Of course not. When someone tells me their name, I don't immediately assume they're lying. Do you?'

'Often,' Greg said, 'but then I'm a policeman.'

'What's all this about?' Marchant asked. 'Are you saying Robyn wasn't who she said she was?'

'Does the name Aoife Cusack mean anything to you?'

'Eefa?' Marchant looked puzzled. Greg spelled it for him. 'Not a name I've ever come across. Is it Irish?'

'Yes,' Greg said, 'and the thing is that your wife's fingerprints exactly match those of Aoife Cusack, who is wanted by the police on six counts of murder and has been since 1981.'

Marchant stared at him, unable to speak for a moment. 'That's not possible,' he gasped finally. 'Robyn was just a child in 1981.'

'She was seventeen. Did you meet any of her family?'

'...No. She said she was alone in the world, which suited me fine, as I wanted to be everything to her. I ... I don't understand. What are you telling me?'

'That your wife was on the run from the police when you met her,' Greg said with calculated brutality, 'that she lied to you about everything to do with her background, her past, her nationality, her name; that she planted a bomb in Windsor twenty-three years ago which killed six people outright and blighted the lives of dozens more.'

'You've made a mistake,' Stephen said firmly. His face was pale but his voice was steady. 'You should be careful what you say, slandering a woman who did nothing but good in the world, who devoted her life to those less privileged than herself.'

'We don't make mistakes like that.' Looking at the older man, Greg could read in his face that he was starting to believe it, just didn't want to. Somewhere, in his mind, odd things were falling into place. He felt a desperate pity for him. How would he feel if someone told him Angie was a mass murderer?

He rose to leave but Stephen said, 'Must it come out?'

'I'm not sure.'

'For the sake of the children, Charlie and Dom. They at least are wholly innocent.'

'For your children's sake, I will do what I can.'

Chapter Seventeen

Daniel Fahey sat slumped in the armchair in his bedroom with his eyes closed. It was not yet teatime but he felt exhausted. It was hard to believe that barely thirty-six hours earlier he hadn't had a care in the world, waving goodbye to the last of his exams with a couple of pints of Marstons best bitter.

Now Robyn was dead and he'd been arrested and questioned by the police because she'd left him her estate. No, of course, he hadn't been arrested – he knew that – but it had felt just as bad and he was sure that the Marchants were angry and upset with him although none of them had given any sign of it. He knew how he would have felt in their place: if Siobhan had died and left everything she had – which was to say nothing – to a virtual stranger.

What had Robyn been thinking of? Whatever it was, he wished she'd had second thoughts.

The tap on his door was so faint that he wasn't sure he'd heard it until a second, louder, knock.

'Come in ... Charlie!'

She was in the clothes she'd been wearing

all day: shorts and a T-shirt, long bare legs, tanned golden by the sun, ending in espadrilles, like a carefree beach child. But he thought that she looked much older; something in her face and the way she held herself said that her childhood had ended. He got up and offered her his armchair but she waved him away and perched on his bed instead.

'How are you?' he asked, and then '–Sorry! What a stupid question.'

'I feel dead inside,' she said. 'She was forty, Dan.'

'I know.'

'She should have lived another forty years.'

He leaned forward and squeezed her hands in his. He could feel the roughness of her palm where she gripped her tennis racket day after day, a callus at the base of the middle finger of her left hand.

'I know you won't believe this now,' he said, 'but it will get better. And you must remember that Robyn did more good in twenty years than most people do in a lifetime.'

'That's some comfort, I suppose.' She attempted a brave smile. 'They do say the good die young.'

'That's my girl.'

'Daniel ... there's something I wanted to ask you, about Mum's will.'

'Oh, Charlie! You have to believe that I

241

had no idea.'

'I do believe you.'

'That policeman – what's his name?'

'Summers.'

'He told me that I can simply refuse the bequest so that's what I'll do. Then she'll be deemed to have died intestate and Stephen will get it all, the way it should be.'

'We don't want you to do that, Danny,' the girl said gently. 'You're welcome to her savings. It's just that I know Dad would like some of her personal things, some mementoes, and as they can't mean as much to you–'

'Oh, God! Of course! He can't have thought for a minute... Of course he must have her personal stuff.' He buried his head in his hands. 'Has he been fretting about that? Why didn't I say something sooner?'

'None of us is thinking very straight.' She got up. 'Thank you, Daniel, for being so understanding.'

She leaned over and kissed him chastely on the brow.

Nicolaides had been working indefatigably on his list of telephone numbers and now had the calls grouped into type: Robyn and Stephen had many friends and the majority of calls were to them; personal calls had also been made to the Marchant children at school at least twice a week and Robyn had called Stephen's London flat at intervals.

'Only thing that's really giving me trouble is this.' Nick pointed to a mobile number. 'I can't seem to find out who it belongs to.'

'Can't the service provider help?' Greg asked.

'The name and address they have for the owner is bogus. The street exists all right but it's a cul-de-sac with just twelve houses and our joker lives at number fifteen. It's a pay-as-you-go service so no one checked it out.'

'And where is this cul-de-sac?'

'Basingstoke. The phone was bought at the local Argos in August two years ago.'

'You've tried ringing it, obviously,' Barbara said.

'I'm not talking to you,' Nick replied. 'You're not here, you bloody madwoman.'

'You've tried ringing it?' Greg said.

'A dozen times, sir. It's switched off, with no voice mail.'

'What do the household say?'

'They deny all knowledge of it.'

'How often did she call the number?' Greg asked.

'Just the once, on the tenth of June. In the evening, a call lasting three minutes.'

The day after her visit from Sullivan, Greg thought, if it had indeed been Sullivan whom Charlie had glimpsed that night, the likelihood of which was greatly increased by Meers's revelation.

'Where was the phone topped up?' he asked.

'Hah!' Nick said, 'that's another weird thing. The service provider says it never has been topped up. It was bought with ten quid's worth of calls but it was never used to make outgoing calls and received none either, until last Thursday week.'

'Curiouser and curiouser,' Barbara said.

'It's as if whoever bought the phone got it solely so Mrs Marchant could call it in an emergency,' Greg added.

SOCO had finally finished with the herb garden and the incident tape had been removed. Greg made his way to a weathered wooden bench that sat in the shade of the wall which marked the boundary with Desmond Chapman's garden, lowering himself on to the rain-scarred slats.

He breathed in the powerful smell of rosemary and basil as he tried to visualise the scene of Thursday night. Had Robyn wandered out into the garden of her own accord or had she gone because she'd seen a stranger lurking in the darkness?

Or had she been summoned out for a twilight stroll by someone she knew? Someone from decades back in Belfast.

He twisted to look at the wall which was all that divided the herb garden from Desmond Chapman's wilderness. It was

244

about six feet high and needed repointing. The old man was as badly delusional as anyone Greg had met. Could he have been out 'patrolling', spotted Robyn enjoying the night air, mistaken her for some ill-defined enemy and killed her? He was small and frail but if he had come upon her from behind, all unawares...

He had no grounds on which he could apply for a search warrant for Chapman's bungalow, look for the missing weapon. Sometimes it felt like the laws were unfairly stacked against him.

He thought that he'd never had a more complex case. It had to be Aoife Cusack and not Robyn Marchant who was the intended victim, surely, and yet it seemed that nobody knew that Robyn was Aoife, that her new identity had been solid enough to fool even her family and colleagues.

He thought he would talk to Chapman some more anyway. If invited in, he might get the chance for a look round and it was possible that the old man had remembered something since their last meeting.

He walked up to the front door of the bungalow and rang the bell. It seemed to echo in emptiness. No footsteps came in response. He tried again, then walked slowly round the garden calling quietly.

'Who's there?'

It was not Chapman's voice but came

from the other side of the wall. He saw the top of Charlie's ginger head and realised that she had taken the place in the herb garden that he had so recently vacated and was climbing on the bench.

'I was just looking for Mr Chapman,' he explained as the rest of her head emerged into view, 'but he seems to be out.'

'He doesn't go out. Hold on.' She clambered nimbly over the wall and joined him, smacking brick dust from her hands and shorts. She looked as if she'd walked out of a poem by Betjeman: furnish'd and burnish'd by Hungerford sun.

'He must go out sometimes,' Greg protested. 'To the post office to get his pension, or to the shops.'

'Most people get their pensions paid direct into their bank account these days,' she said, 'and the local shop still delivers. Also Mum would shop for him.'

'Then maybe that's why he's been forced to go out now,' Greg suggested gently.

She marched up to the front door and hammered on it. 'Mr Chapman? Desmond? It's only me – Charlie.'

Greg knelt and looked through the letter box. All the doors from the hall were closed, as on the night of his visit, and it took a moment for his eyes to adjust. Then he stood abruptly and said, 'Something's wrong. I'm going to break in.'

'Hold on! We have a spare key at Hilltop.'

'Okay,' he said, 'but make it quick.'

She was off before he'd finished speaking, her long, brown legs covering the ground, almost a blur. She was gone for three minutes but to Greg, impatient, it seemed like half an hour. He took the proffered key from her without thanks and opened the door.

'Stay there,' he commanded. 'Don't come into the house.'

This could be a crime scene. Maybe Desmond Chapman had seen more than he knew that night, seen something that made a killer need to silence him.

And the Marchants had a key, no doubt accessible to anyone at Hilltop.

He took out his handkerchief to cover his hand and switched on the light. Chapman lay in a crumpled heap by the door to his 'shrine'. Charlie stood hopping from one foot to the other in the porch, longing to come in but not daring to disobey a direct order.

He knelt to feel for a pulse. It was faint but it was there, the old man's neck warm, dry in the way that ancient skin was. As Greg took out his mobile, Chapman opened one eye and groaned, his left hand reaching feebly for his chest.

'Hurts,' he whispered.

'Ambulance,' Greg said into the phone. 'An old man has had a heart attack. Be quick.' He identified himself to expedite their response, gave them the address and hung up. 'It's all right, Mr Chapman. Remember me – the honest policeman? Just stay calm. Help is on its way.'

He made a swift decision that it was not a crime scene. 'Come in, Charlie. Give me a hand to get him into a more comfortable position.'

Together, they hoisted him into a sitting position with his back against the wall.

'See if you can find some aspirin,' Greg said. 'Try the bathroom or kitchen.'

The girl began opening doors at random and soon found the bathroom, rummaging in the medicine cabinet above the sink.

'It might be quicker if I run home – wait, here's some.' She brought him the packet of white pills and he put one in the semi-conscious man's mouth, poking it into his gullet as you might with a sick animal. Charlie fetched a glass of water and he poured a little carefully down his throat.

Chapman was pale, his breathing heavy and wheezy, but Greg didn't think that death was imminent.

'Can you tell me what happened?' he asked.

The old man shook his head, the smallest of movements. 'Morning visit to shrine,' he croaked. 'Pain in left arm and shoulder. Then nothing. Hurts.'

Five minutes later they heard the distant wail of the ambulance.

When Chapman was safely stowed inside, Greg sent Charlie away and took the opportunity to look round the bungalow. He had to secure the place. Right? The old man might have left the gas on, unlit, or a pan of potatoes boiling over, or a candle burning in the shrine, which might start a fire.

Right?

If he did find the weapon that had killed Robyn, then he would scare up an excuse for a warrant and a legal search.

Half an hour later, he had nothing. He locked up carefully and returned the spare key to Charlie.

He decided to speak some more to Siobhan Fahey. As someone who lived in the house but was not part of the family, her evidence could prove crucial. He had to be careful, however, if he was to keep the dead woman's true identity under wraps.

'Had you any idea,' he began, 'that Mrs Marchant was a fellow-countrywoman of yours?'

Siobhan stared. 'Nonsense!' she said, as if upbraiding one of her charges over an especially foolish remark. 'I've known Robyn Marchant for twenty years. If she was Irish, I think she'd have mentioned it at some point, don't you?'

'Oh, but she was. Belfast born and bred.'

'Well, I'm from Monaghan,' Siobhan said tartly, 'which is in the Republic, so she's not my countrywoman.'

'You never suspected she was Irish?'

The woman hesitated. 'To me, she sounded ... just like anyone else over here.'

'What was your impression of her marriage? Were she and Mr Marchant happy together?'

'I seldom saw a happier couple. They delighted in each other's company.' She smiled. 'It was enough to renew one's faith in human nature.'

Greg thanked her and let her go. He found himself brooding over the fact that Siobhan Fahey's own husband had died in 1981 – the year of the Windsor bombing.

Was it possible that Siobhan's husband had been one of Sullivan and Cusack's victims? But why would she wait all this time before wreaking vengeance? If Aoife knew, then it might explain the bequest to the child she had orphaned.

Charlie had spoken of Siobhan's influence over her mother, 'as if she has some sort of hold over her'. What greater hold could you have over a woman than the threat of twenty years in prison? Had Siobhan been blackmailing Aoife all these years? Had she bullied her into leaving Daniel her estate? But that made no sense either, since Siobhan, apparently, knew that the estate was worth very little.

He groaned, buried his head briefly in his hands and went in search of some more aspirin, this time for himself.

When he got back, he rang Deep's mobile and asked apologetically for the names of the other Windsor victims. He had no sense that the scientist had forgiven him for coming to his flat the other night.

Deepak reeled them off without asking for an explanation and Greg noted them down, especially the men: Peter Mitchell, Donald McLaverty and Adam Mason.

It shouldn't be too hard to find out if any of them had left a widow and small son, or even a pregnant widow.

He let himself out of the front door, just as a black saloon car with tinted windows came to a halt on the drive. He saw the constable who was in charge of the crime scene step forward and talk to someone in the driver's seat through the open window, then glance his way for guidance.

He went over. 'Colin?'

Meers stepped out of the car, a man of seventy with a full head of white hair. He was of medium height and had plumped up since Greg last saw him but still looked tough for a man of his years.

Even retired, he was every inch a senior

policeman, his eyes watchful, his expression giving nothing away. He was wearing trousers in a thin corduroy, brown, with a cream polo shirt open at the neck, two-tone leather loafers. He looked as if he'd just stepped off the golf course.

'Greg.' They shook hands.

Greg said, 'It's okay, thanks,' to the constable, who shrugged and went off.

Before they could say anything further a second car pulled into the drive, a dusty black VW Golf whose speed round the corner suggested a customised engine. The driver switched off the ignition after a short final rev and bounced out on thick-soled trainers.

He was in his late fifties, Greg thought, stocky to the point of pudginess in some baggy khakis and a striped rugby shirt, his mousy hair receding at the front. He was tanned for a fair man, somewhat weather-beaten, and wore a neat ginger beard. Greg thought that his face looked familiar but couldn't think from where.

'Almost lost you round these winding roads, Col,' he said, with a note of reproach.

'Can I introduce Malcolm Fraser,' Meers said to Greg, 'formerly of Special Branch.'

So this was the hero Fraser! Greg shook his hand warmly. 'It's an honour,' he said. 'You've come a long way.'

'Not really.' Fraser had a pleasant Scottish

accent. 'I run a boat yard on the Isle of Wight.'

Greg glared at Meers who laughed. 'He did move to New Zealand twenty years ago,' he explained, 'but he came back, like a boomerang – damn, wrong country!'

'It didn't take,' Fraser said. 'Couldn't get used to having Christmas in the middle of summer and snow in June – it was like a world gone mad. After five years, I decided it was safe enough to return, provided I stayed a good long way from Belfast.'

'You do know that Liam Sullivan is living less than two miles from here?' Greg asked.

'We do,' Meers said, 'and I don't want to tell you your job, Gregory, obviously, but I think we should arrest him right away.'

'Nothing would give me greater pleasure. Now that you're here, I'll send someone to process him right away.'

'Meanwhile, I'd like Malcolm to take a look at your victim, give us another ID. He knew Aoife as well as anybody.'

'Shall we take my car?' Greg said. Meers followed him compliantly, but Fraser called, 'I'll follow you in mine. Try not to lose me!'

As always, the body reminded Greg of a wax dummy, devoid of life or personality. The new morgue attendant – who looked as though he might keep dead bodies in his fridge at home as well – pulled the sheet clear of her face and the three men stared down on her from above.

Nobody spoke for a minute then Meers said, 'Well, Malcolm?'

'No doubt about it,' the Scotsman said, a little sadly. He turned away, his hand covering his mouth, and breathed a long sigh. Meers continued to look at the body, especially the face, and he wore an expression that Greg found disturbing. He had not realised until that moment exactly how much Colin Meers hated Aoife Cusack.

'I feel cheated,' Meers murmured. 'I wanted to see her pay for what she did, pay to the full limit that the law allows.'

'She's paid the ultimate price,' Greg said.

'No, she's escaped. She's got away. *Again.*' Meers turned to Fraser. 'Do you want to sit in with the Sullivan interview?'

'Best not.' Fraser turned back, his face composed now. 'If there's one man in this world Billy wants to kill, it's me. If he sees me in the interview room, you'll get nothing from him. I'll keep a low profile for the time being.' He touched the mobile phone affixed to his belt. 'You know how to get hold of me, Colin.'

'There's one thing that puzzles me,' Greg said, after the Scotsman had driven away. 'If Fraser was so deep in Sullivan's cell, why wasn't he able to prevent the Windsor bombing?'

'The simple answer is that he didn't know about it. Sullivan still didn't trust him enough to make him part of his ASU. We were playing the long game with Malcolm, hoping to round up not only Sullivan's people but maybe many more, show the IRA that Special Branch could make fools of them any time we liked and that there was no one they could trust.'

Greg could see the sense in that: no terrorist organisation could function if they started suspecting everyone of being a police mole.

He had never been sure how far undercover cops were allowed to go in turning a blind eye to crime. Would Fraser have stood by and watched the shooting of an RUC officer or a soldier in the British army if it meant keeping his cover intact? He feared that the answer was yes, that one man could be sacrificed for the good of many.

It was not a decision he would wish to take himself.

They began to walk towards Greg's car as Meers went on. 'After Windsor we realised that Sullivan was more dangerous than we'd thought, so we closed down the operation and settled for hocking him and his mates away for – well, we thought it'd be thirty years.'

His face hardened. 'Who knew the government would go soft on Northern Ireland?

But if we can get Sullivan for this murder, then they really will throw away the key.'

Too hasty, Greg thought. It was a mistake to decide at once who your murderer was and make the facts fit. It was not a mistake that was going to happen on his watch.

Greg had sent Andy Whittaker with a pair of uniforms to arrest Sullivan and process him. That would take a couple of hours and they would ring when he was ready. Meanwhile a warrant was obtained for Wisteria Cottage.

SOCO had already carried out a meticulous search of Hilltop House but Greg thought that he and Colin might as well take a personal look at the Marchants' private quarters. It would give him a better idea of the woman Aoife Cusack had become.

'Nice set-up she had for herself,' Meers growled, taking in the antique furniture, the paintings and a cabinet full of what Greg thought vaguely might be Meissen. 'I wonder what she was up to.'

'I don't think she was "up to" anything,' Greg said. 'She was running a school for handicapped children.' He assumed that the trappings of old wealth were just that: things that had been in Stephen's family for generations.

'Oh, yes?' Meers said derisively. 'Trust me, Gregory: once you've sold your soul to the devil, he never gives it back.'

The sitting room was large and gracious with a grand piano standing to one side of the french windows. On it, a dozen family photos – happy snaps of Robyn, Stephen and the children, individually and in groups. A final snapshot stood alone, as if it were not part of the family. Black and white in a silver frame, it showed a heavy-set man in his mid-twenties, dressed in the fashion of twenty-five years ago with a 'mullet' hair style and flares.

'What have we here?' Meers picked it up.

Greg shrugged. 'I have no idea who that is.'

'No, but I do.' Meers scrutinised the blurred face. 'That's Nessan Cusack, Aoife's brother.'

'The one who wouldn't spit on her if she was on fire?' Greg examined the picture with interest. 'Why would she have a photo of him?'

'Maybe she doesn't feel the same way,' Colin said, 'or maybe she doesn't even know how much he hates her.'

'Excuse me!' Daniel Fahey came into the room at that moment. He marched across to Meers and almost snatched the photo from his hand, placing it reverently back in its former place. 'That's my late father, if you don't mind.'

'Sorry,' Greg said quickly before Meers could answer. 'We meant no disrespect.'

'Only he died before I was born,' Daniel said, 'and I have very few mementoes of him.'

'What was his name?' Greg asked.

'Eamonn John Fahey. Why?'

'No reason. He looks like a nice man. We'll leave you in peace, sir.' Greg steered Colin rapidly out of the room and into the hall.

'I don't buy Nessan as that lad's father,' Meers remarked when they were out of earshot. 'How would he end up here? It makes no sense. And Nessan's just as alive as you and me.'

Greg was thoughtful. Maybe Charlie was right: Siobhan didn't know who Daniel's father was and had borrowed a random photo from her employer for a pious lie.

And yet...

His mobile rang: Andy Whittaker to let him know that his prisoner was ready for him.

'Let's go,' he said.

Chapter Eighteen

Sullivan's lawyer had driven out from London, causing considerable delay. He was a mean-looking man named Stanley Cotton with tight lips and a cold stare. He looked as if nothing would make him laugh except, possibly, the misfortune of others.

Once they were installed in an interview room, Greg introduced himself to the tape. Cotton and Sullivan followed suit and Sullivan added, 'And the wee fellow skulking in the corner is Chief Superintendent Colin Meers of Special Branch, retired. How're yer, Colin, you gobshite?'

'I'm very well, thank you, Billy.'

'Thought you *polis* mostly dropped dead after retirement.'

'I keep very active.'

'Where're you living these days, case I want to drop by one evening, chew over old times? You and your lovely wife – Shirley, was it?'

Meers laughed. 'Don't bother threatening me, Billy. I'm not afraid of you and Shirley even less so.'

Sullivan turned to his brief, spreading his hands in mock bemusement. 'Did you hear me utter anything resembling a threat, Stanley?'

'Can we get on?' Cotton growled.

'CS Meers is observing only,' Greg said. 'Mr Sullivan, can you tell me where you were on the night of June seventeenth?'

'When was that? Thursday? At home, Wisteria Cottage, working on my next book.'

'Alone?'

'Myself alone.' He grinned. The IRA's

259

political wing, Sinn Fein, translated their name as Ourselves Alone.

'I know you're aware that a woman was murdered in Inkpen that night, in her own garden.'

'And how would my client be aware of that?' Cotton said.

'I've seen him standing outside the crime scene with my own eyes,' Greg snapped. 'Gawping. Plus, I told him so myself this morning.'

'Billy likes scenes of mayhem,' Meers put in, 'especially when he's caused them. Chaos, panic, fear, pain, grief – he feeds on them. They nourish him.'

'Now look here–' Cotton said.

'I wasn't the only one rubbernecking,' Liam interrupted. 'It's human nature. People are talking of nothing else.'

'And would it surprise you to learn,' Greg said, 'that the dead woman is a very old friend of yours – Aoife Cusack?'

Cotton blinked in disbelief.

'Little Aoife!' Sullivan threw his head back and whistled. 'Sure, and you're not serious.'

'Spare me the pantomime,' Greg said. 'I think you knew very well that Robyn Marchant was Aoife Cusack. Your coming to settle just down the road is too much of a coincidence otherwise.'

'And yet coincidences do happen.' Sullivan was grinning.

'When we spoke this morning, you must have been very relieved that we hadn't yet identified her. Maybe you thought we never would.'

Sullivan made no reply.

Cotton said, 'Am I to understand that you interviewed my client this morning without a solicitor present?'

'He didn't ask for one,' Greg said. 'He was just helping us with our enquiries at that stage.'

'I'm still making a note of it,' Cotton said, and did precisely that, excruciatingly slowly, in a leather-bound notebook which he took from his pocket.

'You were seen at Mrs Marchant's house late one night,' Greg continued, 'about a week ago, as I mentioned this morning. You had quite a long talk with her. Now, twenty-three years is a long time, but you won't convince me that you didn't recognise her.'

'Really, Superintendent,' Stanley Cotton said with a sigh, 'you're just flying a kite. I don't believe you have a witness to this alleged meeting.'

'It's all right, Stanley.' Sullivan turned to his lawyer. 'Let me answer. I've committed no crime and there's nothing to gain by acting as if I had.' He turned back to face Greg and his eyes were inscrutable. 'Did I know Aoife Cusack was living in Inkpen under the name of Robyn Marchant? I'd been told it.

Did I come to Berkshire to check it out for myself? I did– Shut up, Stanley– Did I want Aoife Cusack dead? No. Why would I?'

'You thought she betrayed you,' Greg said.

'It was Francis Mahoney who betrayed me but, you're right, I had a score to settle with Aoife.' He glared at his brief who was trying to speak. 'I told you to shut up, Stanley. Meers will try to pin this murder on me if he thinks he can get away with it, so I've decided to cooperate with this feller Summers.'

He spoke to Greg. 'I didn't want her dead, though. That's too easy.'

He made his finger into a gun, pointed it at Greg's temple and made a popping noise. 'You put a bullet in someone's brain and half the time they don't even hear it coming. What sort of punishment is that? Besides, I've spent enough time in jail. I have a nice life now and I'm not going to throw it away. Let me tell you, if I had Francis Mahoney here now, bound and gagged and me with a cut-throat razor in my hand, I'd walk away. He's not worth it.'

'But perhaps Aoife was worth it,' Greg said.

'I was going to hand her over to the police, let her go to trial, like me, let her spend twenty years in jail, like me. See how she enjoys it. I was going to give her to you.'

'Then why didn't you?' Greg said stonily. 'After all, you know where I live.'

'There was no hurry. It's nice to let people

stew for a bit. More fun.'

'She might have made a run for it.'

Sullivan shook his head. 'Running is easy when you're seventeen and have nothing to lose. So much harder at forty with a home and husband and two lovely kids. Are you sure she didn't commit suicide?'

'Not unless she stabbed herself in the back,' Greg said bluntly. 'Now can we stop bull-shitting and find out exactly why she tele-phoned you twice – once a few days before the murder and once an hour and a half before she died.'

Sullivan sucked on his lower lip. 'There's no reason I shouldn't tell you,' he said eventually, 'except...'

'That you prefer lies to the truth,' Meers supplied.

'The first time she rang to offer me money.'

'She tried to buy you off?' Greg was inter-ested. It was a logical response for a sensible woman to make. 'How much?'

'A hundred grand.'

'That's a lot of money.'

'Not nearly enough. I told her to stick it where the sun don't shine. I told her that a *million* wouldn't compensate me for what I'd lost.'

'Turning to blackmail now, Billy?' Meers remarked. 'Bit of a come-down for a mass murderer.'

'Rubbish!' Cotton snapped. 'My client has just told you that at no point did he ask Mrs Marchant for money. *She* approached *him* and he turned her down.'

Greg, who agreed that this was a pointless diversion, gave Colin Meers a warning look.

'And the second call?' he asked.

'She rang me Thursday evening and asked me to come and see her. I told her if she was just trying to up the ante then she was wasting her time, but she said she had something to tell me that might make me take pity on her.'

He looked sceptical; so did Meers.

'And what was that?' Greg asked.

'She wouldn't tell me over the phone. She asked me to come up to Hilltop that night, around eleven, like before.' He hesitated. 'I half wondered if she meant to lure me into a trap, to kill me.'

'So you didn't go?'

'But I did. Only you know what I found when I got there – mayhem, police every-where, ambulances, cop cars, talk of a woman found dead – so I turned straight round and went back home.'

There was a pause, then Cotton said, 'As you don't appear to have a shred of evidence against my client, I'd like him released now.'

'Well, I'd like him to take part in a line-up,' Greg said.

'What for?'

'To confirm that he's the man seen at the victim's house on the night of the ninth of June.'

'I've already admitted as much,' Sullivan said. 'I told you I had to make sure it was her and I did. I went to the back door and I knocked like a nice boy and there she was – older, fatter, greyer and unmistakably Aoife.'

'So there doesn't seem to be much point to your line-up, Superintendent,' Cotton said acidly. 'I want Mr Sullivan charged or released.'

'May I have a word, Mr Summers?' Meers said.

'Of course, Mr Meers.'

The two men adjourned to the hallway where Meers said, 'You're not thinking of letting him go?'

'I don't see that I have much choice, Colin. This isn't one of your Prevention of Terrorism cases, you know. I can't just hold him for days.'

'You can hold him for twenty-four hours without charge,' Meers protested. 'Longer, if necessary.'

'Not with that lawyer, not without some evidence.'

'You can't believe that he didn't want Aoife dead.'

'I don't know so much. What he says makes sense... As you pointed out earlier, Colin, it is my case.' Meers made a face. Greg went back into the interview room and looked at both men without enthusiasm. 'Very well. You're free to go, Mr Sullivan. Please don't leave the area.'

The Irishman got to his feet. If he'd been a child, Greg would have called his expression cheeky. 'Don't take it too hard, Summers. Listen. If you want a word of advice, I should look at your man Gupta. He had all the reason in the world to want Aoife dead.'

'And no way of knowing where she was,' Greg said.

'No? I wouldn't be so sure of that.'

'What was that about a man called Gupta?' Colin Meers asked after they were gone.

'Deepak Gupta. He's one of our forensic scientists. His sister was killed in the Windsor bombing.'

Meers thought hard. 'Her name was Sangita. I remember. Not pretty, exactly, but a sweet face, lovely smile. I knew that from the photos her parents showed me, since there wasn't much left of it. He's got motive all right but how would he know where Aoife was?'

'He's been following Sullivan,' Greg said reluctantly. 'The bastard even made a complaint about it and I had to speak to Deep–'

'All official, I trust.'

'I didn't want a blot on his otherwise exemplary record. It was just a friendly word of advice from a colleague.'

'So Sullivan might have led him to Aoife. I think we need a word with your Mr Gupta.'

They found Deepak at home. Indira was settled at the kitchen table with her books while her husband chopped vegetables for a late supper. Greg introduced Colin Meers and asked if the young scientist would come to the station with them to answer a few questions.

What about?' Deep asked stubbornly, drawing a slick knife across the skin of an aubergine.

'There was a murder in Inkpen two nights ago,' Greg said.

'I know. We had the forensics in this morning. What of it?'

'The victim was a woman named Robyn Marchant,' Greg said. 'I wondered if you knew her.'

Deep shrugged. 'Why would I?'

Meers intervened. 'Ever been to her house?' Deep shook his head. 'Big place called Hilltop,' Colin went on.

The young man dug his knife deep in the white, bulbous flesh. 'No.'

'Not even when you were following Liam Sullivan?'

'Is that what this is about? If Sullivan wants to make a formal complaint, then let him.'

'Robyn Marchant was just an alias.' Greg

267

was watching his colleague closely. 'Her real name was Aoife Cusack.'

Indira gasped. Deep leaned heavily on his knife, decapitating the aubergine and sending its head flying across the room.

'Will you come?' Greg asked. 'A few questions.'

'Are you arresting me?'

'No.'

'Then I'll stay right here.' He abandoned his preparations, walked over to the sofa, flung himself down on it and switched on the television.

'Then I'll arrest you,' Colin growled.

Deep glanced up at him. 'What're you? Seventy? I don't know who you are but you're retired for sure.'

'Then Mr Summers will arrest you.'

'So be it.'

'Deepak!' Indira exclaimed. 'The shame of it. What will your poor mother say?'

Her husband capitulated at once, switching off the TV again. 'All right. I'll come voluntarily. But I want Deirdre Washowski.'

Meers glanced a query at Greg, who merely smiled.

Dee Washowski had abandoned her trademark flowing robes that evening in favour of an enormous pin-striped suit and a trilby. She was a woman in her fifties who looked larger every time Greg saw her. She was not

268

impressed by Colin Meers's credentials, nor by Greg's explanations.

'Let me get this straight,' she said. 'You've brought my client in for questioning on the say-so of a mass murderer?'

'Mr Gupta does have an excellent motive for killing Ms Cusack,' Greg demurred.

'Assuming he had the faintest idea who she was! If even Special Branch–' emphasising the words and glaring at Colin Meers '–had no idea where she was, then how is Mr Gupta supposed to have known? What is he – a seer?'

Greg persevered. He and Dee were old friends – or was it old enemies? – and he knew that she was a reasonable woman under the bluster. 'Mr Gupta had been following Sullivan. Sullivan had somehow discovered Aoife Cusack's new identity and her address. It's possible that he led Mr Gupta straight to her.'

'I had been following him,' Deep said, 'but you warned me off, Mr Summers, almost two weeks ago, so I stopped.' He looked Greg straight in the eye without flinching.

'You hated Aoife Cusack,' Meers said stoutly.

'I did, and I'm glad she's dead, but I'm not a murderer. If I'd killed her then I'd be as bad as she was, as bad as Liam Sullivan.'

They couldn't hold him. Greg knew that and Meers had to accept it. After an hour in the interview room, Deirdre stated as fact that her client was going home now and offered him a lift.

'I hate solicitors,' Meers said when they had gone. 'I'd like to put the whole bloody lot of them in a pit and pour boiling oil on them.'

Meers wanted to go public with Aoife's true identity, call a press conference to tell the world that a mass murderer could hide, maybe for years, but that Special Branch would catch up with them in the end.

He had a spring in his step and Greg inferred that it felt good to be back in harness after years of retirement, that the old adrenaline was flowing through his veins.

He disagreed, however, with Meers's view. It was not simply the thought of the sweet girl, Charlie, and her timid brother – he could not afford to be sentimental – but he preferred to keep this vital piece of information on a need-to-know basis, for now.

'It'll muddy the waters,' he explained. 'At the moment, I have a respectable wife and mother, stabbed to death in her own garden. I need to see what we come up with on house-to-house, public appeals for witnesses. If I tell the world who she really was then all sorts of nutters will come crawling out of the woodwork with false evidence.'

'Okay, but–'

'On the other hand, people with useful information may hold back, thinking that she had it coming and the killer's done the world a favour. Also,' he added, as Meers' face spoke of his continuing lack of conviction, 'have you considered the possibility that her murder may not be related to her past, that somebody had a motive to kill Robyn Marchant and not Aoife Cusack?'

Meers's laugh was incredulous. 'Bit of a coincidence!'

Greg privately agreed, but he wanted to keep all avenues open. He looked at his watch. It was gone ten and he'd been up since seven. It might not be quite the summer solstice but today had been the longest day.

'I'm going home,' he said. 'You have somewhere to stay?'

'I'll be all right,' Meers said.

The explosion went off in Deepak's head again: yellow balls of flame tore through brick and glass as if they were paper, searing human flesh and bones. He had not witnessed the blast and the picture that his subconscious made of it was worse than any reality.

Then he was back in the interview room at Newbury police station and Gregory Summers – a man he'd long considered a friend – was looming over him, shouting.

271

'Why did you go to the morgue with some pretext for seeing the body?

'You had no need of more samples, did you?

'You wanted to see the results of your filthy handiwork. Isn't that right?'

'I wanted only to see her face,' he protested, 'to see what the woman who killed my sister looked like.'

'Did you really think I wouldn't find out?'

Deep was screaming now: 'No more questions!'

Then he was back in Windsor, sitting on the hill outside the castle, and behind him he could hear demonic laughter.

He tried Pat's 'trigger' for the first time; a traffic light in the street below turned from red to green, cueing him to wake, to roll over on to his back, gasping for breath as if the smoke and fumes of the bomb choked him.

He was aware of Indira motionless at his side. He thought that she was not asleep but didn't speak to find out. He was sure he hadn't woken her; the screaming had been inside his head. He lay panting; the dim light of a streetlamp outside showed him the white ceiling, the bank of wardrobes on the far wall with their mirrored doors, the clock on his bedside table. He welcomed anything normal.

He reached out his hand to touch his wife's

thigh, to reassure himself, then snatched it back.

It seemed ironic that email had been their method of courtship; now she used it to tell her kid brother of her misery and disappointment. A year ago, Deep had had no thought of marriage. Then Uncle Roshan had come on one of his visits; he came every five years and stayed about a month, visiting the same familiar sights and playing at being an English gentleman.

One evening he had put his arm round his nephew's shoulder and asked, man to man, if he had a girlfriend.

'White English girl, maybe, Deepak?'

Deep admitted that there had been girls in the past, most of them *goris* – white girls – but that he was currently single.

'You remember my old friend Mr Ravi Buhpathi – best bloody heart surgeon in Mumbai?'

'I've heard you speak of him.'

'He has a daughter, a little younger than you, also a doctor, specialises in children. Very nice girl, also pretty. Excellent *rishta* for us.'

Rishta: the alliance between families. Deepak didn't think that way; to him it was man and wife, a nuclear family.

'Of course–' Uncle Roshan grimaced and shrugged his shoulders '–she is dark-skinned like all her family, but you can't have everything.'

Deep laughed uncertainly. As an Englishman he found this Indian obsession with skin colour baffling and a little sinister and was never quite certain that it wasn't some joke he didn't get the point of. It had never occurred to him that his own pale face was a bargaining chip in the marriage game or that that, along with his British passport, made him a desirable son-in-law for a family of high-powered doctors.

'I'm not sure what you're suggesting, Uncle,' he said cautiously, since he knew very well.

'You have the email?'

'Of course.'

'Then here is her email address.' Uncle Roshan handed over a sheet of lined paper. 'Why don't you "drop her a line"? What have you got to lose, dear boy?'

'Nothing, I suppose.'

Deepak put the paper in his shirt pocket and forgot about it until he went to the laundrette a fortnight later. He stood looking at it for a long time, as if scrutiny of the familiar formula would bring enlightenment.

People met on the Internet all the time. Emailing her would not be making a commitment. He sent a couple of lines, introducing himself, joking that Uncle Roshan thought they might click. She wrote back a few hours later. She struck him as happy and busy, funny and warm. Soon they were in daily communication, exchanging their confidences, and he felt as if he had known her for years.

After a month he'd asked her to marry him and she had accepted. He had felt joy and apprehension in equal measure. The wedding had been strange and exotic; he'd decided against riding to it on horseback in the end, but Mrs Buhpathi had knelt in the traditional way to wash his feet and welcome him to the family. He had dreaded it since his feet were ticklish, but it had been oddly moving.

Over the past six months, he'd had to watch the happy girl he had met in Mumbai, surrounded by her extended family and in the highest possible spirits, become daily more morose and withdrawn.

And he had absolutely no idea how to set things right.

Chapter Nineteen

Greg was scrolling through newspaper reports of the Windsor bombing the next morning, examining the photos of the victims. He was most interested in the men but his eyes lingered on the picture of Sangita

Gupta. She looked very like her brother, he saw, neither of them beauties but with kindly, intelligent faces.

Peter Mitchell, assistant manager of The Angel, had been serving behind the bar, not killed instantly but dying of his injuries in hospital two days later. He was a man of forty-five, Greg learned, who left a widow and three teenaged children.

Not him.

Adam Mason was twenty, a student at Reading university, unmarried. He'd been at the next table to Sangita and had died instantly. Could he have left a pregnant girlfriend? Greg did some quick sums: Siobhan was pushing fifty by his calculations, making her in her mid- to late twenties at the time of the atrocity.

Not impossible, but unlikely.

Donald McLaverty was a pensioner who came to The Angel every lunchtime for a pint and his midday meal. Like Adam, he had probably never known what hit him. A widower, he too seemed an unsuitable candidate for Siobhan's husband and Daniel's father.

That left only the two remaining women – Eileen Harris and Sharon Pearson, a middle-aged spinster nurse and a young housewife and mother. Could she have left a babe-in-arms who was now Daniel Fahey, Siobhan her sister or best friend? He examined

276

Sharon's photograph for any family resemblance to the dried-up matron or to Daniel but, with the best will in the world, could see none.

There had been other victims, he reminded himself, people like Rachel Goodman, dead by her own hand because she could not bury the memories and her survivor's guilt. Who knew how many more there might be?

Did it make a difference that the murders had been committed almost a quarter of a century ago? When did human misery become history?

To find out who had been in the pub that lunchtime would be a Herculean task after twenty-three years. And what had he got to go on, after all – that Siobhan Fahey had been widowed in 1981? That she had waited twenty-three years to avenge her loss?

No, it was unlikely that Siobhan was related to anyone in The Angel that day. A policeman's hunch was one thing, but common sense had to prevail.

At 8:59 precisely there was a tap at his door. His secretary, Susan Habib, didn't work Sundays so it was open house.

'Come in!' he yelled.

The door opened and in came Emily Foster and Jill Christie, both in jeans and black t-shirts and, in Emily's case, a black leather jacket in which she looked far too hot.

'We're in plain clothes,' Jill explained.

So much had happened in the past nineteen hours that he'd forgotten their appointment. Otherwise, he would have cancelled them. He looked at them for a moment.

'There've been developments since I spoke to you.' Their faces dropped with disappointment and he got to his feet. 'However, I still think it's worth doing. Come with me.'

He led the way to the CID room along the corridor. 'Now, girls,' he said, 'I don't want you to get too overwhelmed by the glamour of detective work, but I want you to look at these.' He hefted a box of videotapes on to a spare desk.

'What are they?' Jill ventured.

'CCTV footage of the M4 – the Chiswick flyover, to be precise – heading out of London last Thursday evening between seven and ten. It's meticulous work, I'm afraid.' He didn't add, *and terribly dull.* They would find that out for themselves. 'There are only two lanes of traffic on the elevated section,' he went on, 'but you can't take your eyes off the tape for a moment, which is why I've put two of you on to it. Take it in turns, switch the tape off if you need a rest, but don't miss a single vehicle.'

'What are we looking for?' Emily fanned herself, gave up, and took off her leather jacket.

'A silver-grey Jaguar. Here's the registration. I'll leave you to it. If you spot it heading for Hungerford that evening, I want you to call me on my mobile at once. Okay?'

They nodded and Jill put the first tape in the machine. The door opened at that moment and Barbara came in.

'What's going on?' He explained and she grinned and said, 'Rather them than me. Still wondering about the husband?'

'Just being thorough. Let's leave these two to it,' he added, 'and get back out to Inkpen.'

'What happened with the...' She glanced at the two young women and headed out of the door, lowering her voice. 'Our friends from the special services?'

'I'm worried that Meers's ideas are too fixed,' he said. 'He's got his heart set on it being Liam Sullivan but I think that we–'

Barbara's mobile rang. She looked at the display, sighed, pressed the answer button and said, 'Trevor?... Yeah?... 84 degrees in the shade already? Nice. Really?... Squid? Always tastes like rubber to me. No, not yet. Complications have arisen. I can't go into it over an open airwave... Okay. Bye.'

She disconnected. 'Bastard. Ringing up to gloat.'

'You discuss cases with Trevor?' Greg asked.

'Sometimes. He is NCS, and a DCI at thirty-one.'

'Yeah, I know. High flier. Soon be giving all of us orders.' Greg had been over forty before they promoted him to DCI. Not that he was bitter.

'You talk to Angie,' she pointed out. 'I know you do.'

'Yeah ... well.'

'Trevor might have some useful insights.'

'So might Angie.'

'Yeah ... okay.'

He rang the hospital to see how Desmond Chapman was doing. He was in no danger, the nurse told him, but would be kept in for observation for a few days. Given his personal circumstances, they had notified Social Services that he might be in need of care.

Poor bloke, Greg thought. He was in the system now – entered on a computer somewhere – and there was no escape. They'd have him in a home in no time and there'd be no room for his shrine there.

'I don't think I shall be watching telly again for weeks,' Emily complained around noon. 'Have my eyes gone square?'

Jill sighed and paused the video footage. 'Let's get some more coffee.'

'It's coming out of my ears,' Emily moaned. 'We've got to do an eight-hour shift after this, so we'd better make sure we're never more than two minutes from a loo. I thought we'd be working undercover or something, dressed as hookers.'

'They're investigating that murder in Inkpen,' Jill said. 'Where the hell would hookers fit in?'

'Remind me never to apply for CID.'

'I don't really fancy it anyway.' Jill poured two mugs of coffee from CID's filter machine. 'I like being out on the streets, talking to people, helping them with small things. You know?' She handed Emily her mug and restarted the tape. 'And the Super cancelled Barbara's leave.' Jill snapped her fingers. 'Just like that.'

'Yeah, she was going to Corfu with that hot inspector from the National Crime Squad.'

'*Chief* inspector. He got promoted. He can take me to Corfu any time. Or Clacton even.'

'I was surprised by that,' Emily admitted. 'The Super always seems like a decent old geezer.'

'Yeah, reminds me a bit of my dad.'

Emily snorted. 'Can't see your dad getting it on with Martha Childs from SOC, can you?'

'Is that true? I thought it was just station gossip.'

'I had it from Nick Nicolaides and her husband's moved out, for definite.'

Jill's eyes widened. ''Cause he found out

about her and the Super?'

'I dunno.' Emily shrugged. She pointed at the screen. 'I fancy one of those little sports cars. See. Ooh! Is that a Jag?'

'It's burgundy,' Jill said. 'So that's no good.'

'If we don't get finished before two, are we to come back later?' Emily asked.

'Cross that bridge when we get to it.'

When Greg got home that Sunday evening, he found Angie curled up on the sofa reading *Behind the Wire*. She had almost finished it. The television was blaring away too, Angie apparently unable to concentrate without background noise, a generational difference that was likely to remain insurmountable. It was a commercial break and a woman was explaining that her face cream made her wrinkles look ten years younger.

He'd noticed that the volume tended to increase when the ads came on. 'Any supper?' he enquired, raising his voice to drown the sound.

'I cooked it the last three nights. I'm on strike.'

'Pub?' he suggested.

'Good idea.'

Half an hour later, as they settled into a corner of the pub in Hamstead Marshall, he thought that she was unusually quiet.

'Anything wrong, darling?' he asked. 'Sorry I've been out so much–'

She waved his apology away. 'I know what to expect when you're on a murder enquiry It's just something that's bugging me, about that bloke Francis Mahoney, or whatever his real name is. Mr Undercover Hero.'

'Malcolm Fraser,' he supplied.

'Don't you find it a bit odd that Aoife took off just days before the arrest?'

What are you getting at?'

'Suppose whatsizname – Fraser – was in love with Aoife and tipped her off that they were all going to be arrested, told her to make a run for it.'

'That would be incredibly reckless,' Greg said slowly. 'She might have gone straight to Sullivan. Two years of hard work would have gone down the drain and Fraser would have ended up messily dead.'

Angie was silent while a smiling waitress deposited two steaming plates of pasta in front of them, instructed them to enjoy their meal and left. 'That's pretty much my point. It was incredibly stupid, but that's what I think happened. It makes no sense otherwise.'

She picked up her fork and started winding linguine round it, groping for stray pieces and sucking it into her mouth. 'Yum. Wouldn't Special Branch be kinda mad if they knew?'

'Just a bit.' Greg used his knife to cut his pasta into more manageable lengths. Cowardly, but practical.

'Not such a hero, huh?'

'I don't see that it really gets us anywhere,' Greg said.

She put her fork down and sighed at his slowness. 'If Sullivan exposed this woman, the way he said he was going to, and she got arrested, then she'd be bound to spill the beans during her interrogation.'

'I don't like that word,' he objected. 'I prefer interview.'

'Whichever. It'd all come out, his part in helping her evade justice. That sounds like a motive for murder to me.'

Greg gasped. 'I thought your theory was that he was in love with her.'

'Twenty-three years ago! Now it's her neck or his reputation, not to mention his pension.'

Greg thought about it. 'But how would he know that Sullivan was threatening to reveal her new identity?'

She shrugged. 'Happen they've kept in touch all these years. Do I have to do all the work? You should defo talk to him, and get the thumbscrews out.'

He opened his mouth to make a further objection, but then he remembered the unregistered mobile, the one with the false name and address, the single phone call the day after Sullivan's visit. Who needed such a thing? Drug dealers, pimps, undercover policemen.

Or, as he himself had remarked, someone had bought it solely so that Aoife could contact them in urgent need. It had been bought in Basingstoke, in Hampshire. You could drive there and back from the Isle of Wight in a day.

Was it possible? There was no doubt that policemen made good murderers. Keep it simple, that was the key, no elaborate plots, just a quick shove over the edge of a cliff. Or a sharp knife through the ribs and into the heart. Fraser would have been trained to kill in direst necessity and the murder had something of the execution about it.

'Bloody hell,' he muttered, his appetite gone. 'I need to talk to Colin Meers... Um, defo.' He took out his mobile and dialled. 'Colin? I've had a thought.'

Angie snorted into her Muscadet. *'You've* had a thought!'

'Can we meet? Alone. I need to run this by you in person.'

Now, where had he left his thumbscrews?

Chapter Twenty

Meers had checked into the Travelodge just off the M4 motorway and, after dropping Angie in Kintbury, Greg made his way there and met the older man in the cafeteria of the adjacent motorway service station, as arranged.

'Has Fraser gone home?' he asked once he'd supplied Colin with a bottle of lager and bought a mineral water for himself.

Meers shook his head. 'He's staying here too, wants to hang around. He's always taken a very personal interest in the Sullivan cell, especially in Aoife Cusack.'

'That was what I wanted to talk to you about,' Greg said. 'How personal was that interest?'

He explained Angie's theory, which had now become his theory. If it proved nonsense then it might well migrate back to her; if it wasn't, then that would teach Barbara to be sceptical about Angie's insights.

Meers was listening in increasing disbelief.

'Have you any idea what it's like to work under deep cover?' he exploded in the end. 'To spend years cut off from your family and friends with nobody but animals like Sullivan for company?'

'That's precisely why an undercover operative might fall for a pretty girl like Aoife Cusack,' Greg said. 'The way a hostage begins to identify with a kidnapper, like in the Stockholm syndrome. Maybe he began to take pity on her, decided that she was too young and naive to be responsible for what she'd done.'

'And you're seriously suggesting that Malcolm might have jeopardised an operation that we'd spent two years working on by tipping Aoife off.' Meers rose, bristling aggression. 'He'd have known she'd go straight to Sullivan.'

'Not if she was already having doubts about what they were doing. It might all have seemed very glamorous at first – playing the Irish patriot – until she saw what she'd done in Windsor because, from what I've learned of her life since then, Aoife was no psychopath, not like Sullivan.'

'I won't listen to this.'

'Then there's the small matter of an unlisted mobile phone,' Greg said mildly.

'What?' Meers hesitated and sat down again.

'Eight days before her death Aoife made a single call to a mobile number – that's the day after Sullivan went to see her. We've been unable to determine who that call was to. The mobile was bought in Argos in Basingstoke two years ago, on a pay-as-you-go basis, and had not been used for either in- or outgoing calls in all that time. The name and address of the purchaser turn out to be false.'

'Basingstoke? Well, that's...'

'A few hours' drive from the Isle of Wight, there and back.'

'And an even shorter drive from here! You can't go making accusations on a flimsy basis like that. All sorts of people have untraceable mobiles – drug dealers, people smugglers, pimps.'

'Yes, they do,' Greg agreed. 'And what business would a respectable wife and mother like Robyn Marchant have with any of those?'

'Well ... Aoife Cusack was a criminal. Who knows what she was up to these days? That school might have been nothing more than a front. Have you thought of that?'

'I'm certain that it wasn't,' Greg said. 'I'm satisfied that Aoife set up that school to try to earn redemption for what she'd done in Windsor...' Meers was silent for a moment and Greg said, 'I realise how difficult this is for you, but I'd like to talk to Fraser about it.'

'He's not just going to admit it,' Meers said derisively. 'He's trained to withstand torture by terrorists, let alone an interview with a provincial plod.'

'Thank you,' Greg murmured. Now he had a true idea of the contempt in which Colin Meers held him.

'If he got a call from Aoife on an untraceable mobile, then that mobile's now at the bottom of the Solent, dropped off the side of the Isle of Wight ferry not sitting in his house waiting for you to find it.'

Greg got up. 'Let's go and talk to him.'

He tapped at the door of Fraser's room five minutes later and was answered with 'It's open.'

He let himself and Meers in.

The motel room was a spacious oblong with two double beds, a TV and a tray with the makings of tea and coffee. Through a door to one side, Greg could see a bathroom with wet towels strewn around the floor.

Fraser was sitting on one bed, his back against a group of pillows, watching football on television. He picked up the remote as they entered and clicked the sound off. On the bedside table stood an empty glass and a bottle of Scotch, although only two fingers were missing. You didn't last long undercover if you had a drink problem.

'Superintendent,' he said by way of greeting. 'Colin. Can I offer you a drink?'

Meers shook his head and Greg said, 'I'm driving, thanks.'

Fraser swung his legs off the bed and groped under it for his shoes as if he wanted to be ready for sudden flight. 'So what can I do you for?'

'I was wondering if I could ask you a few questions about your time with Sullivan's ASU,' Greg said.

'Fire away.'

'How well did you know Aoife Cusack?'

'I knew them all *really* well.' Fraser grinned, lacing up grubby trainers. 'Billy Sullivan was my best mate – like a brother to me. When you're skipping around the country plotting to murder people, you get very close.'

'Didn't you feel sorry for Aoife?' Greg asked. 'I mean she was just a kid.'

'Old enough to know right from wrong.' Fraser picked up the bottle of Scotch and poured an inch into his glass. He went into the bathroom and added a little water from the cold tap. Greg thought he was creating time to think but there wasn't much he could do about it.

He emerged from the bathroom but didn't sit down again. 'What's this about, Mr Summers, if I may ask?'

'I wondered if you knew anything about a mobile phone.' Greg took his notebook from his pocket and read out the number. He locked eyes with the Scotsman and knew, as he did so, that he was wasting his time. It was as Meers had said – Malcolm Fraser was not going to admit to anything.

'No,' he said now, not too quickly, not too slowly. 'Should I?'

'It's an untraceable mobile bought at Argos in Basingstoke a couple of years ago. The buyer paid cash and gave a false name and address to the service provider.'

'And?'

'And Aoife made a single call to it a week before her death, the day after she got a visit from Liam Sullivan threatening her with exposure. It makes me think that she was calling an old contact, someone she had reason to believe would help her in her time of trouble, since he had come to her rescue once before.'

'And that would be me, would it? What exactly are you suggesting?'

'All right.' In for a penny, in for a pound. 'I put it to you that you were much closer to Aoife than you let on, maybe in love with her, lovers even–'

'She was Billy's girl. No one else would have dared.'

'–That you warned her that Sullivan's cell was about to be rounded up and that she should make a run for it.'

'And risk her going straight to Billy, to tell him I was a policeman? What do you think my life would have been worth that night?'

Greg would not be waylaid. 'You took a

291

calculated risk because you knew she was horrified by the carnage in Windsor. I suggest that, through all these years, you've made sure she had a way of getting in touch with you in an emergency and that she rang you to tell you that Sullivan had tracked her down...'

Fraser was laughing now. He settled himself comfortably back on the bed again, his eyes on the screen, on the antics of twenty-two brightly-clad men against a green playing field. 'You spin a good yarn, Superintendent. You're not buying this, surely, Colin?'

'Course not.' Meers helped himself to a shortbread biscuit from a packet on the tray and nibbled it, but Greg noticed that he was watching his former colleague very closely.

'...And that you killed her because you knew that if she was arrested and questioned she would reveal your part in her escape and your years as a Special Branch legend would be at an end, along with your pension.'

'It has a certain plausibility about it,' Fraser admitted. 'Pity it's so completely wrong.'

'So if I get a warrant to search your place on the Isle of Wight, I won't find this mobile there?'

'Be my guest.' His satisfied smile told Greg that he would find nothing incriminating in Fraser's boat yard; as Meers had said, the phone was long gone.

He got up to leave, frustrated, more than ever convinced that Angie was right.

'One thing,' Fraser called after him as he opened the door. 'Supposing for a moment there was one word of truth in what you've said, supposing Aoife did call me and ask me for help...'

He paused and Greg said, 'Well?'

'Isn't it obvious that I'd have killed Sullivan and not her?'

'I want to go home,' Indira blurted out. 'I'm sorry, Deepak. I have tried, but I don't like it here. The people are as cold as the weather.' She began to cry. 'The food has no taste and I cannot do my work and men live openly with their sons' wives and have no shame.'

He tried to speak but she left no space. 'I know I am an awful person and my parents will probably never speak to me again, but I'm going back to Mumbai and shall get a flat and be a "career girl".'

Deepak thought about it for all of ten seconds. 'I'll come with you,' he said. He took her in his arms to dry her tears and tell her of his love.

Greg was getting into his car when he became aware of a footfall behind him. He spun round, ready for an attack, but Malcolm Fraser, emerging from the shadows behind him, did not look threatening.

'One last word,' he said, 'entirely off the record. I'll deny this meeting ever took place.'

'Well?'

'Aoife Cusack was the love of my life. Okay, so she'd made a new life for herself and I wasn't part of that, but I would never have done anything to hurt her.'

'But she did phone you after Sullivan came to see her?'

'No comment.'

'And you did tip her off before the arrest?'

'You know that's a question I'll never answer, even off the record. Aoife was ready to leave Sullivan. Why don't you accept that she went of her own accord?'

He leaned on the roof of the car, talking across the metal, the way men did in cop shows on TV. 'If Aoife had called me and if I'd suggested to her that Sullivan might meet with a nasty accident, do you know what I think she'd have said?'

'Do tell.'

'I think she'd have said, "I have enough blood on my hands, Francis, without adding his to it."'

'I want you off my patch,' Greg said, 'and nowhere near my case, and that goes for Meers too. Neither of you has any official role here. He's retired and you left the service two decades ago. I was prepared to give you some rope out of courtesy but you've exhausted my patience.'

Fraser shrugged and vanished into the night.

Greg was fairly sure now that Aoife had not asked Sullivan to Hilltop that night to kill him. She'd been speaking the truth when she said she had something to tell him, something that might arouse his sympathy.

Greg thought that, somewhere in the back of his mind, he had an idea what that something might have been, but he couldn't quite tug it out into his consciousness.

He drove away feeling deeply depressed: that was what you got for having heroes.

He had made a mental note of Fraser's car the first time he'd seen it. It was second nature to a policeman.

It was almost ten and, dropping back into the police station, he was in time to intercept Emily and Jill as they ended their shift.

'I assume you found nothing,' he said, 'since you didn't call me.'

'We got all the tapes done,' Emily said, 'but there was no sign of the Jag you wanted.'

'Sick of it yet?' he asked with a smile.

They exchanged looks. Jill shrugged. 'We can always use the overtime with the holidays coming up.'

'Fair enough. Same time tomorrow.'

He would get the tapes of the more obvious routes into Berkshire from Hampshire on Thursday, see if they could spot Fraser's souped-up Golf.

If so, he'd be prepared to arrest the Scotsman, see if he was really as tough as he acted.

Having tried Meers's room and got no reply, Fraser went to look for him in the bar. He found his old boss draining a large whisky and calling 'Same again' to the bartender.

'Steady on, Col.' He perched on the stool next to him.

Meers wouldn't look at him. 'He's right, isn't he? Summers. You tipped off Aoife Cusack so she could get out ahead of the arrests. You told her you were a policeman. You risked everything I'd been working for.'

'Don't be stupid.'

'Is that "Don't be stupid" as in "Of course he isn't right" or as in "You don't seriously expect me to admit it"?'

'Whatever.' Fraser laughed and signalled the barman for a beer. 'You never used to have so much faith in provincial woodentops, Colin.'

'Summers is no fool,' Meers growled. He slammed his palm down on the bar top. 'I trusted you for twenty-five years, Malc, and he had it figured out in twenty-five *hours.*' He raised his voice. 'Where's my bloody whisky? Have you sent to Scotland for it?' The barman hastily brought his glass. He drained it in one gulp and signalled for another. 'Did you kill Aoife? Did you help her escape me again, you little...?'

'I didn't kill Aoife.'

'Yeah, 'cause, obviously, if you had, you'd just come out and admit it.' Meers tossed off his third glass and got up, a little unsteady on his feet. 'I'm off. I don't like the company here any more.'

'Off where?'

'Home. I have no place in this investigation any more. I'm checking out.'

'You can't drive all that way after three double Scotches or you'll be checking out permanently.' Fraser left his beer with a sigh, stood up and put his hand on his old friend's shoulder. 'I'll see you back to your room and you can go home in the morning.'

Meers shrugged off his hand. 'I can find my own way and, if I were you, I wouldn't hang around here either.'

Chapter Twenty-One

'So, you're not going to work today?' Charlie said to her father as they sat at the breakfast table. Each had a bowl of cereal but Stephen's lay untasted before him.

'They can manage without me for a few days,' he said. 'The inquest opens this morning.'

'Mr Summers said it was a formality at this stage.'

'I want to go all the same. I rang your headmistress last night, by the way, put her in the picture. She's not expecting you back till next Monday and she asked me to tell you that you're in the thoughts and prayers of the whole school.'

'Do I have to go back?' Charlie sipped coffee, watching her father closely over the rim of her cup.

'What do you mean?'

'Term ends in a couple of weeks anyway. Can't I leave now and go to the Academy?'

'I thought we agreed that you would stay on and get your A levels first.'

'*Mum* agreed.'

'We all agreed.'

'I didn't agree. Please, Dad.'

298

'Charlie...'

'I thought it was Mum who was so insistent,' she said sulkily. 'I thought you were on my side.'

'It's not a matter of sides, but of what's best for you. And we should respect Mum's wishes, now more than ever.'

'Shouldn't I be the judge of what's best for me? I wish I'd gone to Chiswick on Friday now. It's not like I did any good staying here. She isn't any less dead.'

'I can't discuss this now!' Stephen got up and stood, leaning forward, his head bowed, his hands bunched into fists on the table top, trying to contain his anger. 'For God's sake, Charlie, your mother's not even decently buried and I can't–'

He turned and walked out of the room. He was afraid that if he stayed he might slap her.

By Monday evening Greg was feeling dispirited. Jill and Emily had not found Fraser's car on tape, but the man was trained for this sort of work. He could have made the journey entirely on minor roads or in another car, maybe one stolen just for the operation.

He asked the two young women to check reports of cars stolen in the Isle of Wight, Portsmouth or Southampton on the day of the murder and later found abandoned but none of them struck him as helpful.

House-to-house enquiries in Inkpen had asked about cars seen parked in the vicinity of Hilltop on the day of the murder. Now Barbara was coordinating follow-up visits to ask specifically about the souped-up Golf.

Robyn Marchant – Aoife Cusack – had been dead for four days and he would have hoped for a breakthrough by now.

He thought he deserved an evening off, come back fresh to the problem tomorrow.

There was no sign of Angie at the house when he got home and Bellini was standing in the hall with her lead in her mouth. On the mat were two letters: a gas bill and a white envelope addressed to himself in an elegant hand and franked *HMP Styal*.

'From Mummy. She'll be wanting to know how you are.' Greg showed the letter to the little terrier who looked uninterested, perhaps forgetting that she had once had another home. He pocketed it to read later and, attaching the clip of her lead to her collar, turned straight round and went out again.

'We're only going down to the village and back,' he told her, 'so do your business quick.'

As they reached the end of his close and turned down the road towards the centre of Kintbury, a voice hailed him by name. Some of his neighbours seemed to think that he could get them off a parking ticket, a speeding fine or even a tax audit, apparently under the impression that Superintendent was a colleague of Batman and Spiderman.

'Superintendent. Mr Summers. Super-intendent!'

Since he couldn't go on pretending that he hadn't heard any longer, Greg turned and forced a smile on to his face. The woman with the Pekinese clearly wanted to talk to him.

'Mrs Driscoll?'

Bellini and the Peke started snuffling round each other's rears as if in training for the Olympic bottom-sniffing championship in Athens that August.

'It's about this nasty business in Inkpen,' she began. 'Robyn Marchant. Lovely woman, so selfless – an inspiration to us all.'

'Hmm.'

'If she isn't safe from some maniac, then who is?– Come away, Chairman Mao!'

'Have you some information about the killing?' Greg asked, trying in vain to haul Bellini away from the Chairman who was obviously male and thought he was on a promise. If Bellini was on heat, then no wonder she had been so keen for a walk.

'Yes. No. Well, it was a week or so before-hand but, all the same...'

'Yes?'

She lowered her voice. 'An Asian man, hanging about. And you can't be too careful with all these Arab terrorists and illegal immigrants everywhere.'

Asian faces were still a rarity in the British countryside, though not in Newbury. Mrs Driscoll probably needed to get out more, and read the *Daily Outlook* less.

She pointed. 'He parked his car in our close and he was gone for about an hour but when I spoke to him he claimed he'd been–' she blushed '–answering a call of nature.'

'Rather a long call,' Greg agreed.

'He did seem to speak English like a ... an English person,' she admitted, on a note of disappointment, 'but I bet he was up in Inkpen "casing the joint".'

'It's possible.' Greg tried to keep a straight face at her terminology. 'Can you describe the car?'

'Oh! Just a little hatchback.' As he looked encouraging, she added, 'Light blue.'

'Make? Two or four doors? Did you notice if it was a recent registration?'

'...It might have been a Ford. Two doors, I think. And it was one of the new style of number plate, so it was registered in the last three or four years.'

'That's very good, Mrs Driscoll.' He was surprised. 'We must draft you into CID.'

'I'm a bird watcher,' she said. 'Eye for detail.'

'Now can you remember exactly which night this was?'

She thought very hard, running over her recent itinerary in tedious detail, until she exclaimed triumphantly, 'Wednesday, the ninth!'

Greg thanked her and wished her good evening, picking Bellini up and tucking her under his arm since it was the only way he could get her to leave the love of her life.

He had a pretty good idea who the car belonged to. Even if he hadn't known that Deepak Gupta drove a newish, light blue Ford Escort, it would have been a fair bet that he hadn't kept his promise about not following Sullivan.

Wednesday, the ninth. That was the night Sullivan had been to see Aoife, the night Charlie had spotted him in the sitting room.

Time to talk to Deep again.

Halfway back to his own house, a nasty thought flitted into his mind and he set the struggling terrier down on the pavement to examine it more easily in his mind's eye.

There was no doubt about it: Deepak Gupta was left-handed.

When he got back to the house, Angie's car was in the drive. He let himself in and her voice came floating down the stairs. 'I'm running a nice, foamy tub.' She appeared on the landing wearing nothing but a towel. 'There's room for two.'

'Bollocks,' he muttered. And, aloud, 'I

have to go out again, love.'

'Some other time then.'

As Bellini went barking joyfully up the stairs, he called up. 'But the dog could do with a bath.'

Greg sensed a difference in the atmosphere chez Gupta, as if a weight had been lifted from the young couple, and he was sad to have to break bad news to them again.

Deep once more agreed to come in voluntarily for questioning. When a phone call to Deirdre Washowski's home elicited the information that she'd gone to the theatre in London and was not expected back till morning, he declined a different solicitor and agreed to talk to Greg without her.

Greg called for a SOC team to search the flat and took Deepak down to the station. They walked in the back way together like two colleagues and Greg asked Deep to wait for him in interview room two.

Nick and Andy had gone home after a full day at the crime scene and even Barbara had left murmuring about an early night. She was supposed to be on leave, after all, and Greg wasn't going to ruin her evening.

He needed a second officer to attend the interview, however, which meant somebody from Uniform would have to be drafted in. The ten o'clock shift had recently come on duty and he asked the desk sergeant, Bert

Clifton, who the inspector was on the night relief.

'Bob Holman,' the man replied.

Greg made a face. Holman was a jobsworth with no detective experience. 'Sergeants?' he asked.

'Mistry – no, wait, he went out with the crime squad. Doyle's around somewhere.'

'Can you give her a shout?' Greg asked.

Apparently taking him literally, Sergeant Clifton threw his head back and bellowed, 'Ronnie?'

She came out of the collator's room behind him. 'What? I'm not sodding deaf.'

Clifton gestured. 'Super wants you.'

'I'd like you to sit in on an interview with me, Veronica.'

'You're the boss. Let me just have a pee.'

He laid a hand on her arm as they prepared to enter the interview room a few minutes later. 'This is a confidential matter, Veronica. Our interviewee is someone you know – a colleague – and I don't want it broadcast around the station. Is that clear?'

'Perfectly.' She looked intrigued.

He added, 'Let me do the talking,' and opened the door for her, standing back to allow her through first.

'Deepak!' she said.

'How are you, Ronnie?' He gave her a weak smile.

She sat down. Greg took two new tapes

from the cupboard and put them in the machine. After they'd all identified themselves, Greg said, 'Mr Gupta, we spoke on the sixth of this month, at your flat. Do you remember the conversation?'

He nodded. 'You told me to stop harassing Liam Sullivan.'

'And you promised me that you would.'

'That's right.'

'And yet I have evidence that you continued to follow him, despite your promise.'

He grimaced. 'I suppose it was the old woman with the ratty little dog. She didn't like my face – wrong colour.'

'A neighbour of mine in Kintbury saw you on the ninth,' Greg agreed, 'parked near to Sullivan's house, for over an hour.'

'I kept my promise,' Deep said.

'You what?'

'I promised only to stop harassing him. Before that I'd let him see me. That night he didn't. If he didn't know I was there then I don't see how it can be harassment.'

'That's a fair point,' Veronica said.

Greg gave her a withering look. 'Very much the letter rather than the spirit of the law, don't you think?'

'The letter is what you're paid to uphold,' Deep said.

'That was the night that Sullivan paid a visit on ... on Robyn Marchant.'

'I followed him to the murder scene that

night,' Deep said quietly. 'He went into the house, but I had no idea who he was talking to or why.'

'Why didn't you mention Sullivan's visit to Hilltop when Mrs Marchant was killed?' Greg asked.

'I honestly didn't make the connection at the time. It was dark and I didn't notice the name of the house Sullivan went to, otherwise I would have come forward.'

Greg clicked off the tape recorder. 'I so want to believe you, Deep–'

'Then believe me.'

'–but you've been shifty, lying by omission at the very least.'

'I was afraid,' he admitted. 'When your pal from Special Branch told me who the dead woman was, I was hardly going to admit to having been up to her house, not with the reasons I had to hate her, but like I told him, if I'd killed her then I'd be as bad as she was. I have too much to lose.'

'I'm confused,' Veronica said. 'Who was this woman?'

'Need-to-know basis,' Greg snapped.

'Well, pardon me for living.'

Sergeant Clifton came into the room at that moment and whispered in Greg's ear. Greg got up and followed him out.

Martha Childs was waiting in reception, a look almost of desperation on her face.

Concerned, he said, 'What on earth's the

matter, Martha?'

Apparently too upset to maintain the coldness of their recent meetings she said, 'Gregory, you have to see this.' He took the evidence bag she was holding up and looked at the knife inside. It was about six inches long with an ornately carved handle. The tip was to one side and not in the middle, just like the sketch Dr Chubb had made.

'Deep's flat?' he asked grimly.

'In the bedroom. He has a whole case of them. Mrs Gupta says they're family heirlooms. She seemed baffled by my interest. I've got them all bagged up but this one fits the specifications of what we've been searching for most nearly.'

'Any sign of blood?'

'Not to the naked eye.'

'Get it down to forensics,' Greg said. 'Dr Armstrong can check it first thing. Thanks, Martha.'

He walked slowly back to the interview room, his feet like lead. He sat down in his former chair and switched the tape back on, giving a new time check.

'You have a caseful of knives in your flat, Mr Gupta,' he stated. 'Indian knives.'

'Yeah. What of it? They belonged to my dad – been in the family for generations. Mum gave them to me after he died. They're just ornaments.'

'Ornaments very like the weapon used to

kill Mrs Marchant.'

Deepak looked alarmed. 'That's not possible. I mean...'

'The shape is unusual,' Greg went on. 'Unlike anything found in European culture.'

'But they're not even sharp,' Deep protested. 'I wouldn't use one to cut butter.'

'I'm sorry, Mr Gupta, but until we get some forensic on those knives, I'm going to have to keep you in.'

'Fuck that!' Deep got up. 'I'm going home.'

'Deepak Gupta, I'm arresting you on suspicion of the murder of Robyn Marchant.' He recited the caution and said, 'Do you understand?'

'Will you let Indira know?' was all Deepak said.

'I'll tell her myself.' He nodded to Veronica. 'Thanks for your help, Sergeant.' She reluctantly rose and left them alone.

'Come on,' Greg said, taking the younger man by the arm. 'It's getting late. Try to get some sleep.' He waited while they found a cell for his prisoner, then followed him in, nodding to the custody sergeant to leave them. 'I'm so sorry about this, Deep. My hands are tied.'

Deepak flung himself down on the bed, folded his arms behind his head and said, 'Shut the door on your way out.'

Greg decided it wasn't too late to ring Pat

Armstrong and tell her the news that her assistant had been arrested. Pat listened without comment, then said, 'I don't believe a word of it. I'll be there within the hour. I want to take a look at these alleged knives and I want to see them now.'

Greg went back to the Guptas' flat to break the bad news to Indira. She merely echoed what her husband had said: that the knives were ornamental and not even sharp. Normally he would have asked if she had a mother or sister he could ring for her but he knew that her family were thousands of miles away.

'Try and get some sleep,' he advised her, as he had her husband. 'It'll all be sorted out in the morning. I don't believe for a moment that Deep's a murderer.'

But did he? Didn't they all have it in them to kill if pushed to the limit? He knew he did.

When Greg got back to Kintbury he looked in on Angie. She was asleep, her breathing regular and snuffly; a less charitable and loving listener might have called it snoring. He could have climbed into bed beside her, but he didn't think there was any point.

So good at dishing out advice about the need for sleep, he thought wryly, so bad at taking it.

He sat in the sitting room with the television on but turned down to a low volume. The later the hour, the more awful the programmes. At one o'clock his mobile started to trill. He answered it on the first ring and Pat Armstrong spoke without identifying herself.

'There's no blood on any of those knives, not a drop.'

'If anyone knows how to clean blood from a murder weapon, it's Deep,' Greg pointed out.

'I could do it, for that matter.'

'You're not in the frame. You had no motive.'

'I wasn't aware that Deep even knew the dead woman.'

'We're getting side-tracked,' he said, 'and it's late.'

'Okay, Deep could do the cleaning, but they're all blunted. There's not one that could be used to stab someone.'

'How many knives are we talking about?' Greg asked.

'Martha brought in five.'

'What if there was a sixth knife, specially sharpened, and now disposed of given that Deep, of all people, knows how damning the evidence of a weapon can be?'

'It's not impossible,' Dr Armstrong said sharply, 'but you haven't got it and, without it, you have no evidence on which to hold him.'

Greg felt a sense of relief. For another day he could cling to the hope that Deepak Gupta had not murdered Aoife Cusack.

'It's the middle of the night,' he said. 'With luck, he'll be asleep. I'll see he's released first thing in the morning.'

Chapter Twenty-Two

Greg was at the station at seven and had Deep out of his cell by ten past. It was obvious to him that the younger man had ignored his instructions and not slept at all. 'I should make them give you breakfast before you go,' he advised.

'I've tasted the food here, thanks.'

'Deep, I know you're not in the mood to listen to me at the moment, but you have to give up this obsession with Liam Sullivan, for your own sake. You're hurting no one but yourself.'

'It's okay,' he said. 'I am doing. I won't be around much longer. Indira and I are moving back to Mumbai.'

'You're not serious,' Greg said.

'I very much am. I can't stay in a country where murderers like Sullivan are allowed to strut about as if they owned the place. Also, my wife isn't happy here. I love my wife and if she is unhappy, then I am un-happy. Maybe you don't understand that.'

'I don't know what that's supposed to mean! Won't you have trouble getting a job there?'

'I don't think so. I can always work in a call centre.'

'That'd be a hell of a waste of your skills and experience.'

'Just to tide me over till I can find work as a scientist. Many people are returning to India now, you know. Everything's changed these last few years. It used to be like the 1950s there – any colour of car so long as it was black; any toothpaste so long as it was Colgate – but trade has been opened up and middle-class people can live better there than they can in England.

'We shall have a decent house and a maid. Indira can practise without being told her hard-earned qualifications are next to worth-less. We won't have to wait years to have our children, little Nitin and little Sangita.'

'It's not actually *returning* in your case,' Greg pointed out. 'How many times have you been to India?'

'...Three,' Deep admitted.

'It may seem alien.'

'I'll get used to it.'

'You complained more than anyone when we had that massive heatwave last August.'

'I'll get used to it,' he repeated.

313

'What about your mum?'

'She'll come with us. She'll be thrilled. She'll live with us like in a proper family and see her grandchildren every day.'

'You know I can't let you leave the country till all this is resolved, don't you?'

'Don't worry. It'll take weeks to sort everything out. We have to sell the flat.'

Greg offered his hand. After a moment's reflection, Deepak shook it. Barbara came bustling in the front door at that moment. 'What's happening?' she asked, glancing between the two men.

'Babs, can you run Deep home?'

'I'll walk!' Deepak said.

Greg and Barbara watched him walk out of the front door, pulling himself up to his full five foot five.

'Still not clear what's going on,' Barbara said.

'Come up to my office.'

He explained the latest developments when they were securely closeted. She expressed annoyance that he hadn't called her in for the interview.

'Is there any way on God's earth,' he asked, 'that Aoife Cusack committed suicide? I'm sure I've read crime novels where someone would wedge a knife in a tree or something and then back into it, making suicide look like murder.'

'It could happen,' Barbara said kindly.

'And then, when she was dead, she carefully removed the knife and disposed of it...'

'I hate you sometimes,' he said affectionately.

'Rightbackatcha.'

'Deepak, thank God!' He'd no sooner got his key out of the lock than his wife flung herself into his arms. 'I was so worried.'

'It's okay. I'm okay.' His eyes were ringed with dark circles. 'Uncle Roshan always said those bloody knives were unlucky, which was why they ended up with our branch of the family.' He hung up his jacket and threw himself on to the sofa. 'I could murder a cup of tea.'

'Yes. I will make tea.' When she brought his cup five minutes later, he took her hand and made her sit down beside him. 'I did know that Robyn Marchant was Aoife Cusack,' he said.

'Deepak!'

'At least, that someone at that house was. I wanted to tell Gregory Summers but I was too afraid. I must tell someone and you are my other half.'

He recounted the full story of the night he had followed Sullivan to Hilltop.

'You heard him use her name?' she gasped.

'Just the forename – Aoife – but I had no doubt. It's not like there are lots of them. Part of me had been looking for that woman

315

for twenty-three years and there she was, all the time, a few miles away.'

'I think you did well not to tell Mr Summers,' she said slowly.

'It looks bad, doesn't it?'

She enclosed his plump face in her hands and gazed into his tired eyes. 'Tell me you know nothing of this killing, Deepak. Tell me you did not kill this evil woman.'

'I was so stunned to hear her name,' he said remotely. 'I took to my heels. By the time I stopped running I was sick, literally.' He got up. 'I'm so tired. I must sleep now.'

Nick and Andy had taken statements from all the staff at Hilltop the day after the murder, from the teachers to Mrs Llewellyn who came in twice a day to cook lunch and dinner for the pupils, to the two women from the village who cleaned the house. Even the gardener had been interviewed. Since none of them slept at the school, it had been largely a matter of form.

Now Barbara and Greg spent the rest of Tuesday re-interviewing them, probing delicately to see if any of them knew about Robyn's background. Not wanting to ask outright if anyone knew that she was Aoife Cusack, they ended the afternoon tired, frustrated and none the wiser and Greg began to wonder if it was really possible to keep the Marchants' secret.

When he got home that evening there was again no sign of Angie and Bellini was doing her Highland fling that said, 'If you don't take me out for a walk right now I shall report you to the RSPCA *and* I shall pee on the hall floor.'

This was getting ridiculous. As this rate, they'd have to employ an *au pair* to look after the dog before Social Services came and took her into care.

He grabbed her lead and they set off along the road at a fast pace, pausing only for one of them to relieve herself against the nearest kerb.

At the end of the road, Bellini turned left up the hill and Greg followed her without complaint. At the first corner he could see Wisteria Cottage, the prettiest house in the village, and he hated to think of Sullivan installed there in comfort. He was even more cross to see the man in question luxuriating on a lounger in the front garden, a bottle of white wine in an ice-bucket beside him, a half-drunk glass sweating beads of moisture in his hand.

'Lovely evening,' Sullivan called out.

'Mr Sullivan.' Greg did not slow his pace.

'Why don't you sit awhile?' He gestured at the bucket. 'Have a glass of Sancerre.'

'No thanks. I have things to do.' He cursed himself. Now Sullivan would infer that he might have accepted his hospitality if he hadn't been busy.

'Caught your killer yet?' Sullivan asked.

'...Not yet.'

'What does her sister say?'

'I beg your pardon.' Greg stopped. Sullivan rose and came to lean on the gate, his expression unbearably smug. Bellini whined and strained to continue up the hill but Greg held her head tight.

'The shapeless woman at your Hilltop place,' Sullivan said. 'Ask her what her story is – Aoife's sister.'

Greg stared at him for a moment. 'Why are you telling me this?' he asked finally.

'Well, now, let's see. Maybe I cared about Aoife and I'd like to see her killer punished.'

Greg raised his eyebrows. 'Cared about her enough to turn her over to the authorities?'

He grinned. 'Alternatively, maybe I wanted to see her suffer – dragged off to prison and court, see her own picture in the paper with the words "Spawn of the devil" under it – and she cheated me by getting herself killed.'

'So what – I pays my money and I takes my choice?'

He shrugged. 'Maybe it's a bit of both. I'm not a black and white cartoon character, Summers, I'm a complex human being.'

'Why didn't you tell me this earlier, like when I had you down at the station?'

'You pissed me off by arresting me. Have

you any idea of the memories that brought back?'

'You're breaking my heart.'

'Me and Colin Meers in an interview room with one of his licensed thugs. No lawyer because they didn't have to give me one under the terrorism legislation. They beat me, kicked me, punched me, stripped me and left me naked in a cell on a cold night–'

'I don't believe you.'

'Believe it. And it's not like they needed a confession – Malcolm Fraser gave them all the evidence they wanted. They did it because they enjoyed it.'

Sullivan turned and walked back into his cottage, letting the door slam behind him.

Chapter Twenty-Three

'Am I under arrest?' Siobhan asked.

'Goodness, no.' Greg looked at her with kindly eyes. He hadn't taken to her at first meeting, but now he found himself full of admiration for the way she had stuck by her errant sister, unacknowledged, for so many years. That was true familial love, not like brother Nessan who wouldn't spit on Aoife if she were on fire.

'If we arrest you, we tell you so,' he went

on. 'We say, "I am arresting you." You're here to give us a witness statement as Aoife's sister.'

'How did you know?'

'Liam Sullivan recognised you the other day, when you were having that row with Marie's mother in the drive.'

'And he told you? He helped the police?'

'He likes to make mischief,' Greg said. 'He means no good by it. Why didn't you tell me who you were as soon as your sister was murdered?'

'So many reasons.' She sighed, rotating her head and rubbing the nape of her neck as if she were unbearably weary. 'I hoped that her secret need never be told, for one. It didn't occur to me that you would identify her so quickly, not after all these years.'

'We never close an unresolved murder file,' Barbara said.

'Then I thought that Stephen and the children had had enough shocks for one day. Also I thought I might be an accessory after the fact, or whatever you call it. I kept her secret all these years.'

'I doubt it will come to that,' Greg said. 'Not now, with Aoife dead, but if you'd like a solicitor present, we can get you one.' She shook her head and he went on. 'No one's ever suggested you were connected with terrorism.'

'My God, no! I warned her about Billy

Sullivan. I *begged* her to stay away from him. I knew his sort – so charming and full of the gab and endless second-hand talk about the English occupation and the Struggle. Growing up in Belfast, you hear it all the time from the half-educated idiots who think it makes them somebody, makes them men. Sullivan was worse, though, because he had brains and an education.'

'So who are you really?' Greg asked. 'Roisin?'

'Orla, the eldest of the Cusack siblings. Aoife was the baby of the family and I was a second mother to her.'

'Aoife turned to you after she left Sullivan?' Barbara said.

She nodded. 'I was twenty-five and had recently taken a post nursing at a hospital in Shropshire. Aoife turned up on my doorstep one night, exhausted and bedraggled. She'd run away with no more than the clothes she stood up in and enough cash for the boat, which she stole from Billy since he allowed her no money of her own. She'd hitched from Liverpool and it had taken her two days.

'The following day we heard on the TV news that Special Branch had made a big arrest connected with the Windsor bombing. It turned out that one of the cell had been an undercover policeman. He'd warned Aoife to get out – maybe he had a soft spot for her. I don't know.'

Greg pricked up his ears. 'You're sure about that – that Malcolm Fraser tipped her the wink, told her he was a policeman?'

She frowned. 'He told her to get out,' she repeated. 'I don't know how much he confided in her.'

'Has she been in touch with him all these years?'

'That was my impression,' Siobhan said slowly.

'How so?'

'She never told me in so many words, but once or twice I walked in on her in the middle of a telephone conversation and she would slam the receiver down, tell me it was a wrong number, even though I knew for a fact she'd been on the line for some minutes. A couple of years ago I heard her repeating a mobile phone number as she noted it down on a piece of paper.'

'How did she react to the arrests?' Greg asked.

'She was terrified. She was certain that she'd be next. We waited, both of us, for the knock on the door, but it never came. Aoife had been religious as a child, until she met Sullivan, now it came back. She wanted to atone for what she'd done. She didn't go back to mass, though. I thought at first that she was afraid a priest would turn her in if she confessed, but we both knew that no

322

priest would do that. In the end she told me that she didn't deserve absolution. That she would seek it only when she herself was satisfied that she'd made amends for her past.'

'I wonder if she ever reached that point,' Greg said.

'I know that she didn't. A few weeks ago, she thought she could do it, confess and be shriven, but she came back without receiving absolution. She told Stephen that she had.' She shook her head in despair. 'I think he believes that she died in a state of grace.'

'I'm not sure what that means.'

She smiled faintly. 'It's a Catholic thing. If you've recently confessed when you die – especially if you've received the last rites – then the sins you have committed in life are forgiven and heaven is not denied you.'

'Will you tell him different?' Greg asked.

She thought about it. 'No. What good would that do?'

'It's all so easy, isn't it – for a Catholic – sin and be shriven?'

'Oh, no, Superintendent, that's just what it isn't. All Protestants think that, talk of Mafia chiefs who have a dozen men slaughtered on Friday and confess on Saturday in time to take communion on Sunday and order the next massacre. It doesn't work like that. You have to be truly repentant and genuinely mean not to repeat the sin, or the absolution is worthless. What faith have you, may I ask?'

'I'm an agnostic,' he said, uncomfortable with the subject. Whatever religious faith he might once have had had died with Frederick in a hospice three years ago.

She laughed. 'We'll put you down as C of E then.'

'So what happened next?' Greg asked. 'In 1981.'

'She headed south, took a job in Suffolk, established a new identity. She started evening classes, with a view to doing nursing or social work or something like that, but then she met Stephen. She told me she'd never known anyone like him. Within six months they were married and had bought Hilltop. She asked me to come, to be matron there.'

'Without telling her husband that you were her sister,' Barbara asked.

'I could never do the accent, not like Aoife, and how could she explain me without admitting to being Irish herself? My nephew and niece don't know that I'm their aunt and they care nothing for me.'

'And you're a widow,' Greg said.

'Yes, what of it?'

'And Daniel is your son.'

'Of course.'

'And the photograph in the sitting room at Hilltop is of your late husband.'

'Naturally.'

'Except that it's really a picture of your

brother, Nessan. My colleague from Special Branch recognised him.'

'...I have no photo of Eamonn Fahey, and Daniel wanted to know what his father looked like. It seemed a harmless enough lie.'

'So a DNA test will confirm that you are his mother?' She fell silent and he added, 'Or will it confirm that Daniel is Aoife's son, hers and Sullivan's? Why else would she leave him her estate? Besides, he has his father's eyes.'

After a long silence, Siobhan said, 'That was one of the reasons she wanted out of the life Sullivan had wished on her, so that her baby would not grow up in that world. We hid ourselves away together and, when Daniel was born, he was registered to me. He knows nothing of his true origins. I'm the only real mother he's had. Aoife hardly saw him for the first two years of his life. We were always afraid that Special Branch were watching me.'

'And Stephen?'

'That was the big secret she never told him.'

'Only what I'm thinking,' Greg said, 'is that if Liam Sullivan was threatening to hand Aoife over to the police, then telling him that they had a son together might have made him change his mind.'

'She'd never have done that,' Siobhan said

scornfully. 'She loved Daniel as much as I did.'

'But did she love him as much as she loved Charlie and Dominic?' Greg asked with deliberate brutality. 'Or would she have sacrificed his peace of mind for theirs?'

'She would never have exposed him to that man's poison.'

'Really? Not even if she was desperate?' Greg leaned forward, holding eye contact with Siobhan. 'Only she rang Sullivan just a couple of hours before she died, asked him to come and see her that very night.'

'She was trying to get him to take money to let her go.'

'No, that was earlier. He'd made it clear that he wouldn't take her money. This time she had something to tell him which might make him take pity on her.'

'Why would you believe a word that man says?'

'Because he has no reason to lie about it.'

'He doesn't need a reason. He's in league with the father of lies.'

'Only it seems to me that that gives you a very strong motive for doing away with your sister. As a trained nurse, you would have some knowledge of anatomy. You would know where to strike the blow for a quick death. Are you sure you don't want a solicitor?'

'Another person to know Daniel's secret? I

don't think so.'

'Can you look me in the eye and tell me that it didn't go through her mind to use Daniel as a weapon?'

'She would never have gone through with it.'

'So you knew she was considering it! Daniel's a grown man, after all. He has the right to know his true parentage and he'd handle it.'

'You're a grown man,' she replied. 'How would you feel if you learned that your mother wasn't really your mother and that your father was ... Jack the Ripper.'

'I'm not that old!' he protested.

'All right. Ian Brady. Yes, let's say Myra Hindley is your mother. Your whole life would have been a lie, your very identity a fraud. No mother would inflict that on her child.'

'Brady is certifiably insane,' Greg pointed out. 'Whatever else you may say about Liam Sullivan, he isn't mad.'

'Which makes it worse! To commit atrocities without the excuse of madness.'

She was right, he thought, he would be devastated. He leaned back in his chair, folded his arms and looked at her.

Something she'd said bothered him.

Stephen Marchant believed that his wife had been absolved from her sins before she died. Also, Aoife didn't have a hundred thousand pounds in the bank. The money she'd offered Sullivan could only have come from Stephen, which cast doubt on his claims that he knew nothing of his wife's past. The most indulgent husband, when asked for blackmail money on that scale, would want to know why.

And he found himself reflecting on what Siobhan had said, that Daniel was the big secret Robyn had kept from her husband. Meaning that she had told him the others?

'Did Stephen know who Robyn was?'

'Ask him yourself.'

'I did and he denied it.' She made no reply and he said, 'Do you know Mr Marchant's uncle?'

'Guy? Of course. He's one of the old school who think he's better than other people because his family are rich and he went to the "right" school. He's never got over the fact that Britain doesn't have an empire any more and thinks the world's a worse place for it. He makes no secret of his disdain for Hilltop and for "freeloaders" like me and Daniel.'

'That must be galling.'

'In the good old days, according to Guy, if a woman gave birth to a child with an obvious handicap such as Down's the midwife would quietly stifle it and pronounce it still-born. He can't see why that doesn't still happen.'

Barbara looked shocked but Greg had heard such stories from his own mother. 'You must dislike him a lot,' he said.

She smiled faintly. 'Actually, I rather like him. At least he's no humbug.'

'He said something to me about Stephen having tried a number of careers before going into the family business. Do you happen to know what those were?'

'Some.' She frowned in concentration. 'He actually thought about going into the church at one stage – which was taking his religion a bit too seriously as far as his parents were concerned – but he left the seminary after six months. Then he tried medicine but, again, he dropped out.'

'He was training to be a doctor?' Barbara's voice was sharp and urgent.

'Only for a couple of years. He even did a spell in the army – I suppose he must have been a lot fitter in those days – but he ended up buying himself out. I think he was just kicking against the inevitable – Marchants Marine Insurance – making an attempt to assert his individuality the way you do when you're young. He's seemed happy enough running the firm for all the time that I've known him.'

Greg realised that he now had the final confirmation of his suspicions. He said, 'Will you help me catch your sister's killer?'

'Of course.'

'Even if it's Daniel? Or Stephen or Charlie or Dominic?'

'That's... I can't believe... What do you want me to do?'

'What I want you to do,' Greg said, 'is to go to the canteen with Sergeant Carey here and have some supper. Stay with her until I tell you different. Don't call the school or communicate with anyone there in any way.'

'You don't think she's in danger?' Barbara asked, puzzled.

'Not in the least. I just want her kept out of the way. I'll call you later with further instructions.'

'May I speak to you in private, sir?' Greg said.

Stephen Marchant looked grey and Greg, noticing a family photo which showed him with rosy cheeks, would hardly have recognised him as the same man.

'Of course.' Stephen led the way into a cluttered room which was clearly his private study.

'I wanted to let you know right away,' Greg began, 'that we've charged Siobhan Fahey with your wife's murder.'

'What!' Some colour came back into his face but it wasn't a healthy hue. 'I don't understand. That's impossible.'

'I gather you weren't aware that Siobhan is, in truth, Orla Cusack, your wife's eldest sister.'

330

Marchant groped for a chair, collapsing into it with a sigh. 'There seem to have been a lot of things I didn't know,' he said distantly.

More than you think, Greg thought, since he had no intention of telling the man that Daniel Fahey was really his stepson. That truth was none of his business and something for Siobhan to decide.

'You never suspected?' he asked.

'How could I? Siobhan was clearly Irish and Robyn, equally clearly, not, or so I thought. But what was her motive? What proof have you?'

'It's complicated,' Greg said. 'It seems that it was, in its way, a mercy killing. Siobhan knew that Liam Sullivan was about to expose your wife as Aoife Cusack. Her crimes were still unresolved and she would certainly have faced trial and imprisonment. For Aoife's sake, and for the sake of the nephew and niece she couldn't even acknowledge, Siobhan – Orla – decided to kill her.'

'No!' Stephen said.

'There would be no point in Sullivan denouncing her then. He would have nothing to gain by it. She loved her sister that much.'

'No.'

'Robyn Marchant's name – the good name she'd spent two decades building up – need not be sullied, bandied about the front

331

pages of the tabloids.'

'No.' Stephen clutched at his chest and Greg feared he was having a heart attack. He stepped forward urgently.

'Mr Marchant, do you need a doctor?' Marchant waved him away. 'I'll get you a glass of water,' Greg said firmly.

When he got back, Marchant seemed more composed. He took the water without thanks and gulped it down.

'What evidence have you?' he asked finally. 'She surely hasn't confessed.'

'It's all circumstantial at the moment,' Greg admitted, 'but I think we can build a case the Crown Prosecution Service will be happy with. Then you can watch your wife's killer go to jail for a long time.'

'Has she got a solicitor?'

'She refused one. She's still trying to protect Aoife and the children.'

For a couple of minutes, neither of them spoke, then Greg said, 'Well, I wanted to set your mind at rest. You can all sleep easy in your beds tonight, knowing that the murderer is behind bars. Do you happen to know where I can find Mr Fahey?'

'He ... um, he went out on his bike earlier today.'

'As next of kin, he needs to be told,' Greg explained. 'Shall I tell him or would it come better from you?'

Stephen looked up at him and Greg could

see his shrewd mind ticking over behind his mild eyes. 'Can I sleep on it, decide what to do for the best?'

'Of course, sir.' Greg hoped he wasn't making a stupid mistake about the type of man Stephen Marchant was. 'Perhaps you'll let me know your decision first thing tomorrow, since Daniel needs to be told before I put his mother up in front of the magistrates for remand.'

Chapter Twenty-Four

Greg got to the police station early the next morning – arriving via the back door on the dot of eight – but Stephen was waiting for him, alone.

He looked grey and old and defeated.

Greg, relieved that he had not made a terrible error of judgement, led him into an interview room and made sure he was comfortable while he fetched Barbara to sit in as second interviewing officer.

He also made a phone call to a local B&B.

Finally, they were all ready and the tapes were running.

'You must release Siobhan,' Stephen began.

'Why's that, Mr Marchant?' Greg asked.

When the older man didn't immediately reply, he continued, 'Could it be because it was you, and not Siobhan, who loved Robyn *that* much...You knew all along that she was Aoife Cusack. Didn't you?'

Stephen whispered an answer and Greg said, 'I can't hear you. Loud enough for the tape, please.'

'I said yes. It was me. I killed Robyn and for those reasons you attributed to Siobhan – to save her from the consequences of what she had done. What she *did*, so many years ago.'

He looked at Greg in mute appeal, seeking not mercy but understanding.

'Stephen Marchant, I'm arresting you for the murder of Robyn Marchant. You do not have to say anything...' Greg completed the caution and said, 'Do you understand?'

His 'Yes' was barely audible.

'Are you sure you don't want a solicitor? We can phone your uncle, but you might do better with a specialist in criminal law.'

'I don't want a lawyer.'

'You should have one, given the serious nature of the charge,' Barbara advised him.

Greg sensed animosity in the set of her shoulders and her compressed mouth – the sympathy of a woman towards a comrade betrayed; contempt for the eternal male enemy who used his superior strength to control and even to kill – but still she was the consummate professional.

Marchant dismissed the advice with a shake of his head. 'You will release Siobhan now?'

Greg glanced away, suddenly embarrassed by his necessary subterfuge. 'Siobhan was never under arrest. She spent the night at a B&B in Newbury and is now on her way back to Hilltop. I knew that if you were guilty, as I thought, and for the reasons I surmised, then you would never let an innocent person be accused in your place.'

'Did your wife tell you her history before you married?' Greg asked. Half an hour had passed, during which Marchant had been processed by the custody sergeant, deprived of his belt and shoelaces and delivered back to the interview.

'No,' Stephen said. 'As far as I knew, she was Robyn Simpson, and always had been, an orphan from Suffolk. I didn't even know she was Irish, not till our tenth wedding anniversary, when she told me everything, every last detail – or so I thought, since she never told me about Siobhan.'

No, Greg thought, in case you guessed the truth about Daniel. Aloud, he said, 'Must have been a hell of a shock.'

'You could say that.'

'Would you have married her if you'd known?'

He shook his head, though not as a negative to the question. 'I can't answer that. I can't imagine not having been married to her all these years, not having Charlie and Dom. She was just Robyn, the best thing that had ever happened to me. I was never much good with women, you see. They found me ... unexciting.'

Aoife had had enough of bad boys with Sullivan, Greg concluded, and Stephen had the money to make her dream of redemption come true.

Marchant was still speaking. 'This woman – this terrorist, Aoife Cusack – was a stranger I never met.'

'And yet you killed her,' Greg said evenly.

'He was going to reveal her identity,' Stephen said. 'Liam Sullivan. He was going to brand her a psychotic killer to the world. You know what the newspapers are like. The wonderful work she's done these twenty years – all she's done for society and the community, for the children we have now and hundreds of others – would be nothing. She'd just be another Paddy terrorist who deserved to rot in jail and the school would never survive the scandal.'

He paused, sucking in breath in quick gasps; his face turned red, then purple.

'Are you all right?' Greg asked.

'Asthma inhaler,' he gulped. 'Was in my pockets.'

'Get it!' Greg snapped at Barbara. It bothered him that people were forced to leave vital medication at the desk, but the custody sergeants insisted, implacably if implausibly, that an asthma inhaler could be a gun in disguise. The sergeant left the room swiftly and was back in two minutes with the piece of blue plastic in her hand.

Marchant snatched it and sucked gratefully on it, once, then again.

'Dr MacDonald is in the station,' Barbara reported.

'Mr Marchant? Shall I get the doctor?'

'I'm all right,' he said and laid the inhaler on the table. His face had lost its alarming purplish tinge and looked grey and saggy.

'Let's take a break,' Greg said. 'Why don't we get you a cup of tea? I don't suppose you had any breakfast before coming in, did you?'

'Perhaps some strong coffee,' Marchant said. 'They say it helps open the airways.'

They switched the tape off and the two men sat in silence while Sergeant Carey fetched coffee for them all. It was a peaceful silence, with none of the usual crackling of hostility between murderer and interrogator.

When Barbara returned, Greg gave another time check and asked Stephen to continue with his story.

'Where was I? Yes. Sullivan. He was going to tell the police who she was, and for what?

337

If it had been revenge then I could understand – sort of – but he knew she didn't
betray him, just ran out because she'd realised that what she was doing was wrong.
He had no reason to denounce her, only for
the pure pleasure of it.'

'Nobody's ever claimed that Liam Sullivan
is a nice man,' Greg said.

'With her dead, there was no point in his
exposing her. In fact, he wouldn't dare as
he'd be an obvious suspect. That way my
children would be safe from the knowledge
that their mother was once – in another
lifetime – a terrorist.'

They would now have to live with the
knowledge that their father was a murderer
instead, Greg thought. How could he make
them understand what he had done, gain
their forgiveness, without telling them the
truth?

'So you stabbed her in the back,' he said
evenly.

'In the back?' Stephen looked astonished.
'Oh, I see. No. It wasn't like that. I was holding her in my arms as she died. I timed my
arrival carefully. I thought that on a hot summer's evening, she'd be alone in the sitting
room, at dusk, with the windows open and I
could surprise her there.

'Except that I came upon her in the herb
garden instead. It was her favourite place and
she was always so happy there but that night,

as I stood watching her, she was drawn and careworn, terrified of what Sullivan would do. I stepped out of the shadows and she exclaimed at seeing me because I was supposed to be in London.'

'At the theatre in the Barbican,' Greg said. 'Watching Marianne Faithfull. Nice bit of detail, by the way. As a matter of interest, why doesn't your car show up on the CCTV footage on the Chiswick flyover earlier that evening?'

'Because I came along the A roads,' Stephen said. 'There was no hurry after I left the office since I didn't want to arrive until dusk. I know there are cameras on the motorway – not just speed cameras but the ones the television stations use to do their traffic reports in the morning. I knew you could get access to them if you suspected me, as you must.' He looked apologetic. 'Not much to do on long evenings in the Barbican except watch telly and there's a police show on practically every night.'

'So what happened when you found Aoife?'

'Please! Call her Robyn. Aoife Cusack died a long time ago. I went up to her and took her in my arms and she began to sob. I comforted her and kissed her and told her it would be all right, that I would make it all right. I would have given anything for there to have been another way. You must believe me.'

'I do,' Greg said. 'I believe that *you* thought there was no other way.' He would never know how Sullivan would have responded to the news that he and Aoife had created life together, if the man had an ounce of pity in him.

'I slid the knife in between her ribs and into her heart. She stared at me with eyes so wide...' His voice grew thick and he swallowed hard. 'Then she made a little choking noise and died.'

Greg and Barbara sat in silence, envisaging the scene he conjured for them. For a violent death, it had been oddly peaceful. Stephen was right-handed, but he had not sneaked up behind her in the darkness to strike from the left; he'd looked her in the eyes without shame as she died.

It had not occurred to Greg until yesterday that the killer had been facing his victim. 'You knew where to strike after a brief flirtation with medical school,' he stated.

'Yes. How did you know about that?'

'And then?' Greg said. 'You must have got some blood on your clothes.'

'A little. I went back to where I'd hidden my car and drove straight to London. There I changed and showered and disposed of the clothes I'd been wearing. It was while I was doing that that your officer rang and left a message for me. I waited another couple of hours before ringing back, until the performance in the theatre was over.'

He'd kept it simple, Greg thought, the best way to do murder. 'And the weapon?' he asked.

'Nicked, I'm afraid to say, from Uncle Guy's flat in Knightsbridge.'

'He keeps weapons lying around?'

'It was an eighteenth century Samurai knife he picked up in Tokyo before the war. He's got quite a collection of souvenirs from his misspent youth – including, rather gruesomely, a shrunken head. I have a key and, as he's not getting any younger, I drop in on him at least twice a week on my way to or from the Barbican. It was the easiest thing in the world to help myself to a suitable weapon while he was out at his club one day. I doubt he's missed it. If he has, he's not mentioned it.'

From what he'd seen of Guy, Greg thought, if he had noticed, he would have drawn his deductions and kept his own counsel. 'And where is it now?'

'You know those artificial lakes just off the motorway near Slough, used by windsurfers and such like?' Greg nodded. 'I chucked it in one of those. Pity. It was beautiful as well as valuable.'

'Yeah, that was what was worrying me most,' Barbara said.

Stephen sighed and wiped his hand across his face, moving sweat. 'She paid for what she did a hundred times over. There are people living happy, productive lives because of her. Isn't that better amends than sitting in jail, growing ill and bitter? But I underestimated the pain. It was unbearable, but I had to bear it. I had no choice.'

'One thing I don't get,' Barbara said. 'Why didn't you just kill Liam Sullivan?'

Stephen stared at her in astonishment. 'I'm not a murderer! A man like me ... a man like him ... I wouldn't know where to start.'

It made a kind of sense, Greg thought. Marchant didn't see what he'd done to his wife as murder but as mercy: releasing her from suffering as if she'd been terminally ill and in unbearable pain. And he probably knew Robyn well enough to know that she wouldn't want Sullivan's blood on her hands, as she'd told Malcolm Fraser.

But there was one thing that still bothered him.

He said, 'Tell me something, Mr Marchant. Who did you think was going to get the blame for your wife's death? If you didn't get caught, then some innocent person might have been arrested.'

'I didn't think about that,' Stephen admitted. 'I thought the case could remain unsolved. I mean, it happens.'

'Yes,' Greg agreed. 'It happens.'

'I hoped you would never find out her true identity but you did, almost at once. That was a terrible shock to me.'

'Your exclamations of surprise were convincing.'

'It helped that I was so stunned when I realised you knew who she was. I was able to use that to manufacture my incredulity. And, after that, things just seemed to unravel at high speed and this morning I realised that I had no choice but to hold my hands up.'

He added, 'Is there any way we can avoid the truth about her coming out?'

'Hard,' Greg said.

'If I plead guilty?' he begged. 'That's why I didn't want a lawyer, so as few people as possible know. If it never really comes to a trial? If the truth comes out then it will all have been for nothing. She will have died for nothing.'

'I can make no promises ... I will do my best, for the children's sake.'

'She preferred death,' Stephen said.

'Did you ask her?' Barbara demanded icily. 'Because if that was the case there was always suicide.'

'But that would have been a mortal sin! Don't you see? Even *asking* her would make it a sin in her complicity.'

More of that complicated Catholic stuff, Greg thought.

'And murder isn't?' Barbara was saying.

'Oh, it doesn't matter about me.'

'I think Sergeant Carey was referring to

the murders your wife committed in 1981,' Greg said, 'not yours.'

'Oh, but she'd been shriven of those. Finally, after all these years. Three months ago she went to confession. She was gone for ages but she came home at peace.'

He looked from Greg to Barbara and back again and his eyes shone with tears but they were not unhappy tears.

'Robyn died in a state of grace.'

Epilogue

'I give up.' Greg raised his hands in surrender. 'I'm not a philosopher.'

'But, sir.' Barbara was never afraid to persevere with an argument. 'Surely it was better for her to devote her life to helping others than to rot in jail.'

'It depends what you think prison is for,' Greg said. 'It's not entirely a process of redemption or rehabilitation. It has to carry an element of punishment too, and of deterrence.'

'Can't have people choosing their own punishments,' Andy agreed. 'That would be chaos. I mean, the woman was doing a form of community service, which isn't much of a sentence for killing six people.'

He lifted one buttock and farted in Barbara's direction.

She punched him in the upper arm. 'Oh, that's right – get in touch with your inner pig.'

'Sorry, Sarge.' He massaged his arm. 'Better out than in.' Barbara appealed to her other colleague. 'What do you think, Nick? … Nick?'

'Huh?'

'What do you think?'

'About what?'

'Nick's on screensaver,' Andy remarked.

Greg laughed and got up. 'My round, I think. Same again, everybody?' He began collecting up their glasses. He was feeling full of the party spirit with another case closed. True, the morning's post had brought a congestion charge fine from his trip to London, but he could shout at someone about that tomorrow.

'What's the matter with you?' Barbara asked Nick in annoyance. 'You've been miles away all evening. We're supposed to be celebrating a case solved.'

'I'm engaged to be married,' Nick blurted out, looking surprised at his own announcement.

Greg, setting off for the bar, turned back. 'To your nurse? Congratulations.'

'Yeah,' Andy said. 'All the best, mate.' He tried hard to sound pleased for his colleague, although his own foray into wedded bliss had ended with his wife leaving him for a racehorse trainer.

'Is she up the duff?' Barbara asked.

'No,' Nick replied, with dignity.

'I could buy champagne,' Greg said, 'but I'm sure we all prefer beer.'

He went to get their drinks, musing as he did so about Hilltop and what would become of it. Siobhan – or Orla, as he must now think of her – was willing to go on running it while Stephen was in prison and he had appointed her guardian to his children.

He hoped that Robyn Marchant's good work in the community would continue.

So far, the press hadn't got hold of the truth about Aoife, although Stephen had had to confess all to Charlie and Dominic since the alternative – that they should think him a domestic murderer – was worse.

Charlie, a daddy's girl if ever he'd seen one, had forgiven him; Dominic was slower to accept what had been done and inclined to take upon himself a guilt that did not belong to him, reasoning that, if his father had killed his mother to protect him and his sister, then it was somehow his fault.

He'd told the children that their mother had died shriven of her sins; it was the truth as he knew it and Greg wasn't going to tell him different. He wasn't a Catholic – or even a believer – but if there was a God, then surely He would show mercy to Aoife Cusack. That was part of His job description.

There was something in Portia's 'Quality of Mercy' speech in *The Merchant of Venice*; he couldn't remember the exact words but it was to the effect that if justice ran its true course then no one could expect salvation.

Stephen would plead guilty at the trial and no mention of motive need be made, although Greg hoped that somebody would have a private word with the judge before he handed out his tariff, that he might err on the side of leniency.

Not that he in any way condoned what Marchant had done, but he did understand it.

It was a sad reflection of the times that 'domestic murders' tended to get a lesser tariff, anyway, perhaps with the justification that the perpetrator was not a threat to society in general, just to his family.

Both Marchant children were surprised to find that they'd had an aunt on their doorstep all these years and, in Charlie's case, not that pleased. Orla, as far as he knew, had told nobody the truth about Daniel's parentage and he respected that decision.

An inconsolable Marie had been taken away from Hilltop by her mother and placed in another institution.

There'd been no sign of life at Wisteria Cottage for the past few days, confirming

Greg's view that Sullivan had come to Berkshire solely to torment his former lover.

He had made a courtesy call to Colin Meers who'd been disappointed that the murder had been 'a domestic'. Greg hadn't gone into detail about Stephen's motives as he didn't think Colin would understand.

He'd also made a full report about Malcolm Fraser to the Home Office but knew that there wasn't enough evidence to accuse him of having jeopardised the operation. Special Branch wouldn't want to poke that sleeping dog, lest it bite their hand off.

The Queen didn't like having to ask for her police medal back; it made her look stupid.

'So, when did this happen?' he asked Nick, depositing a pint of extra-strong lager in front of the young man a few minutes later.

'This morning.'

'Are you happy?' Greg asked.

'...Yeah. I really am. I never thought it'd happen to me.'

'Will Nadia be commuting to the West Middlesex every day?' Barbara asked.

'No, she's handed in her notice and signed up with a freelance agency. They've already found her a job locally, looking after an old bloke in a big house on the downs. He's dying of pancreatic cancer. Poor sod.'

'It's been a good week,' Andy remarked. 'Nick's getting married, we arrested a murderer and England are through to the quarter finals of the European cup.'

'So are Greece!' Nick said.

Greg raised his glass of Fuller's best bitter. 'Well, here's to Nick and Nadia, to the England team and to a murderer brought to justice.'

'To Nick and Nadia,' Barbara echoed. 'And here's to the few who forgive what we do.'

'To England,' Andy said with a grin.

'To justice,' Nick said.

When Greg stopped at the village shop to buy his *Times* the following morning, his eye was caught by a headline in one of the red-tops.

Exclusive, he read, *Murdered wife was terrorist*.

He snatched up the paper and shook it open. The subtitle read: *IRA death-dealer meets justice 23 years after Windsor outrage*. A quick scan of the story predictably told him nothing about its source. He folded the paper slowly and replaced it on the rack, letting out a long breath of dismay. He'd made no promises to Stephen Marchant but he'd allowed him to hope.

Why did he always forget that hope was only disappointment deferred?

But who, exactly, had taken the *Outlook*'s thirty pieces of silver? Sullivan, Meers,

Deepak? Or somebody else at the police station who had picked up a lucrative piece of gossip and didn't mind profiting from it?

He couldn't even contemplate the possibility that it was one of his own CID team.

After driving to Newbury in something resembling a daze, he pulled into the car park at the Sainsbury supermarket opposite the police station and bought himself a double espresso to go from Starbucks.

Walking back to his car, he raised his cardboard cup to the dim rim of the sun as it tried to force its way out from behind a pewter cloud.

'To justice,' he said, startling a young woman in a business suit, who hurried away, 'whatever that is.'

He went to find someone to yell at about his congestion charge fine.

The publishers hope that this book has given you enjoyable reading. Large Print Books are especially designed to be as easy to see and hold as possible. If you wish a complete list of our books please ask at your local library or write directly to:

Magna Large Print Books
Magna House, Long Preston,
Skipton, North Yorkshire.
BD23 4ND

This Large Print Book, for people
who cannot read normal print,
is published under the auspices of

THE ULVERSCROFT FOUNDATION

Please Leave in Book

CA
CH
HE
KI
LH
LU
M/C
PA
PE
RI
SB
SO
TA
(TE) June 106
TI
TO
WA
WI